IMMORAL CODE

IMMORAL
CODE

LILLIAN CLARK

Alfred A. Knopf
New York

THIS IS A BORZOI BOOK PUBLISHED BY ALFRED A. KNOPF

Visit us on the Web! GetUnderlined.com

Educators and librarians, for a variety of teaching tools, visit us at RHTeachersLibrarians.com

Library of Congress Cataloging-in-Publication Data
Names: Clark, Lillian, author.
Title: Immoral code / Lillian Clark.
Description: First edition. | New York : Alfred A. Knopf, 2019. | Summary: Told from five viewpoints, high school friends Bellamy, Nari, Reese, Keagan, and Santiago team up to hack into Bellamy's absentee billionaire father's business accounts to skim enough money for her MIT tuition.
Identifiers: LCCN 2017058212 (print) | LCCN 2018004322 (ebook) | ISBN 978-0-525-58046-1 (trade) | ISBN 978-0-525-58048-5 (ebook)
Subjects: | CYAC: Friendship—Fiction. | Stealing—Fiction. | Fathers and daughters—Fiction. | Hackers—Fiction. | High schools—Fiction. | Schools—Fiction. | Family life—Oregon—Fiction. | Oregon—Fiction.
Classification: LCC PZ7.1.C59413 (ebook) | LCC PZ7.1.C59413 Imm 2019 (print) | DDC [Fic]—dc23

The text of this book is set in 11.5-point Goudy Oldstyle Std.
Interior design by Jaclyn Whalen
Jacket art used under license from Shutterstock.com

Printed in the United States of America
February 2019
10 9 8 7 6 5 4 3 2 1

First Edition

For Erik and Owen.
It's all for you.

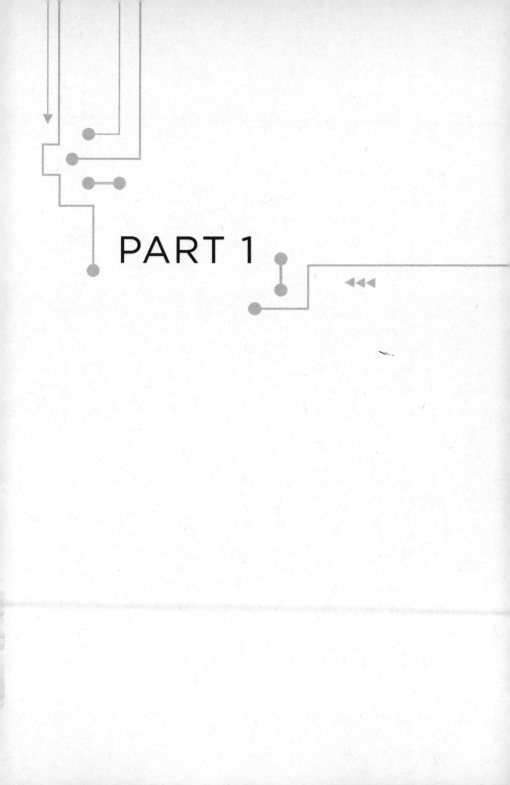

PART 1

NARI

Saturday, February 16, 11:32 a.m.

Reese and I sat on the top bleacher against the back wall to watch the season's last home swim meet. The announcer called the first heat of the first event, and the medley relay teams began to assemble. Keagan waved to me from his towel-and-snack nest on the far side of the pool deck. I stood to give him a proper Swim Fast Salute (elbow up and arm bent; fingers kissed, then flung wide). He pulled on his swim cap and wandered over to the rest of his heat-three relay team. The butterflyer helicoptered his arms. The freestyler held his above his head, stretching onto his toes, elongating his body. Keag tucked stray pieces of his straw-blond hair under the edges of his cap.

The first-heat backstrokers jumped into the water, fixed goggles one last time, adjusted hands on block pegs, foot stances on the wall. The buzzer chirped once and they readied, pulling up tight, waiting for the start. Twice, and they dove. Arms flung, backs arched, legs pushing away from the wall.

I sat down. "It's kind of pretty, you know?"

Reese, hunched over her work—i.e., a blank white Adidas

3

sneaker she was carefully making less blank for her Etsy store—made a sound in her throat. "Teenage-boy junk crammed into tiny Speedos?"

"No. That's less 'pretty' and more . . . what do you call a perpetual almost-wince?"

Reese pushed her hair (half shaved and electric blue with dyed-black roots) over one shoulder, then blew on the fresh lines of ink on the less-blank sneaker. "Pre-wince?"

"Permacringe?"

"Dear all that is holy, don't let that thin patch of spandex slip?"

"Yeah, that one." The swimmers completed their first length, one after another except for the two slowest ones in the outside lanes, and flip-turned on the opposite wall. The breaststrokers mounted the blocks at the other end. "But also no. I meant the way they all take off like that at once. *Synchronized*."

"Except for the ones that back flop."

"Truth."

Shouts echoed off the water, the concrete walls, the tile floor, as the backstrokers touched the wall and the breast-strokers dove into the water.

"Butterfly is pretty," Reese said. She stared down at the pool, half-finished sneaker in her hand. This one was covered in a collage of tiny cartoon characters, all a little ugly-cute. Ugly-cute being Reese's specialty.

"Or looks like drowning," I said.

"Right. No middle ground with that one."

Santiago joined Keagan on the deck, where they alternated cheering on their teammates and laughing about something with the other accumulated relay team members. San, being the team's fastest butterflyer, wouldn't swim till the last heat half an eternity from now, but he stood with Keag and the other guys anyway. "Santiago looks pretty doing fly," I said.

"Yes, well, San looks pretty doing everything. He is a pretty human."

This was true. Apart from his generally pleasing aesthetic, Santiago's one of those people who are good at basically everything physical. Like swimming the fly and running cross-country and playing basketball, if he were to, in fact, play basketball. Even walking. He's a very good walker, smooth, graceful, which is totally not a talent worth remarking upon, but hey. It's the diving thing. While San swims the fly beautifully and fast, as in he's top three in the state, he's also a diver. First and foremost a diver. As in, top three not just in the state but in the *country*. As in, fosters Olympic dreams that are not in the least bit pipe-like despite what his parents think.

I fidgeted on the metal bleacher. Fleece-lined leggings were proving a poor choice for swim-meet attire. In retrospect, obviously. Even if it was mid-February. The butterflyers mounted their blocks. "You should tell Bellamy that."

"I'm pretty sure Bells is aware."

"Yeah, yeah, I know."

Reese looked up. "Yes, you do. Like how you know that . . ." She stared me down, waiting for me to finish her prompt.

I rolled my eyes. "That it's none of my business." Someday Reese's steely gaze shall be a thing of legends. Legends! "Even though they would be so freaking cute together and Santiago already—"

"Nari."

"Okay! *Fine.*" I fluttered my hands into the balmy chlorine air. "Farewell, brilliant intentions! You're fate's problem now."

"Good." Reese bent her head back to her work in progress, adding a pair of googly, unmatched eyes to a tiny, roundish something-or-other with a yawning mouth and single tooth.

The freestylers followed the butterflyers, the faster teams nearly lapping the slowest. One of the doors to the lobby opened and I turned, looking for Bellamy, but instead of my favorite aspiring astronaut it was a herd of freshman girls followed by Keagan's mom wearing a T-shirt with the quote "If I only have one day left to live, I hope to spend it at a high school swim meet, because those things last FOREVER," printed over a watermark of our school logo. *Preach, Autumn Lotus Breeze* (not her real name, but you get the idea). I waved at her, smiling my biggest I-love-your-son-like-mad smile. She waved back, then got waylaid by another swim parent in the third row. No sign of Brent, Keagan's dad. Which meant he was probably in his pottery studio or off selling his wares, leaving Paisley Star (yes, *that's* her real name) to represent.

I watched the second heat of the relay and the concurrent filling up of Reese's white sneaker to the beat of the pool drains gurgling, the water splashing, the crowd cheering, until Bellamy clomped up the bleachers and sat beside me.

Yes, clomped. *Like a Clydesdale?* you say. Isn't that a bit, you know, *rude,* Narioka? This is our first impression of dear Bellamy Bishop! Your oldest and bestest friend! Don't you want her portrayed in a more, dare we say, *attractive* light? To which I reply, *Pish-posh.* And *balderdash!* Bellamy is beautiful *and* she clomps. Just as Reese is beautiful *and* she wisps. And I am beautiful (and terrifying, like a Siren, luring the unsuspecting to their demise) *and* I pirouette or flit or even storm.

So!

Bellamy clomped up the bleachers in her heavy-soled shoes and sat beside me in her jeans and too-big Goodwill T-shirt, today's being adorned with a faded picture of the Backstreet Boys worn without intent and utterly unironically. ("Clothes are for warmth and adherence to social constructs concerning the inappropriateness of nakedness, Nari." Actual Bellamy quote, btw.) Her brown hair was pulled back into a ponytail.

Bells and I met in the second grade after I moved to Oregon from Minnesota. My dad got a job at the university, and the whole lot of us (Mother, Father, Older Brothers One and Two, and seven-and-a-half-year-old me) packed up and migrated away from the Midwest. I was devastated. Truly. As only a slightly melodramatic seven-and-a-half-year-old can be. At least until I learned I was swapping epic winters for epic coastlines. Plus my new room was awesome. And then there was Bellamy, who, seated next to me in our second-grade class, replied to my glee over our matching Darth Vader folders with a lecture about the way sound travels (or, better, doesn't) in space.

The rest is history and context, but it should be entered into the official record that Bellamy is brilliant. Mensa brilliant. Talked about the physics of space at age seven brilliant. IQ of 165 brilliant. Has been riding the high of getting into MIT, early action, since before Christmas brilliant.

She sat down beside me on the bleacher as the third heat of the relay stepped up to the blocks. Keagan and the other backstrokers jumped into the water, and I heard Paisley shout, "Let's go, Keag!" from her seat down below. I stood at the first buzzer and cheered along with everyone else as Keagan swam his leg of the relay. Reese joined me, shoe and pen in hand, as he passed below the flags fifteen feet from the end, half a body length ahead of the next-fastest swimmer. He took his final stroke and touched the wall, and the breaststroker dove over him off the block.

As he climbed out of the water, pulling off his goggles and cap, I wolf whistled. Chest heaving, water dripping off him, he looked up at me in the bleachers, bowed, then turned to cheer for the rest of his relay team. Reese and I sat down.

Bellamy hadn't moved. She stared at the water with a vacant expression, brow tight.

"Solving differentials in your head for funsies?" Reese asked before pulling the cap back off her pen with her teeth.

Bells shook her head. "No. Deadline for the MIT financial aid paperwork was yesterday."

"Didn't you and your mom turn that in weeks ago?" I asked.

"In January, yeah."

"Then . . . ?"

"My dad had to fill out some forms, too."

Reese tipped her azure head to one side. "You think he'd miss the due date?"

Bellamy shrugged, but I knew her worry was less of the Missed Deadline variety and more of the Ragingly Wealthy Estranged Parent sort. I looped my arm around her shoulders and squeezed. "Worry not, dearest Bellamy. You deserve this. The money will work out."

REESE

Friday, February 22, 11:15 p.m.

It was hot. Airless. Scarlet, cardinal, crimson.

Eyes closed, muscles moving, bass thrumming up through the ground into my feet, I danced.

I danced till my skin was slick with sweat. Till I lost autonomy, lost full sense, feeling liquid, elastic, stretched, dissipated. The music was me and I was the crowd. No outlines. No beginnings. No ends. Only a beat, stronger than the one set by my heart, filling my chest and my joints and my head. Just the pulse of lights, the push of bodies, and—

My phone, vibrating in my pocket.

Again.

I should've left it in the car. Screw 'em. You get your crisis, I get my catharsis.

I stopped and the dancers were a writhing mass around me, red-hot and vibrant. It felt like waking up. Or stepping back on land after a few hours on a boat. You know you're standing still but your insides sway to the rhythm of the waves. I wove through the crowd, avoiding elbows, skirting couples, heading for the doors.

Outside, the night air was frigid. Damp shirt, damp skin, no coat, plus Portland air in late February? Yeah. I freed my phone from the side pocket of my pants, hunched my shoulders, wrapped my arms around my chest like that did anything, and walked a few paces down the sidewalk away from the club's door. Other people milled about smoking, laughing, checking phones, watching the icy clouds of their breath. I unlocked my phone: Six texts, four missed calls, two voicemails.

Rad.

The first voicemail was from my dad: Concern and a touch of understanding. The second was from my mom: *Delete*

The texts, in chronological order, were as follows:

(1) Dad: *Please check in getting late*

(2) Nari: *Where are yooouuuuuu???? Answer your phoooooonnnne. Please and thank you.*

(3) Mom: *Your dad called to ask if I'd heard from you, which of course I haven't. Reese, you have to stop doing this to him. I know you're angry, but acting irration—* And . . . *Delete*

Really, I deserved a medal for reading even half of it. And no, I didn't feel sorry for being rude. She'd earned rude. Therefore, I would not regret it. Also, regrets are a waste of time. For real. Even about the bad shit—not intentional rudeness but the stuff that makes you go, *Damn, I really shouldn't've done that.* Regret is pointless. I'm not saying, *Here's a free pass to be a complete asshole and do stuff you know is shitty before you even do it.* I mean *regret:* feeling sad or sorry about something you did or did not do. Key word: did. As in, already happened, in the past. And since all you can do is fix the fallout or learn from your mistakes so you don't repeat them in the future, *why waste your energy and time on regret?*

I'm totally still pro consequences, though. Particularly the well-earned kind, since regretting a thing only because your consequences suck is shitty. Also because some consequences, like the deep teal of my resentment in response to the electric turquoise of my mom's fuckup, are kind of poetic.

(4) Nari: *Majestic Friend of the Newly Aquamarine Hair, CALL ME. Remember how Bells was a walking ball of sulk all afternoon? Well, I finally got the Why out of her. And it's B-A-D.*

(5) Dad: *Answer your phone.*

"What's so interesting?"

I looked back. He was standing too close, peering over my shoulder, smiling like his attention was a gift he'd chosen to bestow especially upon me. I took a step away, turning to face him. Ecru. Him and every other guy like him. Bland, unoriginal, the paint people throw up on a wall because they're dead inside and/or *just that boring.* The color of hospital hallways, schools, and the patriarchy. "Oh, just some hard-core porn," I said. "The usual."

His lip twitched. Then he smiled. "Funny. I like a girl with a sense of humor."

"Yeah?" I grinned and tipped my head to the side. "I like a guy who minds his own business."

He glared. "Fucking bitch."

I held the back of my hand to my forehead, faked a swoon. "Ah, my delicate sensibilities!" And turned away.

I could feel him hovering behind me for one, two, three seconds before he bailed back to whatever dank pit of sexist fantasies had spawned him, and I relaxed. And yeah, I was there alone. And yeah, I get that that's a risk. But I'm not in the habit of letting risks dictate my choices. Catch a ride with some

11

rando in a windowless panel van? Probably not. But no way will I let the fact that the world is home to pervs and douchebags alongside all the awesome people keep me from doing something, going somewhere, being whoever I want to be.

Because this is me. Reese Ethel Gregors, out by myself an hour-plus drive from home because I felt like it, and not giving a shit. Well, no. I give lots of shits about plenty of stuff. But I can't give even one tiny baby shit about pretending to be anyone other than who I am. And who I am is an eighteen-year-old who hates pretense and loves dance music and dyeing my hair. Also art. And bad horror movies, especially ones about Sasquatch. And Julia Kristeva's theories about abjection. Plus my family, even if I don't currently like one of the fundamental members. And my friends, even when Nari and Keagan's perfect teenage love song and Bellamy and San's will they/won't they dynamic make me a fifth wheel?, third wheel?, unicycle?, whatever because being me also equals enjoying my own company. And being ENFP. And Sagittarius. And five foot seven with overly long arms and that thing where my second toe is longer than my big one. Plus stubbornly independent. Oh, and acearo and not all that worried I'm missing out. Not on what Keag and Nari have. Not on whatever Bells and San may or may not have. And definitely not on the epic dumpster fire that is my parents' marriage. Not that any of that is mutually inclusive. My parents could be the human equivalent of swans or termites or barn owls or some other kind of animal that apparently mates for life and I'd still be asexual and aromantic. Does anyone walk away from the explosion of their hetero parents' marriage, pick out all that emotional shrapnel, and say, "Whew, guess I'm not straight anymore!"

No.

They don't.

So anyway, let's just say I give some shits, and one of those involves me *not* giving a shit about things I don't care about even if the world is screaming, *CARE!* Things like feeling sexual or romantic attraction. Or respecting curfew. Also assholes. And hypocrites. And Sasquatch deniers because have they even heard about *Gigantopithecus?* I mean, come on. *Come on.*

I looked back at my phone.

(6) Nari: *Fine! Don't text back! See if I care! Also? Bells heard back about her MIT financial aid, and, thanks to her rich asshole King of Prebirth Abandonment biodad, GOT ZIP. As in $0. As in up shit creek without two dimes to rub together. As in CAN'T GO. Because also again? She's REFUSING TO MAKE HIM PAY.*

Wait. *What?*

SANTIAGO

Sunday, February 24, 3:07 a.m.

"A toast!" Reese raised her skewer, complete with flaming marshmallow, out of the fire.

Nari giggled. "Toast. That's punny."

"Puns are the discharge of humor, Nari," said Reese. "Goldenrod and olive's diseased baby." The firelight lit her turquoise hair, exaggerating its green tint. Her marshmallow, now a flaming ball of char, fell off her skewer into the fire. "But, seriously. Congrats, guys. Senior swim season over!"

Keag, lounging across from me on a bench made of old downhill skis with Nari tucked in tight to his chest and staring at her phone, lifted his skewer out of the fire and knocked the end with Reese's. I did the same, then grabbed a marshmallow out of the half-empty bag, stabbed it onto the end of my stick, and held it over a cache of coals. The heat and color and flames, the February night air and quiet company, were mesmerizing. It didn't hurt that it was also a little after three in the morning and I'd been up since around six a.m. with everything in between: the actual swim meet where I swam in two relays and won the individual hundred-yard fly and diving; the last bus ride back; the party at Mike's that we'd all left around one, piling into Reese's dad's car so she could drive us back here for one final post-State huddle around the fire pit in Keag's backyard.

I rolled my skewer between my fingers and thumb, spinning my marshmallow in a slow rotation near the coals. The air was cold and obvious, a tangible weight, a heavy curtain held back by the dry swell of the heat from the fire. When I turned my face away from the flames toward the darkness, my breath clouded. *Senior swim season over.*

I felt . . . I felt both enormous and diminished, proud and deflated. I'd swum my career-best times in every event today, had won diving by a double-digit margin with my career-best score. When I climbed out of the pool after my final dive, dripping water, muscles shaking, as the crowd and I waited for the judges' scores, when they finally held up their cards, near-perfect numbers securing my win, when the crowd cheered, I'd felt full, brimming. I'd held my chamois to my face, overwhelmed, and when I dropped it found Bellamy's eyes in the crowd. On her feet, cheering for me between Reese and Nari, she met my eyes, too. Her smile made my heart swell.

It was bittersweet, a contradiction, a double-edged sword. Because Bellamy smiling at me, cheering me on beside Reese and Nari while my parents hadn't come to State at all, was a reminder of that schism, of how my successes are tinged by their disapproval. Disapproval for succeeding. I know how unreasonable that sounds. But it isn't the concept of my succeeding they take issue with, it's the breed of my success, a success that leads to more opportunities for failure than it does opportunities to succeed.

It's my dream, a dream so big it requires a semidelusional level of devotion, the confidence to know I can do it and the humility to accept how many times I'll have to fail to get there. A dream that is literally, according to Bells's math showing that the odds of winning a gold medal at the Olympics are around twenty-two million to one, a bad bet. A dream that lives behind a wall in my head, a wall so coated in doubt, the layers so thick, so robust, that no matter how many times I try to knock it down, the wall still stands. Because it's my doubt and also my parents'. Because it's my dream, but it isn't theirs. Because according to my parents, my dream is utterly impractical. An unnecessary risk, an expensive, time- and energy-consuming risk. Because más vale pájaro en mano que cien volando, *one bird in hand is worth more than a hundred flying,* or a bird in the hand is worth two in the bush.

Whatever language you say it in, the idea is the same. They don't think I should risk realistic goals chasing an unrealistic one. To them, you don't risk guaranteed moderate success by pursuing uncertain grand success. You don't leave your friends and family and all you know in Mexico to move to a new country, to build a stable and secure life for yourself and your future children, only to watch one of those children risk the accessible opportunities you worked hard to earn on likely inaccessible ones. You don't get into Stanford on a diving scholarship only to risk the education you'll get there stretching yourself too thin with extra practices, extra competitions, extra distractions, trying to qualify for the Olympics. You do your best, get good grades, earn your degree, then come back home and get to work.

You don't reach for the stars when you should keep your feet on the ground.

My marshmallow bubbled and browned. I pulled it from the heat and held it out to Bellamy, slouched back in the camp chair to my left, the flames reflected in her glasses. She pulled the toasted outer shell off the end of my skewer, leaving the wad of uncooked middle, and put the whole thing in her mouth.

I tried and failed to read her expression in the dim light. More bittersweetness, another of life's dichotomies to have had her worst day and my best back to back. Keag and I had been so busy with State that this was the first time we'd all been in the quiet together since she'd heard about not getting funding, and now the subject felt taboo. Too much between Bellamy and me felt taboo, or at least tentative. As though there was some form-less barrier between us, one that'd been changing texture for the last six months and that I couldn't quite overcome. Some-times it felt like trying to motivate myself to get out of my warm bed on a cold morning. I wanted to start the day, to get moving toward all the possibilities of what could happen next. But our friendship was so comfortable, so easy, so certain, and what if the morning ended up only being cold?

But that was just courage and timing, willing myself to fi-nally take a chance. This thing with her dad and MIT was . . . devastating.

I took a slow, deep breath and held the gooey innards of my marshmallow back over the coals. "It feels like the first of the lasts."

My friends nodded, even Nari, finally looking up from her phone. Reese snuggled deeper into one of the wicker chairs we'd moved over from the porch, wrapping her blanket tighter around herself. "The end of the beginning," she said. "And the start of the middle, where the story finally gets good." I noticed her flick a glance at Bellamy to see if her comment had unintentionally stung, but Bells's expression didn't change.

"I'll toast to that," said Nari, and held up an imaginary glass from within her and Keag's cocoon. They got together sophomore year and have been inseparable ever since. Keagan-and-Nari, Nari-and-Keagan, a pair made singular, like pants.

I pulled my marshmallow away from the coals, blew on it, and popped it into my mouth. It was perfect, crisp and sticky and almost too hot. A log shifted, emitting a puff of sparks into the still air. Beside me, Bellamy yawned, covering her mouth with her hand, then said, "Painted Pig."

Reese smiled wide. "Yeeess."

Painted Pig, or Split Pig, depending on the mood, is our very own role-playing game of hypotheticals. It works like this: The winner of the last game poses the hypothetical, sets the parameters; then we each take turns adding a layer, continuing the story until someone "wins." Usually, with Painted Pig, winning means achieving the most innovative version of success, such as we all win the lottery and whoever does the coolest, most original thing with the money, while avoiding the pitfalls of sudden wealth, is the winner. In Split Pig, the winner is whoever survives. For example, in the last game, Reese was the only one of us to survive a hypothetical zombie apocalypse after setting our stronghold on fire and waiting out the barbecue of the reanimated on the roof atop an elevator shaft that remained structurally sound. Nari and I weren't so lucky. Keagan and Bellamy, by that point, were part of the horde.

Keagan shifted, sitting up straighter on the bench. Nari checked her phone again, then tucked it into the pocket of her hoodie. "Who won last time?" he asked.

"Me!" Reese cheered. She leaned forward, still swaddled tight, and tapped her lips with a finger. Her eyes glazed as she stared at the fire, deep in thought. "Okay, got it. Brain tech. Like *Feed.*"

So, Split Pig for sure. We'd all read *Feed*, a book by M. T. Anderson set in a future where the population is permanently plugged into a consumer communication network through a chip in their brains, in English last year and Reese had been obsessed ever since. She even did a whole series of organic/mechanical mash-up paintings that were both impressively disturbing and plain impressive.

Reese took a sip from her water bottle, then continued, "How about, say, half of Americans already have it. Shopping, entertainment, news, social media—everything's moving to it. So. Do you want one? Do you not? Do you resist until the inescapable pressure to conform and join the masses finally gets to you? Do you go full-on paranoid and start digging out a bunker in the woods? Nari, go!"

Half an hour later, we were in the midst of a cyborg-versus-human civil war after the tech was hacked by a cadre of ecoterrorists. Hypothetical Nari, the leader of said ecoterrorists, whose hack accidentally created the cyborgs, was killed when her lair was overrun by one of the first cyborg gangs, or "death by irony," as Bells called it. Hypothetical Bellamy was overtaken by her tech when it erased her personality after the network spawned its own AI. Hypothetical me met the same fate. The remaining players, Keagan and Reese, squared off on opposite sides of the divide, brought together by a clever trap devised by Keagan at the cyborgs' epicenter: their main server. Keagan, using software written by Nari before she died, spoke to Reese through one of her own hijacked minions.

"We are few, but we're powerful, Reese," Keagan said. "You and your ilk—" He looked to Nari. This was a game of theirs: Keagan stretching his vocabulary with words that he learned from a word-a-day app and that no one really needs to know or use beyond taking the ACT or SAT, while Nari awarded him imaginary points.

"Five and half," Nari said.

"—should surrender while you still can."

Reese scoffed. "There are, like, eight of you left, Keagy. And while this hijacking software's cute and all, I'm master of the AI, which means I'm the master of every surviving cyborg. You should just give up already and join me."

Keagan shrugged. "Nah. I think instead I'll pull out this *dart gun*." He threw off his and Nari's blanket and mimed pulling out a gun. "Filled with darts armed with *microchips*. That I then shoot you in the face with! Spreading a computer virus to the hardware in your brain, which then destroys your precious cyborg army through your own network!" He jumped up and down, pumping a fist in the air, then faked a show of meekness and uncertainty. "You know, if that sounds like it works."

"Jury?" I asked, looking to Bells.

"As we're already assuming the existence of biologically compatible nanorobotic technology, a dart carrying nanobots coded with the necessary malware to an area of skin near the original brain implant?" She lifted a shoulder. "Sure, could work. Nari?"

20

"What she said."

"Fine! I give up! You win!" Reese threw her hands up. "Also, yeah. Good one. And people?" She stood, shedding her blanket and leaving it wadded up in the chair. "It's like four in the morning. I'm out."

With that, the rest of us started moving, slowly unfolding, stretching, standing. The fire had burned down to coals. Keagan doused them with the bucket of water he always kept on hand, and they hissed and steamed. The cool air seemed to push in around us, like it'd been waiting impatiently to take the place of the heat. Keag offered his hand to Nari, who waved at us and followed him inside.

Reese pulled her dad's car keys from her pocket. "Either of you need a ride?"

I shook my head. "I left my car here before State," I said. Bellamy looked to me, and the fact that she did tightened my gut in that nervous, delighted way reserved for Bells. "And I can give Bellamy a ride. Bells?"

Bellamy nodded. "Sure. 'Night, Reese."

Reese gave us a quick salute and turned to leave as Bells and I looked back at the fire pit, watching the last of the smoke and steam rise from the extinguished coals with the porch light at our backs, the sky overcast and the clouds glowing with the town's light above us.

"So," I said.

Bells grinned and turned her attention to me. "So." She's beautiful. Unlike Nari, who's striking and so carefully tailored, or like Reese, who's interesting and hyperconfident, Bellamy is beautiful in an effortless, sky-is-blue, water-is-wet way, and I'm in love with her.

It's her lips, full and soft and petal pink, and more so the brilliance that comes out of them. Bellamy is one of those people you "knew when"—utterly exceptional, an outlier, the kind of person who will help change the world. And one of my favorite things about her is that if I told her I thought as much, she wouldn't argue. She might offer qualifications or caveats, but she wouldn't wallow through a mire of faux humility, which isn't to say she's arrogant or acts as though she's superior, but when you tell her she's extraordinary, she'll accept that you're right, then remind you that "the first definition of 'extraordinary' is more literal than the colloquial sense of excellence."

It's also because being with her is like the moment I hit the water after a successful dive. In that second, my nerves still. The water catches me, holds me. My heart, thrumming as I bounded off the end of the board, as I tucked and twisted and turned, slows. My body is the exhale after a held breath, the quiet after a clap of thunder, the steam rising off the rain-soaked sidewalk after a storm. Being alone with her like this, I felt it, the passion, the triumph, the calm and relief and quiet. I felt all of it.

"Do you want to talk about it?" I asked.

"MIT?"

I nodded. "Sorry to bring it up if the answer's no."

She inhaled deeply and heaved a full-body sigh. I stepped closer but didn't reach for her even though I ached to. The barrier felt thick, viscous. "I don't—" She shook her head. "I don't know what to do about it."

I scrubbed my hands on my beanie, using it to scratch my newly shaved head. "You haven't tried to call your dad or anything?" All I knew, from Keag, who'd been the recipient of

Nari's flurry of angry texts over the last day, was that because of Bellamy's dad's apparently impressive finances, she'd been denied any need-based funding. And because of that, she'd decided she wouldn't be able to go to MIT after all.

"Nari told me to call him up screaming," she said, and huffed a half laugh. "Force him to pay my tuition since he's the reason I can't get aid."

"But?"

"But." She hugged her arms tightly around her chest. "I've never talked to him, San. Not once. Biologically, I'm his daughter, but . . ." She shrugged, not loosening the circle of her arms around herself. "I'm an automatic child-support debit from one of his accounts. And now I'm supposed to call him up begging for a shitload of money?"

"But. Isn't he some big-deal investor or something?" *Big-deal investor or something* was a bit of an understatement. According to one of Nari's texts, there was a building in San Francisco's financial district with his name on it. We'd all known that Bells's dad was and always had been out of the picture. But before Friday, I honestly couldn't remember ever wondering anything about him, let alone what he did or how much money he had. He was a nonentity in Bells's life. Until now. "And, he's still your dad. Doesn't he . . . owe it to you?"

"He's not my dad," she said. "He's a genetic component, a spermatozoon. It doesn't matter who he is. His contribution's done."

KEAGAN

Sunday, February 24, 9:48 a.m.

I kissed up Nari's neck from her shoulder to the spot beneath her chin that's so ticklish. She squirmed beneath me, giggling, then laughing harder until she started doing that quiet gasping thing she hates but is cuter than a puppy and a baby hippo being best friends.

I moved my weight to my elbows, hovering above her with the blanket pulled up over us. The flannel snagged on the sandpaper that was my recently shaved head. Her long dark hair spread out in a tangle across my pillow. The T-shirt she wore—mine, my first uniform tee from my job at the pizza shop, now super soft and faded from half a million washes—was wrinkled.

I pressed the tip of my nose into the hollow beneath her ear. "How late can you stay?"

She ran her hands up my bare back. "Forever."

"Aw!" I pulled my head back and batted my eyelashes. "I'm blushing."

She leaned up to inspect my cheeks. "Liar." Then she flopped her head back onto my pillow. "But really, ten? Or whenever. They think I'm at Bells's, so . . ."

So I leaned down and kissed her some more. This time there was minimal giggling.

Later we lay on our backs, her head on my shoulder, me staring at the water damage above my window and she at her phone. Ah, Nari and her phone. Or should I say *d0l0s* and her phone? They, whoever "they" are, say the average person checks his/her/their phone every three minutes. I saw that somewhere or someone told me or who really cares, but basically most people are totally addicted to their phones. A-dick-ted. But while most people are, I don't know, playing games? Scrolling through Twitter? Making a Snapchat story about the number of rainbow marshmallows versus clover marshmallows in their cereal? Do I sound middle-aged yet? Ha ha. Nari calls me a Luddite, but I don't *hate* technology. And even my grandma tweets now. So it's not really my premature elderliness either. More that if I'm going to waste my time, I'm going waste it by, like, staring at nothing or going on a hike or playing an Xbox game with Bells that we've both already beat. I'm a purist like that.

Anyway, my point.

My *point* is that Nari stares at her phone as much as or more than most people, but it's not like she's taking quizzes to find out which Disney princess she'd be post apocalypse based on her dessert preferences or anything. No, she's doing d0l0s stuff involving . . . uh, yeah. Coding? Minor espionage and extralegal social justice on the Darknet with the members of her oh-so-secret Internet Relay Chat group? Or reading the news. She reads lots of news.

"What're you looking at?" I tapped the back of her phone with my free hand.

She locked it, brought it to her chest, and sighed. "Secrets."

"Scintillating secrets?"

She flipped over onto her stomach, rested her crossed arms on my chest, and grinned. "Scintillating?"

I lifted my head to fold my flat old pillow in half, propping myself up a little. "Five points?"

"Seven-five."

"Kick-ass! You can tell I'm happy from my *dazzling* smile."

Nari shifted her head off her arms to lay her ear on my bare chest.

"Seriously, though," I said. "What's up?"

Another sigh. "It's just so *unfair*."

"What? State?"

She scoffed. Probably because we'd gotten an altogether expected and respectable third at State. I even placed ninth in the backstroke. Career best and a rather satisfying end to my swimming tenure, if I say so myself. I was going to miss swimming. Not the getting-ninth-place part. That was cool and all, but I don't have that competitive organ that people like Nari and San and Reese have. Though Reese's is more, uh, combative? Not so much violent, more like aggressive. Reese versus Bland Mediocrity. What I liked was the team part. Winning together, losing together, pushing ourselves so hard during peak that at least five of us puked together. You know, camaraderie.

But I digress. "Right. Not State," I said. "Bellamy."

She sat up. "Yes, Bellamy! Jesus, do you *know* how rich her dad is?"

"No. Wait. Do you?"

"*Rich* rich, Keagan. Private islands rich. Island-*za*. Plural."

"Nari. You said Bells told you not to—"

"I didn't do anything. Not yet. I just—"

And my door swung open. No knock, no heavy footsteps, just "Good morning!"

I yanked the comforter up to our chins, covering Nari's and my bare, um, everything. "Uh, good morning, Mom."

"Hi, Paisley," Nari said, blushing. Though on a scale of parent-mortification from one to set me on fire, this was barely a three. Three-point-two, tops. Meaning we'd been through worse. Oh, had we been through worse.

My mom leaned against my doorframe. "You guys have a good night?"

Dear God.

Nari smoothed her hair with both hands and nodded.

"Use protection?"

Yup. There it is.

"Because I haven't checked the box in the bathroom in a while, and if you need more condoms, just—"

"Mom."

"Keagan, I know some people find it embarrassing, but if you're prepared to have sex, you should be prepared to talk about the logis—"

"*Mom.* We get it. We got it. We're good. Okay?"

"O-kaaay," she sang as she turned back into the hallway, voice receding as she continued, "*I don't want no gra-and-ba-beeees,*" to the tune of "Satisfaction" by the Rolling Stones. Then, from the kitchen, she yelled, "Not yet! Someday in the future? Ten years? Fifteen? Fine!"

Nari curled into a ball on my bed, burying her face in my comforter. I got up to close the door.

Again, three-point-two. Because no, this was not the first time Nari had stayed over. And no, this was not the first Sermon of the Prophylactics, as Nari affectionately called them, that we'd suffered through. Though, for the others—one Nari titled The Pill, or Thanks, We Already Know Where Babies Come From, and another, less prevention-based, that she called Mechanics: Don't Be Selfish Just Because the Media and Entertainment Tell Everyone That's the Default If You're a Guy—we were both fully clothed. And not in my bedroom. Or in my bed. Okay, four-point-seven. Maybe a solid five.

But that's my mom. And my dad. It's the peer-parenting thing they do. The mostly hands-off, friend-parent vibe they're always aiming for. It's cool. For the most part. The trust me and treat me as an equal part? Grand. The walk in on me and my girlfriend in bed sans knocking, then start up a convo about condoms part? Less grand.

I closed my bedroom door. "Uh . . . sorry?" I crossed back to my bed. "Yeah, I'll go with 'sorry.' "

Nari sat up, mouth open, hands on her cheeks in a spot-on impression of *The Scream* by Edvard Munch. "Wow," she breathed.

"Hey." I leaned down and kissed her forehead. "At least it wasn't as bad as Anatomy. There was no diagr—"

"*Erh! Erh! Erh!*" Nari sounded off, mimicking an alarm.

I laughed. "Okay, okay. Never to be repeated."

Eyes wide, she mouthed, *Ever.*

"Ever," I said. "Promise."

She crawled out of bed, pulled a fresh set of clothes—neatly folded leggings, flowy shirt, even a different pair of shoes—from the bag she'd brought, and started to change.

"Leaving?" I asked.

"Dressing," she countered.

I watched her. Which sounds totally creepy, but I wasn't *watching* her watching her, more like waiting for her to fill in her own blank. The one that started with "I just—" and ended with something along the lines of "did a little hacking, cyber-spying, morally gray digging using less-than-legal means."

"You gonna make me ask?"

She finished buttoning her blouse and pulled a hairbrush from her bag. "Nothing big, okay? I just poked around a little. Answered some questions."

"Questions like?"

Using the black screen of my ancient desktop as a mirror, she brushed through her long hair, then bound it up in a knot with an improbable twist of her wrist. "He wouldn't even notice. It'd be like one of us buying a pack of gum. Freaking *pocket change*."

I grabbed a pair of shorts and a clean T-shirt from the pile of laundry on the back of my desk chair. It was a shirt from State sophomore year. The screen-printed swimmer decal was starting to crack, which was a total bummer as it's my favorite of my very many swim tees, since sophomore year was the season I first qualified to actually swim at State. It was also the first year San scored first in diving, so double favorite? Because I'm one of San's proudest fans. Like, I'll *proudly* tattoo GO SAN and the Olympic rings on my forehead if—no, *when*—he makes that dream come true. He will. Which might make a friend of lesser moral fiber than myself jealous or at least a little competitive if not slightly bitter, three things I'm solidly not. Mostly because swimming is not my capital-D Dream. It was a thing to do that I for the most part enjoyed. But truthfully, I don't really have any dreams or even goals, for that matter. Maybe to have a job I like that pays me more than I need to cover my bills? So I don't have to work two jobs like Bells's mom or pick through the stack for whatever's most urgent and/or overdue like my parents do some months?

Wow. That took a turn, right? Where'd this even start? My T-shirt?

I pulled the shirt over my head. "He wouldn't notice what, Nari?"

She paused while applying fresh mascara in the computer screen's reflection and looked at me. "Paying for her tuition, Keagan."

My eyebrows rose. "He wouldn't notice a quarter-million dollars?"

"Island-za, Keagy. His vacation home in Jackson Hole cost twenty times that much."

"Great! Then all Bells needs to do is call him and ask."

Nari tilted her head and arched an eyebrow at me.

"Why is that not the answer?" I asked. "She's his daughter. He's her father. If he really has that kind of money, why wouldn't he help her out?"

"It's not that simple, Keagan. She doesn't want to. And why should she have to? He bailed. He's gone. Why should she have to beg for anything from the guy who abandoned her? Plus he filled out that paperwork. Or one of his minions did, at least. Which means he knows she's trying to go to MIT and has still done shit-all."

"So, a couple phone calls, then." I smiled. "Okay, maybe some light coercion."

She pursed her lips, utterly unamused, then carefully packed yesterday's clothes into her bag. I waited for her to argue with me, to push her point. Which she didn't. . . . Well, know that saying about hindsight?

She finished tucking her stuff into her bag and turned to me. "Which wins, waffles or pancakes?"

I grinned. Apart from the vocabulary thing, Which Wins was my favorite of our games. "Pancakes. Perfect pillowy pancakes."

She opened my door and started down the hall. "You think alliteration will trick me? Waffles win, no contest. Built-in mini syrup troughs!"

I followed. "Scrumptious circular sugar stacks!"

"*Sugar* stacks? Foul. Point deduction. Automatic waffle win."

BELLAMY

Sunday, February 24, 2:30 p.m.

There are an estimated 100 billion planets in the Milky Way, roughly ten percent of which are terrestrial. A minimum of 1,500 of these are within fifty light-years of Earth. Taking observable conditions into consideration, such as quiet versus active stars and mass and temperatures comparable to Earth's, one of the closest terrestrial planets with a possibility for human habitation, however slight, is Ross 128 b, located a mere eleven light-years away. But as a light-year, a unit of distance calculated using the speed of light in a vacuum, i.e., how far light travels in one year, measures approximately 5.88 trillion miles, those eleven light-years set Ross 128 b around 64.68 trillion miles from Earth. Which means that traveling at, for example, 36,000 mph, the speed at which the *New Horizons* probe left Earth's orbit, it would take current technology around 1.8 billion hours, or nearly 205,500 years, or, at eighty years per, over 2,500 human life spans to reach it.

In other words, the obstacles between us and the colonization of another Earth-like planet, between us and shifting the course of human existence, expanding it beyond the confines of our singular planet, are utterly insurmountable. The stuff of fiction and wishes. But I don't believe in wishing. For progress. For change. Just as I've never wished for my life to change. Not because I've never wanted anything, like narrower hips or higher cheekbones, or possessions like my own car or a Celestron CPC 1100 Catadioptric telescope, or different circumstances so my mom could make more money and quit her second job. I want those things, but I won't wish for them. Because wishing is passive. And impractical. And a substitute for actual effort. I'd like to have my own car, but I can ride the bus. It'd be nice to own a Celestron telescope, but I can use the equipment at the university where I take courses after school and during the summers. I don't like that my mom has to work such long hours, so my plan was to pursue my passions into a career where I'd make enough money that she wouldn't have to.

What I believe in are real actions facilitating real solutions. I believe in processes, in making observations, formulating hypotheses, gathering data, developing theories. I believe in identifying problems and designing solutions. In taking steps, such as from our current interplanetary travel technology toward the near light-speed technology we'll need to expand our species' reach. Such as from my current circumstance with its big goals and financial restrictions toward a future with bigger goals and fewer restraints.

MIT was my solution. It was my next step. Was.

"What would you name your direwolf and what color would it be?" Nari asked.

"Throat Opener," I said, "and black. So the blood wouldn't show."

"Nice." She reached for the tray of Oreos on the coffee table and took three. We were at my apartment, watching the first season of *Game of Thrones* for maybe the seventh time while we waited for everyone else. On the screen, Tyrion rode the elevator up to the top of the Wall.

"You?" I asked, though I already knew her answer.

"No wolf," she mumbled, mouth full, and together we said, "I'm Daenerys."

She stuffed another cookie into her mouth and smiled at me, cream filling and black crumbs in her teeth. "Minus the 'sold into marriage by my dick brother' thing, of course," she continued. "Death by molten crown is cool and all, but screw character development. I'd have taken him out first thing."

"What about Drogo?"

She shrugged. "I'd arrange that business myself. Or find a less rapey and gruesomely tragic way to get my dragons."

"So it's all about the dragons, then."

"Obviously. Bitches with dragons get shit done!"

Nari is the original reason we're friends, which is unsurprising as Nari is the reason for a lot of things. We met in Ms. Mitchell's second-grade class when Nari noticed we both had the same *Star Wars* folder and decided we should be best friends by declaring, "We're best friends now." Ten years later, we still are.

She took a few more cookies from the tray, split one, and licked off its filling. Her knee bounced, shaking the couch.

"Nervous?" I asked.

She narrowed her eyes at me. "Anxious."

34

"Near synonym."

She rolled her eyes and popped the licked cookie halves into her mouth. "Excited, then."

"About what?"

Nari shoved two whole additional cookies into her mouth and chewed. And chewed. And chewed.

"Was that necessary?" I asked.

She finally finished chewing and swallowed before leaning over to loop her arm through mine. "Patience, dearest Bellamy. All will be revealed in good time."

"Fine. I'll wait," I said, and she gave me a sloppy kiss on the cheek.

Nari seems a contradiction. The polished way she dresses and her self-possession are at odds with her humor and tendency to eat cookies until she makes herself feel sick. I've wondered what it's like to be able to tailor oneself for different circumstances. Narioka, the daughter and student; d0l0s in the IRCs; Nari, the friend and girlfriend; Dr. Okada, Narioka Diane, and whoever else she decides to be, while I'm only me.

The door opened and Keagan and Santiago walked in. Keagan leaned over and kissed Nari before sitting in the narrow space between us on the couch. Santiago pulled a chair over from the kitchen table and set it by the end near me. They both wore beanies over their shaved heads. San smiled at me, arched one thick black eyebrow, and nodded toward Nari in silent question. I shook my head to answer that I didn't know what was going on either.

"Where's Reese the Piece?" Keag asked, and Nari elbowed him in the ribs.

He flinched, knocking into me. "Hey! She said she's taking

it back! Owning it." "Reese the Piece" is a nickname Barret Tundle gave Reese when she turned him down after they went on a date freshman year. It rhymes, so it stuck. Which is a proud testament to the intelligence of Barret and his friends. "Besides," Keag continued, "I didn't say a piece of *what*. How about Reese the Piece of *Molten Titanium*?" He said the last two words in the dramatic voice of a wrestling announcer.

"Molten titanium is, um, you know, *molten*, Keags," Nari said. "Less than intimidating."

"But she could burn someone, right, Bells?" He looked at me, eyes widened, asking for help.

"Titanium has a melting point of about three thousand degrees Fahrenheit."

San breathed a laugh and smiled his wide, beautiful smile at me again. My stomach flipped. "How do you know that?" he asked. "How is that a thing you just *know*?"

I shrugged. "Molten titanium also explodes when it reacts with water. Or, it breaks down the water, absorbing the oxygen and releasing the hydrogen, which then explodes when it comes into contact with air. So, really, the hydrogen explodes, but still."

Reese stepped into the apartment through the door the boys had left open. "What explodes?"

"Molten titanium," said San.

She closed the door and crossed the small living room to the kitchen nook to grab another chair. Keagan grinned at her. "That's your new nickname: Reese the Piece of *Molten Titanium*," he said, using the voice again.

"Kick-ass," she said, pulling her chair up next to San's. "I should figure out how to dye my hair like quicksilver and put that on a shirt."

I looked at Nari while the other three laughed. The episode had circled back around to Tyrion's narrative, but though she was staring at the screen, she didn't seem to be paying attention.

"Nari," San said. He leaned forward to rest his forearms on his thighs. The chair was too small for his height. He'd pulled it up close enough to the couch that his clasped hands nearly brushed my knee. "What's up? I mean, I love you guys and all, but I'm also kind of sick of you? So this better be good."

"Freaking *epic*," Reese said.

"Legendary," added Keagan.

"Is 'legendary' a one-up from 'epic'?" San asked. "Because it seems like 'epic' "—he flashed his hands—"is, you know, *epic*."

"Yeah," Reese said, "and I was planning on binge-watching some early seasons of *Game of Thrones*." She waved at the TV. "Not whatever *this* garbage is."

"Ha ha—you're all so very funny," Nari said. She made a show of sitting up and squaring her hips on the sagging couch cushion. "Okay. Prepare yourselves."

Keagan leaned forward for the remote on the coffee table and turned off the TV. The rest of us waited while she let the suspense build.

"So," she finally said. "You all know how Bells's dad is a point oh-one-percenter, and how as of Friday that's basically screwed Bellamy out of MIT?"

I froze.

The others nodded.

A few points of context: One, my mom and I are poor. I understand that "poor" is a loaded term with a range of connotations and interpretations. I don't say "impoverished," because my mom's income, from two jobs totaling an average of sixty to sixty-five hours a week, sets us solidly above the Federal Poverty Level though still definitively within the lower class.

Two, my parents conceived me as teenagers. My mom was seventeen and about to finish her junior year of high school. My father, Robert Foster, a senior, was preparing to attend Columbia in the fall. He left five months before I was born and, other than sending a monthly child-support check of a minimal amount, agreed upon in my infancy and never amended, has never had any contact with me. My mom dropped out of high school to raise me, eventually earning her GED and entering the workforce. Robert Foster went from Columbia for his undergraduate in finance to Yale, where he earned an MBA, to Wall Street, where he earned his first millions short trading high-risk stocks, to Silicon Valley, where he began Foster Innovations, a venture capital firm with primary interests in tech startups and luxury lifestyle brands.

Three, after finding out I got accepted at MIT, my mom and I filed my financial aid paperwork, including requesting, through my mom's and his lawyers, that Robert Foster fill out some forms of his own, which skewed my supposed familial contribution to MIT's nearly $50,000 yearly tuition to one hundred percent. Which is fiscally prohibitive. Loans might've been an option, but my mom's bulk of credit card debt and bad credit rating inflated our interest rates. And I refuse to risk a guaranteed debt of $70,000 after adding room and board, or more than a quarter million total, depending on changes in aid after the child support stops when I turn eighteen, plus living expenses, on the inevitably uncertain nature of my future. I also refused to beg for a handout from a man who clearly wanted nothing to do with me, and not only because the idea of asking Robert Foster for anything was debasing but because I . . . I'd done it *right*. I had done *everything* right, solved every step, worked for every correct answer, passed every test. Only to end up at a dead end of someone else's making. Only to end up here:

"Well." Nari took a dramatic deep breath. "I have an idea."

PART 2

BELLAMY

Sunday, February 24
33 Days

"Hell yes!" Reese cheered once Nari finished outlining the fundamentals of her plan. "The adventure to win all adventures!"

"*Adventure?*" Keagan was on his feet. Soon after Nari had started talking, he'd moved from the couch to pace the worn carpet between the hallway and the door. "This is a felony! *Multiple* felonies. Don't encourage her, Reese."

"Don't 'encourage' me?" Nari snapped. "Are you *kidding?* It's a good idea. The *only* idea!"

"Hey," San said, hands raised, palms up and placating, "let's just—"

"It is *so* not the only idea." Keagan scrubbed his head with his beanie, then pulled it off and threw it on the floor in agitation. "How about *talking* to the guy. Bellamy, he's your dad. Why not just *call* him?"

Call him.

I felt it in my head, in my ears. It's a chemical reaction. I know this. But it felt like heat and shrinking. It'd felt the same when Nari first suggested the idea on Friday, the same again

43

when she'd volunteered to call him up herself before I talked her down and she, apparently, shifted focus. And it was equally intense now, equally repugnant. Calling Robert Foster, not only claiming him as my father, certifying myself as his daughter, but then asking him for *anything,* let alone an enormous sum of money, was something I physically did not want to do.

"Again, Keag. *Why?*" Nari challenged. "She's not the one who bailed!"

"This is *stealing*, Narioka. Grand theft."

"Like he'll even notice," Reese said. "He's not the victim here—Bellamy is."

"I'm not . . ."

San glanced at me, but I was still trying to swallow and breathe properly, so I looked away. "It's not about being a victim," he said. "It's about fixing a wrong."

Keagan's eyebrows rose. "'Fixing'?"

"You think it's right that Bells's dad has helped them out so little?" San asked gently. "And that he's the reason she can't go to MIT now?"

"No, dude. Of course not. But, come on! *This?*"

"This" was Nari's plan to steal my college tuition from Robert Foster using malware she'd code to skim a fraction of a percentage off transactions made by the various bank accounts of Foster Innovations. "I saw it on some nineties movie," she'd said as she explained.

"A movie," Keag repeated, expression slack.

"Yep."

"And how'd that work out in the end?"

She'd shrugged. "A building burned down. Or one of the characters set it on fire. I don't know. Can't remember, doesn't matter." Because, she'd stressed, the idea was to do it all remotely. For her to infiltrate Foster's online banking accounts from her system at home, route the stolen money into an account opened with a false identity, buy Bitcoin with those funds, then sell the Bitcoin for USD and deposit the balance into an account in my name. The fact that she was telling all of us, instead of doing it on her own or only telling me, was proof of our friendship.

"Listen," Nari said. "Can we just calm down? Keag?" They met eyes, communicating in that way of theirs, and he sat on the floor, cross-legged and fidgeting with his beanie in his lap. "I get it, okay? It's illegal. It's scary. But think about it. If it's reparations? Is it really *wrong*?"

I cleared my throat. It still felt thick. "Yes."

Nari turned to me, looking betrayed. I broke eye contact and leaned back into the couch. Still turned toward me, she said, "Jeremy and Evan Foster."

"Who?" Reese asked.

"Jeremy and Evan Foster," Nari repeated, still speaking directly at me. "Jeremy's eight and Evan is ten. Their mom is Emily Foster, mid-thirties, beautiful. She and your dad met at Yale when he was getting his master's and she was doing her undergrad in art history or English or some other M.R.S. degree. She does charity work now. Very cliché. The boys go to private school. Expensive, pre-pre-Ivy private school."

"What does any of that matter?" Keagan asked. He stared at the carpet, head down. Like San's, his shaved scalp was paler than his face and neck.

"It matters because he could give Bells everything she's ever wanted in the world and then some, but he doesn't. He knows she's here, he knows she's trying to go to MIT, yet he *still* doesn't help. And now, because of him, she can't afford to go." She paused. When she spoke again, her tone was fervent. "But we can fix that."

We quieted. Someone crossed the living room in the apartment above mine with a heavy tread. I tried not to, but I pictured my half brothers. I wondered what they looked like, if they were short like me, had brown hair like mine. But they wouldn't, would they? Because I looked like my mom, and maybe they looked like theirs.

"I'll call."

"Bells—"

"I'll call," I said again, looking Nari in the eye, and reached for my phone on the coffee table.

"You know his number?" Reese asked. Her voice, though a normal volume, sounded loud against the others' quiet.

"No. But the internet will."

For a dollar and his full name and zip code, finding the number for Robert Foster's landline at his San Francisco home took less than a minute on one of those people-finder sites.

I held myself as still as possible on the couch, staring at it, feeling my heart rate, plateaued at around one hundred ten beats per minute, in my chest. I'd never thought waiting could be so *loud*. The five of us breathing. Reese suppressing a cough. Keagan picking at a threadbare patch in the carpet. Santiago's chair creaking as he shifted, even the dry sound of him rubbing his palms together nervously. Silence like this is never truly silent. It's the absence of talking. It's quiet. But it's also the hum of our old refrigerator and the cars driving past on the road outside, the downstairs neighbor's TV and someone slamming a door down the hall.

Silence, true silence, the silence of a near-perfect vacuum, was the first thing I loved about space.

When I first read about it, in a book about the basics of space my grandma gave me in the first grade, I felt my tiny world explode. Learning that the construct of my reality, what I understood of it and took, as a six-year-old, duly, for granted, was not the *only* construct, that the universe was so huge, so varied, so incredibly *possible*, made me feel infinite.

This did not make me feel infinite.

This made me feel minuscule.

I tapped the number, clicked call, and lifted my phone to my ear as it rang.

And rang.

Sunday afternoon. What were the chances that he was even home? That if he was, he'd be the one to answer?

Another ring. San, Keagan, Nari, and Reese were so quiet, they might've been holding their breath.

Another, and my thoughts stalled, white noise.

"Hello?" A man's voice.

I opened my mouth.

"Hello?" he asked again, slightly annoyed.

"Mr. Foster?"

"Yes?"

"It's —" I cleared my throat. "This is Bellamy Bishop?"

No answer.

"Lauren Bishop's daughter?"

A pause.

Then:

Click.

He'd hung up on me.

A breath caught in my throat, half inhale, half exhale. I brought the phone down from my ear. Held it in my lap. Waiting. For . . . him to call back? For him to have not hung up on me? I tried to talk myself through the processes of my nervous system, the names of the hormones rushing through my blood.

"He hung up on you?" Reese asked, shrill.

My head felt hollow.

"Bells," San was saying, soft and close, while Nari leaned forward to look at Keagan where he still sat on the floor and said, *"See?* Is that enough now? He *deserves* to pay."

The way she said it, almost righteous, almost validated, I— I swallowed. My spit tasted like bile.

Keagan didn't answer, didn't look up at Nari or me. I knew I should've answered for him. No. The answer was no, it wasn't enough. Not for this. Not for a felony. Not for me.

But I couldn't make my mouth and jaw and vocal cords work. Not when Santiago said, "Okay. We know the why. Time to tell us the rest of the how."

Not when Nari's expression lifted.

Not as I listened to her talk about code and accounts and firewalls and percentages, about timelines and security cracks and how she'd tried Friday night but hadn't managed to root the system yet. Not as she talked about how deep she'd already gotten into his life, how she'd traced Foster Innovations' bank statements back for six months and figured that by coding the malware to skim .01 percent, one cent of every one hundred dollars, off transactions over a million dollars to avoid detection, assuming FI did business comparable to the previous two fiscal quarters, that "We should hit two hundred fifty thousand within a year. And definitely have enough for Bells to make her first tuition payment by the deadline."

"A year?" Keagan asked. "*That's it?* So FI makes *how much* in a year?"

"Two-point-five billion," Nari answered. "Which is a moderate assumption and doesn't include transactions below the million-dollar—"

"Seventy thousand." When I finally managed to speak, I didn't say no, stop, enough of this. I said, "Seventy thousand, not two hundred fifty. Just the first year's tuition and room and board. After that I'll be eighteen, the child support will stop, and I can try to reapply for aid." My voice sounded separate from me, as though I were listening to it from the outside. A recording, or someone else using it to speak.

"What about everything else?" Nari asked me, frowning. "Books? Fees? Life? What if aid doesn't come through after that?"

"Seventy," I repeated. "That's it."

My mom works nights at the twenty-four-hour Walmart, usually getting home around three unless she's covering or switched a shift with someone. Most of the time I don't wait up. It isn't reasonable with high school and college coursework, summer internship applications, and my research project on the hypothetical physiological effects of simulated gravity on the human body during prolonged space travel. Some days I wouldn't see her at all except that she wakes up every morning to have breakfast with me before either going back to bed or getting ready for her other job as a maid at the local Holiday Inn Express.

That day, long after everyone left, I waited up.

"Bells," she said, closing the door, keys in one hand and purse over her shoulder. "Why aren't you in bed?"

I folded my legs up under me on the couch and picked at the fraying hems of my sweatpants. The pant legs were too long, and stepping on them with my heels for however long had worn holes in the cuffs. I could've told her then. I probably should have. At least about calling my dad. But the sound of that click, of him realizing who I was and hanging up . . . Maybe it was cowardice, but instead of telling her, I said, "I want to talk about him. Robert Foster. It's time."

She sat down next to me, still in her coat, and slipped off her shoes. "Three-sixteen a.m. on a school night is time?"

"Metaphorically, it's time. Or emotionally?"

"Bellamy."

"I've been thinking I should call him. About college." I heard the click in my memory again and felt embarrassed. Deeply embarrassed, ashamed. Which I knew, objectively, was wrong. The feeling, my reaction, was wrong. It shouldn't have been *my* embarrassment. It wasn't *my* shame. *He'd* hung up on *me*. He'd *abandoned* me. It wasn't logical to blame myself. Yet. "Or you could?"

She was quiet for so long I looked up. Her eyes were wet. "Oh, Bluebell. We can't."

I swallowed. My tone was flat. "Of course we can. We already have, to get him to fill out the financial aid forms."

"No, that was through the lawyers. And who even knows

if he—" She sighed. "You know I don't mean we can't *literally*, Blue."

"Then you mean I shouldn't."

"I mean you aren't allowed."

I watched her wipe her pinky fingers along her bottom eyelids, where her makeup had smeared. "How am I not allowed?"

She looked away, her cheeks flushed. "Legally, Bellamy. He, *we*, wrote it into the child-support agreement. That you and he would have no contact, that he and *I* would have no contact except through the lawyers. And only when unavoidable."

"And me not getting funding because of *his* money is 'avoidable'?"

She didn't answer, still wouldn't meet my eye, and my embarrassment turned to anger. My future, forfeit for a phone call. Thanks to tangential wealth. Wealth that wasn't and had never been mine. The irony of it was enough to make me sick.

Maybe Nari was right. Maybe he did deserve it.

"Why agree to that?" I asked.

"Because." She slumped back into the couch and stared at the ceiling. "Because it was what he wanted. To move on with his life. And because I was angry and very good at spiting myself." She smiled a little—at what, I didn't know. Then the corners of her mouth turned down and her eyes filled. "Oh, Bluebell. I've failed you in so many ways."

NARI

Monday, February 25
32 Days

Cowards! Skeptics! Nonbelievers all! No, not really. Except for maybe the skepticism part, of course. But this was some serious shit. Some *next-level* shit. Life-defining, pivotal, tipping-point, radioactive-spider *shit*. (Plus the whole class-A felony thing, yeah, yeah, Keag, I know.)

But!

As of 3:27 this morning, i.e., when I received a text from Bells that read simply, *OK*, it was official. Which was why I was using my golden hour, that time between school and my parents' coming home from work (dad) and CrossFit (mom), to do some serious conspiring with the members of my tiny hacktivist cadre in our personal IRC about how to root Robert Foster's system. I'd spent most of last night trying to untangle this mess, fueled by my rage at the guy who'd abandoned his kid before her birth, then spent seventeen years never once looking back. Seriously. And yeah, in case it isn't obvious, I was still super freaking pissed that it'd come to this. The way Bells looked yesterday after Foster hung up . . .

Swear to God, if anyone ever makes her feel like that around me again, I'm going to develop laser vision on the spot and burn the offender to the fucking ground.

Anyway! Rooting the system was . . . not going well. But two of my group were online and helping me brainstorm. (Per usual, I kept the more incriminating specifics of my plan to myself. Not that what we were discussing was strictly legal, but, well, yeah. . . . Each member's ops were their own until they decided to tag others in, and this was an altogether extra-curricular activity.)

<d0l0s> this some dragon shit yo
<Formular> u still tryna pwn that op??
<f8ters> . . . PoD?

But the problem wasn't the regular firewalls. I got into parts of Foster Innovations' network just fine. *Parts.* The email parts. The client list and quarterly report and employee roster parts. But not the finance allocation conveniently linked to FI's many sumptuous bank accounts part. Meaning I could see the money. I could count it, add it up, fantasize about paying all of Bells's bills with it. But I couldn't *touch* it. What f8ters was suggesting, breaking it down for the plebs, was a Ping of Death DoS (Denial of Service). But I didn't want to just shut the system down. What I needed was a zero day. The difference between overrunning a shop with so much business they're forced to close and pull down their security gate (the DoS) and finding the one carelessly unlocked window in a building that was otherwise sealed up tight (zero day). I ran my fingers through my hair and typed back:

```
<d0l0s> select block frag pings.
<f8ters> shit
<f8ters> . . .
<f8ters> Life is really simple, but we insist on making
it complicated.
<d0l0s> wut
<Formular> Confucius?
<f8ters> here phishy phishy
<d0l0s> done done done. email, passwords. got
keystroke. But
```

There was a knock at my door. I closed the window.

"Hey." Reese let herself into my room, closing the door be-hind her.

I spun around slowly in my desk chair, legs crossed, palms together, fingers drumming, chin down, and wearing my Dr. Okada face. (Yes, Okada. Yes, that's Japanese. Because I'm Japanese American. Or, half Japanese—my dad's, like, sixth gen and half French-English, my mom's third gen and all American, aka "from here, yes, really, here, Oregon, by way of Minnesota, so kindly shoot that racist question into the fucking sun.")

"Why, hello, Dr. Okada," she said, and dumped her canvas messenger bag on the floor and sat on my bed. "Playing at evil genius today?"

I spun back to my computer. "A little. Evil-ette."

Reese kicked off her shoes. "Ahh. The cute and fuzzy ver-sion of evil."

"Precisely."

"Something that rhymes with Shmellamy and Shmem-Eye-Tee?"

"Shmes?"

Reese shook her head. "Nope. Too much. Starting over." She resituated herself on my bed and cleared her throat. "Ahh. Cute, baby evil. Anything to do with Bellamy and MIT?"

I laughed. "Yes."

"How's it going?"

I sighed. "I'm thinking we're going to have to enact plan B."

"Like birth control?"

"Har har. No. The other kind. The one that comes after plan A."

"Gotcha. So, what's plan B?"

"It's . . . involved." I opened some of my research, being a couple thousand emails (ninety-nine percent useless so far), years of financial records (proof), client lists (alternate ins and more proof), Robert Foster's personal info (in case I started feeling doxxy, which wasn't likely to happen; I mean, I'm not a troll, I'm a freaking *vigilante*), and staff files.

Reese tucked her legs beneath her on my bed. Her hair was no longer just turquoise but turquoise that faded into neon pink. And she'd buzzed the outline of a lotus flower into the shaved side because Reese has talent. Raw, sprung from her mother's now-adulterous womb that way, *talent*. (Can a womb be adulterous? Probably not. "A womb, being an organ, is not a sentient entity capable of making choices," Bellamy would say. "Or having thoughts.") "What color of 'involved'?" she asked.

I reopened my IRC. "What color would breaking and entering with a side of cybercrimes be?"

Her eyes went wide for a fraction of a second; then she pursed her lips and considered. "Graphite. With a smear of vermilion."

"Cool. Then that color of involved."

<f8ters> . . . but
<d0l0s> separate systems. One's cracked. One's locked. Like LOCKed.
<Formular> any overlaps? a fence is thinnest when there's only one side.
<d0l0s> yeah, ill look

"What're you doing?" Reese stood behind my desk chair, watching over my shoulder as I opened a series of windows.

I answered, "A smear of vermilion."

So, there are some things I'm good at. I mean, I'm pretty good at lots of things. Things like basketball and soccer, though I hate team sports so don't bother joining. Math things and science things and history things because I have almost perfect recall. And kissing-Keagan things (wink wink). There are also some things I'm not so good at, like Government, mostly because I hate that class and think it's full of hypocritical revisionist-history bullshit. Like, why are we learning about all the things the US government is supposed to be when it's really a kleptocratic cesspool of special interests and corrupt pseudo-"statesmen" actively refusing to do actual work while getting their pockets lined? Also, saying as much doesn't make me "argumentative and disruptive," it means I'm *paying attention.* I'm also not good at physics because uuuugggghhhh it's sooooo booooorrrriiinnnngg. I am more than fine with that being Bells's thing. Oh, and English lit. Blah. Okay, I like reading as much as the next person. But freaking *Romeo and Juliet? The Scarlet please-oh-please-why-are-we-reading-this-damned-book Letter?* How about swapping that mess of mixed messages for *The Handmaid's Tale* or some Octavia Butler? So, yeah. I'm bad at some stuff. Mostly whatever I find boring or a waste of my time.

As far as contextually relevant skills go, one of the things I'm *best* at is hacking. You think your shit's safe? Nope! Bank account passwords? Credit card numbers? SSN? Mother's maiden name and that of your first pet? That nudie you were gonna send your girlfriend/boyfriend/both, then thought better of it? Yeah. I can get all that. *Loads* of us can. Maybe you know that. Maybe you're careful. Maybe your password isn't P@ssw0rd but wf5TNo09ihtsk8. Doesn't matter. I can get it.

Thanks to my skills, I knew that Robert Foster got his hair trimmed every two weeks for two hundred bucks. I knew how often he took clients out for drinks (on average, three times a week); the mortgage payment on each of his five homes (Pacific Heights, New York, Martha's Vineyard, Vail, and Jackson Hole. Vail *and* Jackson Hole. Freaking redundant much?); which were his favorite weekend getaways (Sonoma and Santa Barbara); the last time he and the fam had vacationed abroad (the Antilles at Christmas) and when they planned to again (this coming May, Tuscany). I knew where he got his suits dry-cleaned; the name, age, education, and browser history of his personal assistant; and what he'd gotten little Evan for his last birthday.

That's the thing about living our lives online. I can *know* you without ever having met you. I can mine the data of your life. And use it.

But! Soapboxes and PSAs aside, all that still wasn't enough. I didn't care about Jeremy's love of elephants or where Mr. Foster had taken Mrs. Foster for dinner on their last anniversary. What I needed was the gap in his (well, FI's and their banks') rather exceptional cybersecurity, a super-secret back door into his financial dealings in order to install the sleek—elegant! Bloody brilliant!—bit of fund-diverting code I'd started working on.

"Full disclosure?" I asked Reese.

"Always."

"So, I've hacked all this—" I waved a hand at my computer screen, windows piled more than a few layers deep. I pulled one to the front: black background with lines of code listed down it. "But I haven't gotten into the parts that count."

"Which parts?"

"The parts that let me actually *do* the grand theft."

"Okay . . ."

"Okay," I said, and looked at her. "So, Foster Innovations works in venture capital, investing huge chunks of money in all these different companies, mostly tech startups and lifestyle ridiculousness, like gourmet toast delivery services or whatever, right?"

Still watching my screen, Reese nodded. I turned back to the window, buzzed through the lines of code, again. Looking for a way in, again. Again, again, which was bordering on the definition of insanity, if you know what I mean. "All of which they do online. Which means I can find it. I can *look* at it. Some of it, at least. But I can't actually tap into the vein yet. At least, not in a way that'd work. I mean, okay, sure, I could try using Foster's passwords to log in to his personal bank account and transfer a lump sum out of his savings, but."

"But that'd be as subtle as throwing a grenade through his front door, then trying to steal his refrigerator?"

"Exactly."

Tap, tap, keystrokes: No go.

Clickety-clack, code pirouettes: No go.

Furious palm-smashing (jokes): No go.

Every time I tried a different route, I hit a wall. Like I'd said to Formular and f8ters, *dragons*. A ring of fire-breathing, d0l0s-deflecting dragons catching my shifty shit and lighting me on fire. Or, more simply, I still couldn't find any unlocked windows—there was no gap.

(And why "d0l0s"? Well, Dolos is the spirit of trickery and guile in Greek mythology. An apprentice of Prometheus, the Titan who created man and then bequeathed the gift of fire upon us and blah, blah, blah, it doesn't really matter because I liked the name and voila! Also, most people think d0l0s, as in me, is a dude. Probably a *white* dude. Probably an *American* white dude in his twenties, which, you know, isn't exactly a bad thing to pretend to be. Or at least to let people assume I am. Because hey, if you don't think the world pays more attention to youngish Western white dudes, then hahahahaha I can't help you. Case in point. Wanna know who Dolos's mythological female counterpart is? Apate. The freaking *personification of deceit*. I mean, how's that for some entrenched misogyny? Like any of us ladyfolk needed more proof that we've been fighting this biased shit since The Beginning.)

I growled and shoved away from my desk.

"What?" Reese asked. She stared over my shoulder at my screen with her arms crossed and one eyebrow arched. "No luck?"

I slumped back in my desk chair with an appropriate level of drama, i.e., I threw my head back, arms out, and groaned a thousand syllables of annoyance into the air beneath my ceiling. "Yeah, no luck."

"What's this one mean? Formular. About one-sided fences."

I sat up. I shouldn't have left that open. Not that Reese's were prying eyes, but still. "He—or she or they—means that I should find the place where the security is thinnest. Seems obvious, right? And I guess it is. FI works with all these other institutions, banks and such, to spread their money out. So maybe I could get in through them? But if I want my precious leech to suckle at the main artery and not just a few peripheral veins . . ."

"Then you need the source."

"Exactly. I need to latch onto FI's primary account. Or better, *be* Robert Foster for a bit so I can get past this shit like I belong there."

"Which is proving difficult."

"Which is . . ."

I opened a new window, feeling my grin spread even as I fought it.

"Nari?"

Fuck it. It was my last idea. My last go at keeping all this a satellite endeavor, aka keeping it digital instead of risking our actual, physical necks.

"Narioka Diane, you're wearing your Destroyer of the Universe face."

I turned my grin on her. "Pull up a seat, most colorful

buddy." She brought over the little upholstered bench from my vanity. "Have you ever seen a botnet work?"

"'Botnet.'"

"Horde of zombie computers programmed to do my bidding?"

She snorted a laugh. "Um, no."

"Well, then." I fired it up and watched the window as computer after computer after computer, located all over the world, logged on, surrendering its computing power to me. (Cue maniacal cackle followed by exclamations of "Mine! All mine!")

Reese rested her elbow on her knee and her chin in her hand. "On a scale of one to very, how illegal is this?"

"Very. With italics."

"You sound super nervous about that."

I didn't sound nervous because I wasn't. I wasn't some skid. I knew what I was doing. And I knew that what I was doing was, yes, *very* illegal, but also very morally gray. Because commandeering a bunch of computers that were, you know, not mine, without their owners' knowledge or consent, was objectively wrong. But *subjectively?* What about doing the "wrong" thing for the *right* reasons? What about the hypocrisy of the powers that be deciding that me doing this was illegal while them doing the same exact things in the name of security (*cough*, power and money, *cough*) is A-okay? But, hey, that's a different argument for a different day.

"Isn't this beautiful? I mean, look at it! *Look!*" My beauty. My baby. The list was so long.

She leaned in closer to watch the growing list. "You mean, all those are computers . . ."

"Primed to do my bidding."

"And what is your bidding?"

"If I told you—"

"You'd have to kill me?"

I shook my head. "You'd have no plausible deniability."

Reese's eyebrows rose. "Ah. Yeah, then don't."

But really, my bidding was a targeted DoS attack on the financial arm of Foster Innovations, specifically the finance department. Using my botnet, I'd overload FI's server with bogus access requests, hopefully allowing me to slip through their firewalls unnoticed. Basically, f8ters's PoD suggestion plus Formular's bit about thin fences. A sort of distraction and sleight of hand. Watch the shiny while I steal your wallet.

My botnet finished logging on, and I dove in.

This is what power feels like.

I remember thinking that, those exact words. No hyperbole, no gimmicky vernacular (I do know how to be serious sometimes). I felt electric and expanding. Like nothing could touch me, while all I had to do was *look* at a thing to make it burn. I commanded an army of tens of thousands. A singular, obedient horde. All from the comfort of my bedroom.

Except.

I disconnected the botnet and covered my tracks.

"What happened?" Reese asked. "Did it work?"

I took a deep, defeatist breath. "Nope."

"Time for plan B?"

"Time for plan B."

Reese smiled. *"Awesome,"* she said. "I love vermilion."

SANTIAGO

Friday, March 1
28 Days

The cafeteria was the same as it always was, too loud and too crowded. I picked up the orange from my tray and started peeling it. Across from me, Keagan ate a bean sprout, rice noodle, and tofu concoction out of some glassware from home. Glassware because it didn't have BPA, or whatever'd replaced BPA now that everyone knew it was basically poison, which was one of the things Paisley crusaded about alongside Monsanto and Roundup and industrialized farming and bovine growth hormone and nitrates in lunch meat. Reese sat beside me, eating a slice of pizza. Her hair was new today, bright red with a dark-gray color in the shaved part and her roots.

"How do you do that?" I asked, waving at her head.

"Sorcery." She took a bite of pizza. "And dye I buy online. My bathtub looks like bad tie-dye." She looked toward the entrance of the cafeteria, maybe waiting for Nari and Bellamy, who sometimes took a few extra minutes getting to lunch from AP Physics on Fridays, or her friend Maddie, who sat with us sometimes.

I finished peeling my orange and licked my fingers, which

tasted bitter from the peel. "I should've let you dye mine teal or orange or something before State."

Chewing, she studied my head. My hair was beginning to grow back, covering the weird paleness of my shaved scalp. She swallowed her bite. "Dark hair's hard. You have to bleach it first. Plus the chlorine would wash it out." She took another bite, still focusing on my head, and said, mouth full, "But you probably would've left a kick-ass color streak in the water."

Keagan looked up from his food. "Like a contrail!" His own eighth inch of hair, so blond it turned nearly white during the summer, caught the glow of the room's fluorescent light like a halo of peach fuzz. "You could do mine! Neon pink. Or *green*. But it *has* to be neon."

"Had," Reese said.

"Right." Keagan pouted theatrically, turning down the corners of his mouth and widening his eyes. "No more practices. No more meets." He shook his head, feigning despondency. "No more Speedos. No more blocks. No more coaches' dirty looks."

Reese groaned.

Keagan turned and sang at her at full volume. *"Swimming's out for summer!"* He pumped his fist to the beat in his head. *"Swimming's done for-EV-ER!"*

"Stop it. It's horri—"

"Poooooool's been blown to pieces." Facing her, he did a few air-guitar power chords, then abruptly turned back to his food. "Okay, I'm done."

"Praise the Lord," Reese said, and took another bite of pizza. "That was obnoxious."

Keag grinned at her. "You're welcome."

"Alice Cooper?" I said. "Your dad would be proud."

He shrugged. "He'd be prouder if I performed a forty-five-minute air-guitar rendition of some rambling Gov't Mule jam."

"Government mule?" Bellamy asked. She and Nari walked up behind Keagan with their trays.

He looked back, beaming, and said, "¡Hola, chicas! ¿Cómo están? ¿Qué pasa?" He turned to me, eyebrows raised and eager for validation that his Spanish was reasonably correct.

"Bueno," I said. Keagan was coming off a phase of having me speak to him almost exclusively in Spanish when we were alone, because that's the kind of thing Keagan does. He loves learning new things, usually with an all-in sort of gusto that burns out after a week or two, but during those two weeks his interest is genuine and infectious. With this one he'd even tried to keep it up during dinner at my house, leaving my little sisters in tears from laughing at his declaring he was "un poco embarazado" after knocking his water glass over at the table.

"Really, Keagan?" my dad had asked in English. "Only a little?"

"Lo siento, Mr. Ramírez," Keag said, mopping up the water with a napkin, and I'd finally clarified that embarazada means pregnant. Which made Keagan laugh, which started my youngest sister, Teresa, up again, giggling so hard she'd snorted milk out her nose.

"Just great and not much, Keagy," Nari answered, sitting beside him. "What's up with you lovelies?"

"Nothing," Reese said, "except for a bit of Keagan's theatrical flair."

Nari nodded and opened the salad she'd bought to doctor it, picking out onions, adding dressing, but didn't ask what Reese had meant, maybe because Keagan was often theatrical so outbursts weren't rare, or maybe because things between them, between all of us, had been a little shifted, a little off center, since Sunday.

For five days, no one had said a word, not when we were all together, not when it was just Keag and me, and if any of the others were discussing or planning elsewhere, they hadn't felt the need to tag me in. Instead, everything we'd left unacknowledged since Sunday had grown all week, with each lunch and class and hangout when we'd pointedly turned away from the increasingly bloated elephant in the room, as though if we let the sleeping dog lie, we could ignore the cat we'd let out of the bag, nos habíamos ido de la lengua, like *it'd all escaped our tongues,* and pretend like it'd never happened. But haciéndonos de la vista gorda, *making our eyesight thick,* or turning a blind eye, didn't mean there was nothing to see.

I get why there are so many idioms about secrets and avoidance, because the greater the insistence on something staying ignored, the more obvious it feels, just as our avoidance made us twitchy and uncomfortable, turning the quiet a little crisp, brittle with everything we left unsaid.

"I love the new hair," Nari told Reese, her tone and smile together seeming almost conspiratorial.

Sitting beside me, Bellamy opened her can of Dr Pepper with a hiss and a crack. "Reminds me of a nebula," she said.

Reese beamed. "Reese the Space Ace!"

We laughed.

"You could put *that* on a shirt," Keag said. He held his hands up, miming like he was reading from a theater marquee. *"Reese the Piece of Molten Titanium, an Ace from Space."*

She smiled; then the silence went embarazada again while

we all chewed and swallowed and collectively ignored any and all suggestions of grand larceny. Nari ate her salad, Reese finished her pizza and pulled out her phone, Bellamy ate bites of her turkey sandwich, and Keagan started fidgeting, jiggling first one then both knees beneath the table, while I finished my own ham sandwich and wished the weirdness was something I could fix.

Part of me wondered if Nari was doing it on purpose, ignoring what she'd started only to keep working on it quietly behind our backs, or not exactly behind our backs, but privately, without argument or oversight. I might've wondered, if that was the case, why she'd bothered telling us at all, but Nari exercised a strange mix of almost anarchistic self-determination and respect for permission, which—paired with her concoction of selflessness and love of attention—made her kind of predictable. She'd hate knowing I thought that, but she is. Maybe we all are; Reese's enthusiasm on Sunday, Keagan's disapproval, Bellamy's silence, even my calm agreement, readily supporting the plan because of my feelings for Bells. It was all true to character.

Except that my feelings weren't the only reason, and I doubted the reasons I assumed were behind the others' knee-jerk reactions were their only ones either.

I swallowed the last bite of my sandwich and drank from my water bottle. Beside me, Bellamy had pushed her half-eaten sandwich away and sat slowly sipping her soda. Reese still stared at her phone, and Nari had pulled out hers as well, staring at it in one hand while eating her salad with the other. Keagan's legs still bounced arrhythmically under the table. "So," I said. "How long are we going to act like Sunday didn't happen?"

Nari finished chewing and set her phone down. "Yeah,

about that." She shared a look with Reese. "Operation Justice for Bellamy has hit a wall."

"What wall?" Keagan asked, frowning. Nari opened her mouth but Keag interrupted, "No, wait. Rewind to 'What are you doing to have hit a wall?'"

Nari narrowed her eyes. "What do you mean?" It wasn't rhetorical, but she also already knew what he meant. Sometimes I understood Bellamy's impatience with artifice . . .

"You know what he means," Bellamy said, and we all looked at her. "Why don't you ask the question you really want the answer to?"

This is what I meant about predictability and how we all both are and aren't. Nari taking liberties after Bellamy said okay was as predictable as Bells's annoyance with Nari's question. Bellamy voicing that annoyance was not.

"O-kay," Nari said, over-enunciating. "I mean, weren't we all in agreement? Why's anyone shocked that I've been doing what I said I'd do?" She and Keagan shared a look. Then he shifted focus to his lunch, packing his fork inside his empty container and shoving it into his backpack.

Reese spread a wide game-show smile on her face. "Let's try this again," she said. "What wall, Nari?"

Nari clicked the plastic lid shut over what was left of her salad. "I can't get all the way into the system. Which means I can't do the thing remotely."

Bellamy sighed and frowned at the table, already getting it. For the rest of us—or Keag and me since Reese seemed to already know—I asked, "Which means . . . ?"

Nari shrugged and answered, "Time for plan B," as Reese cheered, "Road trip!"

REESE

Friday, March 1
28 Days

"You want us to *what?*"

"Keep your voice down, Keag," said Santiago, always calm, always collected, always smooth and deep like pewter. Keagan shot him a glare.

"I can't get in from here," Nari said. "I've tried everything I can think of and a few things other people thought of for me. But"—she shrugged—"Foster's security is too good. Well, his and his banks'."

"Explain," San said. "Please."

Nari huffed a breath and, in a low voice, obliged. "Okay. So I've been doing some midgrade spying to see what, exactly, it's going to take to get the code I'm working on to do its thing. And what I really need is access to FI's bank accounts, right? Which, best-case scenario, I'd get Foster to unwittingly give me himself. Passwords, et cetera. So I tacked some keystroke spyware onto a link in an email, and ta-da! Except his antivirus software caught and flushed that. Like, in a day. Before I could get all his bank-account log-in info. And while he didn't seem to notice and so didn't change any of his passwords this time, if I try to get him to reinstall the spyware so I can get the rest of it, his virus protection will punt the program and probably alert him."

"Meaning he would notice," Santiago said. "And change his passwords."

"Locking you out," I said, "and leaving us shit out of luck."

"Exactly. And not getting all his bank log-in info nixes the easy install-the-fund-diverting-malware-by-logging-on-and-pretending-to-be-Foster option. And no way the Trojan horse approach'll work after my spyware got trashed so quick, because the malware file will be *way* bigger and *way* more noticeable.

"Which leaves two options. One, break into each and every financial institution FI utilizes either digitally, or, more likely, physically, thanks to the aforementioned issues, to install the malware. Or I code it to multiply and latch onto each bank account as Bells's dad uses them, and we download it directly onto Foster's computer. In person. As in, plug a flash drive into a port," she said, miming it. "And click download." She shrugged again. "Once it's installed, I'll be able to watch it or kill it from anywhere. But I can't install it from here."

Keagan was shaking his head, had been the entire time Nari talked. "Neat," he said. "That's all just super cool." He kept his voice low this time, but he was pissed. "And, really, a fabulous list of reasons to, you know, *not do it*. Really, Bells? I'm sorry. Your dad's a first-class piece of shit, but this is—"

"Not your decision." The muscles in Nari's jaw flexed. She stared Keagan down with one eyebrow arched.

He narrowed his eyes at her. "So it's *yours?*"

"It's Bellamy's," I said.

Bells shook her head. "No. Not just mine."

"Right. It's each of ours," Santiago said, eyes on Bellamy, who was staring at her can of soda, trying to balance it on one side of its bottom edge. It tipped toward its side, top-heavy. She took a sip and tried again.

Bells is . . . I don't get Bells. I love her. She's kind and loyal and honest and brilliant. But I don't always understand the way she thinks. I appreciate it, but, like, how I appreciate fractals. I am often in awe of fractals. But I don't *get* fractals. They're amazing, but I have no clue how they work.

I don't get Santiago's thing for Bellamy either. Or hers for him, if she has one. It's all very opaque. Not that I've tried to un-opaque, de-opaque?, *clarify* it. Because I don't care. Well, ugh, okay. I don't not care. But we've been over this. Sort of. Say you don't care about enough stuff and people get all, *Check out the misanthrope!* But I am not a misanthrope. I don't hate *people*. I hate *assholes*.

Basically, what I mean is that I care about Bells's and San's happiness, not what makes them happy.

I think it's how different they seem. Keagan and Nari? Fine. They're both bright and glowing and in the yellow-orange spectrum. Just, Nari's glittery to Keag's matte. But Bells is so cut-and-dried and exact, like a checkerboard of black and white, while San is dye dropped in water. A twisting cloud of pigment, all graceful curves with no straight lines.

But maybe that's me and my aesthetics. Maybe it's me being acearo. To make a flippant analogy, it's like not liking chocolate. Almost everybody likes chocolate, right? All kinds, some kinds, one kind. Or they at least like chocolate on occasion. Or if they spend a careful amount of time getting to know a certain preparation of chocolate, a soufflé or something, they like that specific one. But when you don't like chocolate at all, people are like, *How can you not like chocolate?* And I'm like, *(Shrug) I just don't.* And they're like, *But have you even* tried *it?* And I'm like, *Have or haven't, what does that matter?* And they're like, *What about x, y, z kinds of chocolate? What about brownies and cake and mousse and and and—* And I'm like, *Hold up, why do you care that I don't like chocolate?* And they're like, *But not liking chocolate is weird! Chocolate's the best! I wouldn't want to live without chocolate!*

For real, the world is chocolate *obsessed*. It's everywhere, all the time. Which can make people look at chocolate-indifferent me and decide I'm

(A) Lying

(B) Broken

(C) A partial person

(D) Better off ignored

(E) All of the above

I have to not care. Example: *Reese the Piece.*

Freshman year I dated a guy. Barret Tundle. He asked me out. I said, "Sure, okay." We went to a few movies. Sat on the beach watching his older brother and a few of his friends surf in the frigid October water. Then one night he kissed me. I kissed him back. His hand went up my shirt. I pushed it down. He tried my pants. I shoved him off. He got pissed and said a bunch of shitty things, which should've been the end, right? Except the next day at school some guy asked if he could try me out now. Someone else stopped while I stood at my locker and asked if I'd give him head in the bathroom. Another cornered me at lunch to say he didn't care I was so flat-chested, he'd take a turn anyway, which is how I met Nari.

I was new. We'd moved closer to the coast that summer for my dad's job, and because my mom, the once-upon-a-time aspiring actress turned real estate agent, was unhappy or something, so I didn't really have friends yet. Maybe that's why I said yes to dating Barret? Though I think I just said yes because I wasn't sure yet how to say no. Anyway, Nari heard the "take a turn" comment and snapped. Even then, Nari was a force. She verbally laid the guy out. Shrank him to about two feet tall, then folded me into her and Bells's friendship like I was the arm they'd been missing. Then came Keagan and Santiago, and here we are.

Despite that, "Reese the Piece" stuck. People decided I was a slut, and I didn't argue. Because screw them and their sexist heteronormative bullshit. Because to Barret it was the "no" that mattered and not whatever color of "because" I could've given. Because I don't owe anyone answers or explanations about who I am. And having to convince someone who I'm *not* is the same as having to convince them who I *am*, which isn't my burden. It's theirs. I've never wasted my time begging people to have an opinion about me, so I'm sure as hell not going to waste my time trying to change whatever opinion they've decided to have.

So, yeah. Long story short-ish, I dated a tool, and kissing that tool confirmed what I already thought I knew: I don't like or care about chocolate, however you want to define "chocolate": sexual attraction, romantic attraction, sex the act itself, which I haven't tried and am not sure if I want to though I'm not touch averse or incapable of desire. Do I reserve the right to want some kind of chocolate in the future? *Yup.* Or to never want any kind of chocolate at all? *Yup.* But do I want it now? Even if not wanting it makes some people think I'm a lying/broken/ignorable/partial person? *Nope.*

So when Santiago said that this decision, to do or not do the thing, was "each of ours," I was like, *Yes!* Because while I didn't get his feelings for Bells or vice versa, or if that was why he was willing to risk his version of everything for her, I didn't need to. He had his reasons. And I had mine. And that was enough. No explanations needed.

"Right," I said. "It's each of ours. So the same grand theft main course, now with a road trip appetizer and a side of trespassing. Everybody still in? Speak now or forever hold your peace."

Silence. Brittle, ice-blue silence. Even from Keagan.

It was on.

Smash cut to Saturday at Bellamy's apartment with the Fab Five—

"Fab Five?" San asked. "Can we vote on that?"

"Okay . . . Quintexcellence?" I said.

"Pentawesomeness," Keagan suggested.

Then Bellamy, "Pentaderanged."

Nari clapped her hands. "People! Focus! We can brainstorm names for our amazingness later. Now"—she pulled a fat folder out of her bag and slapped it onto the coffee table—"we have work to do."

And work we did. It felt surreal. *Magenta.* We were doing it. Really doing it. An adventure. A *heist.* Nari was the brains.

Santiago the acrobat. I was the diversion. Bellamy the reason. And Keagan?

"Getaway driver."

Nari pursed her lips, watching him cautiously. "You're okay with that?"

He fidgeted with the corner of a piece of paper on the table, rolling it up, then flattening it again under one finger, and shrugged.

Fade out to the following Thursday, twenty-two days to go, with me standing inside the door of school's main office, watching the hall through the narrow window. I'd say don't ask how Nari and I ended up in the office, alone, with access to the admin's computer and ID printer, but Nari had everyone convinced she was allowed to do whatever she wanted and could break into almost any computer system by breathing on it. As for me, Mr. Roberts had given me permission to use the art rooms in perpetuity sophomore year, so Reese-spottings in the empty after-school halls were a common occurrence.

"Clear?" she asked.

I peered through the window. "Yup," I said, and left my post to join her.

Nari plugged the flash drive into one of the computer's USB ports and opened the file I'd loaded on it. This was the easy part, printing Santiago's fake Foster Innovations employee ID. The hard part had been the hours it'd taken me to make the thing. Graphic designer, I was. Magician, I was not. The hologram wasn't real. The magnetic strip and QR code were fake rather than existing ones lifted from the FI system, since using those might—inadvertently, *of course*—frame an actual

FI employee. But at a glance, hell, under pretty close scrutiny, it looked damn good.

I turned the ID printer on, and we let it warm up. Nari saved the ID image into its queue and hit print.

Yep, damn good.

She printed a spare, just in case, then went to eject the drive, but I stopped her.

"Wait," I said. I reached for the mouse and added five more image files to the printer's queue. She cocked her head in question, and I wiggled, waggled?, wriggled? my eyebrows at her. "Just in case."

Star wipe to the next Tuesday, March twelfth, seventeen days left in the countdown and my friend Madeline and me walking down the hall toward my locker after pottery, our last class of the day.

"You meeting Nari this afternoon?" Maddie asked. She leaned against the next locker as I loaded my chem and AP English books into my bag.

"Yeah." I'd have told her we were headed to Marty's Closet, but since I couldn't invite Maddie along and she loves the place almost as much as me, I didn't. "What about you?"

"Driving down to Eugene to see Emily."

Emily is Maddie's girlfriend, a year older and studying . . . something at UO. "Kick-ass," I said, and shut my locker. We wove our way through the crowded hall toward to the main doors. "Did she stick with Design this time?"

Madeline laughed. "No. She's officially 'undeclared.' Her adviser told her to stop switching her major after the third time. This semester she's taking everything from a business management class to sculpture with some intro to history and biology sprinkled in. Dropped calc last week, though, so she's crossed engineering off her list at least."

"A Renaissance woman!" I cheered.

"Ha, yeah," Madeline said. "Or just fickle as hell. She's waiting to feel inspired by something."

"Hey. That is capital-V *Valid*." We reached the door and I used my hip to shove it open. "Tell her I say hey. And maybe see if there are any cool shows or anything we could see down there this weekend."

"Will do."

Bellamy and Nari waited out front beneath Nari's umbrella. They waved, we waved back. Maddie peeled off toward the parking lot, in a hurry to get on the road toward Eugene, and I joined Nari and Bells under the umbrella.

"Ready for this?" Nari asked, beaming. "This" was a search for, drumroll, *props*. I was neon-level excited.

"Does a chow have a blue tongue?"

"I dunno, do they?"

I smiled wide. "Yup!"

It was drizzling. *Drizzling*. What a ridiculous word. Though I guess it's better than saying "the fat gray air fizzes all over you like it's telling you some pointless and infuriatingly boring story and spitting while it talks." Because brevity.

"How's Maddie?" Bellamy asked.

"Good. Going to visit Emily." I looked around. "Keag and Santiago didn't want to come?"

We started toward the parking lot and my dad's car. He'd let me borrow it that day, like he did plenty of days, since he likes to ride his bike to work anyway. Keagan and San are the only of us with their own cars, but San's is a two-seater, which leaves

Keag to shuttle us all around most of the time, or at least when he isn't working. My parents offered to buy me one, 'cause I'm privileged like that, which sounds shitty, I know, but shittier is not recognizing that I'm privileged. I asked them to spend the money on marriage counseling instead, or to put it in my Europe fund. They went with the fund. Nari's parents can afford to buy her a car but won't because they're very much "the world doesn't owe you anything; earn it yourself" and "just because *we* have money doesn't mean *you* do" people.

"San's teaching swim lessons," Bellamy answered, and looked to Nari for Keagan's whereabouts.

I jumped off the cement retaining wall that separates the slope of the school's lawn from the parking lot. Bells jumped after me while Nari crouched and stepped down daintily in her skirt. We rehuddled under the umbrella, and Nari shrugged. I widened my eyes at Bells. She widened hers back. Because

(1) Nari *always* knew where Keagan was.

(2) That's it. They're basically conjoined. Nari and Keagan. Narigan.

"So . . . ," I started. We kept walking, narrowing to single file with me in front and Nari in the middle to pass between the cars. "What's that about? The shrug."

I knew they'd been fighting. What with Keagan hating this whole idea and all. But it wasn't *fighting* fighting. At least not what I'd call fighting. Voices screeching, doors slamming, tires squealing as the car ripped away in a cloud of selfishness and abandonment. But a burnt sienna sort of fighting, teetering between a tangerine-colored normal and a sludgy discordant brown.

"I don't know," Nari said. "Maybe I don't care where Keagan is right now."

"But you always care," Bellamy said behind her.

"Well, so, I'm taking a break."

"From?" I asked.

"Caring?" she said. "At least about trying to change his mind."

I glanced back. Nari watched the ground, carefully avoiding the puddles between the cars to keep her shoes dry. Bellamy watched Nari, looking guilty. I guess I could've said something, but I didn't know what, if anything, would help.

I stopped short in the lane in front of my dad's Honda. Nari bumped into my back. "Oh, for—" I groaned. There was a condom on the antenna. Again.

"Fantastic!" Nari said, sarcastic. "Nothing like a bit of light harassment to round out the day."

I reached into my bag and ripped a blank piece of paper out of a notebook. "Bully Lite," I said, using the paper to pull the condom off and throw it on the ground without touching it. "Misogyny for calorie counters."

"Diet Sexism," Bellamy added. "All the flavor of torment with none of the guilt."

Nari glared down at the condom, nose wrinkled in disgust. "Barret?"

"Barret, Derrick, Martin." I unlocked the car. "Who even cares anymore?" Condoms on my dad's car and in my locker, wrapped those times at least. A picture that made the rounds every so often, some porn star with my head photoshopped on her body. The rumors that resurfaced every few months like someone was spinning a chore wheel of who to harass and I was one of the brightly colored wedges.

And spare me the "you do it to yourself" argument. Trust me, I've heard it. "If only you'd smooth your edges a bit, Reese," my mom would say, gesturing to my hair and clothes and me in general. "You could at least *try* to fit in. No one's making you wear such a big target on your back." For real, folks. My mother. The queen of throwing boulders inside her glass house while standing on a soapbox made of toothpicks and adultery.

And even better than her acting like I earn my own harassment? Like she has any room to criticize how I conduct my life? I'm the one who caught her.

You think the idea of walking in on your parents is bad? Try doing it when the man in the bed isn't your dad.

"I care," Nari said, opening the passenger door. She shook the rain off her umbrella and collapsed it before climbing into the car. We closed our doors in three metered beats. I started the car and waited, letting it heat up.

"Which is noble, Narioka Diane. But also pointless. Remember what happened when I reported that picture? I'll give you a hint. It rhymes with 'schmothing.' So it seems like there's two options." I flipped on the windshield wipers. "One, spend a bunch of energy trying to get Barret in trouble for crap I can't prove he did, thereby proving to people whose opinions I already don't care about that I'm not actually a slut. Which is doubly shitty because that's like acknowledging I've been slut-shamed and that being a 'slut,' as in a female person who likes to have sex, is something worth feeling ashamed about. Sprinkle in the choice to either keep my being ace out of it, which means erasing part of myself, or add it to the conversation and open myself up to a bunch of aphobic bullshit, and it's triply shitty.

"Or, second option: Ignore it. Bide my time. And in a few short months, never look back."

"Okay," Nari said, pulling her lip gloss out of her bag. She flipped down the visor to use its mirror and gave me a quick Dr. Okada side-eye. "Or *third* option, you finally let me use d0l0s."

I cranked up the heater and held my hands in front of the vents, funneling the warming air up my jacket's sleeves. "If I ever want their identities sold or to have them framed for murder or cyberespionage or something, I'll let you know."

I pulled into the parking lot at Marty's Closet, and we piled out. On a list of Reese's Favorite Places, this one, being a costume shop–slash–consignment store stuffed full of amazingness, was like number four. Which was extra nice right then as the latest Barret strike had left me feeling like my whole body was covered in one of those peel-off face masks that I'd left on too long.

Marty, or whoever the actual buyer was, as I don't know if Marty is even a real person, culled the best and the weirdest from the armies of old tracksuits and mom jeans that usually end up in thrift stores, stocking only the finest of oddities alongside some choice new stuff. Case in point, that day the mannequins in the window were dressed as an authentic vintage disco dancer; an exorbitantly priced stormtrooper; an utterly inauthentic, utterly latex, utterly X-rated nurse; and basically me: leggings with a loud and colorful print, oversized tank with a kick-ass graphic, vintage waist-length leather jacket, and scuffed suede riding boots. Though my ankle boots weren't suede and had those rad neon-colored stretchy laces that curl up all tight so they don't need to be tied. Thanks, eBay!

We walked through the door into the dry warmth of the shop, and my skin relaxed. Like peeling off the mask all at once, revealing that deliciously clean feeling beneath it. The left wall was a majesty of wigs. Short, long, curled. Blunt bangs, shaggy, A-line. Black, brunette, blond, red, purple, green, rainbow. More costumed mannequins lined the other walls on a shoulder-high shelf. There was an old-fashioned deep-sea diver, an eighties punk rocker, a mod princess, a cop. Racks of clothes and spinning displays with an incredible assortment of additions and accessories crowded the floor.

I went for the wigs, Nari for the fake eyelashes, Bellamy for the masks.

"What do you think?" Bellamy asked, voice muffled by the full unicorn head she wore.

Nari clapped, demurely, like a beauty queen. "Glorious."

Bells pulled the mask off and brushed her staticky hair from her face. "Hard to see out of, though. And breathe in," she said, then walked away.

Nari held up a set of neon-orange lashes with gold stars glued to the tips. "What do you think? My new everyday wear?"

"Do it," I said. "I bet you the glitter wishes of a thousand mischievous pixies that the following day no fewer than six underclassmen will be wearing them."

"If I'm going to start a trend, I'd rather do it with *these*." She grabbed a set of chrome lashes with matching press-on nails from the display.

"Those would get you *five* thousand glitter pixie wishes."

"Deal."

Bellamy came back, now wearing an epic tiara and a pair of demon fairy wings, and asked, "What's the plan?"

"The plan"—Nari plucked a wand with purple fluff and a glittery plastic star out of a bin and handed it to Bellamy—"is for Reese to wander, to steep, to *season*, to await Inspiration with a capital I."

Inspiration. For the part of the plan I was, as previously mentioned, neon-level excited for. Performance art as distraction. The chance to have an entirely purposeful public meltdown.

I wandered, trailing my fingers along the racks of costumes and clothing, skirting the spinners and other displays. Until I saw the bottles of fake blood.

I picked one up, handle looped over my finger, and held it up for Nari and Bells to see. "Inspiration achieved."

Simple right-to-left wipe to Thursday, March twenty-first, and a sunny-ish late afternoon in my backyard with Nari, eight days till the doing of the deed.

"How much did these set the slush fund back?" I asked, curling the clear plastic earpiece over my ear. I set the small two-way radio she'd given me to the right channel and clipped it to the pocket of my jacket. We'd all been pitching in what we could to cover the expenses of this scheme: my props, San's disguise, gas and supplies for the trip, the hotel room in San Francisco, and, apparently, spy gear for her and Santiago.

Backing away across my yard, Nari put on her headset and pulled the mic down in front of her mouth. I heard the click of her radio turning on, followed by her voice in my ear: *"Like eighty bucks."*

I lifted my mic to my mouth, pressed the button to speak, and said, "Not bad, Dr. Okada."

She dropped into a quick curtsy, then finished crossing the lawn.

Speaking of money, aka the whole point of this plan, why worry about a slush fund at all, right? Why scrimp? Why not go all in on a few credit cards in preparation for taking as much from Foster as we want? Why not enjoy an advance on those ill-gotten gains? Also, why stop there? Why not a backpack of bullion for each of us, slung over our five separate shoulders, heavy beneath five separate satisfied glances back, as each of us boards our plane/train/bus/ferry toward our separate corners of the earth, where we'll hide, swaddled in luxury, until it's safe to reunite and plan our next job?

Well, because we're not greedy thieving assholes; we're opportunistic thieving avengers! For real, though, the money isn't the point. The point is Bellamy going to MIT, which, yeah, takes money. A lot of it. Also screwing over Bells's dad for screwing over her and her mom, though this part is more "perk" than "purpose."

Really, that's it. And I'm cool with that. I don't need the money. Bells does.

"Why don't I get one of these?" I asked.

She turned on her toe to face away from me, skirt flaring as she spun. *"Because you are the bait. And bait doesn't wear a wire."*

I pressed the little button again. "Nope. Try again. The bait *always* wears a wire. Or, if we're going with fishing, you know, a *hook.*"

"Fine. The distracting spectacle *never wears a wire."*

"In case I get caught."

I watched her back. She stilled, staring at the fence along

the back of my yard that needed new stain, or the neighbor's tree across the alley or something. A light click preceded her voice. *"Yeah. In case you get caught."*

That was a fun thought. Orange. Like kumquats and, uh, oranges. And jumpsuits.

"So. What *is* my plan? To, you know, *not* get caught."

Nari turned around to look at me from across the yard. *"You just need to give San enough time to get in unnoticed, since that's when the lobby'll still be full. After that . . ."* She lifted her shoulders. *"I don't know. Run?"*

"Run."

"Yeah. And hope they don't chase you."

Pixel fade to midmorning Sunday, March twenty-fourth, also known as five days until The Thing That Shall Not Be Named, but only because we couldn't agree on a name, and when I'd get to use that fake blood, *huzzah!* Tomorrow we'd leave for Redwood National Park, where we'd be "camping" all "week" for "spring break." Okay, not all of those quotes were strictly necessary, but you get the idea. Camping was a cover. We'd stay a night for authenticity and to break up the drive, then move on.

We sat around Bellamy's little four-person kitchen table, Keagan in a chair pulled over from the living room, each of us nursing some version of coffee courtesy of Nari, munching on bagels courtesy of Bellamy's mom, who was at work, and stared at blueprints.

Yes, actual blueprints. Or, well, copies. Plus security-guard schedules, employee records, timetables, Robert Foster's personal schedule, and that of every person connected to it.

"So," Keagan said, smiling like an idiot, laying it on thick. "How's everyone's morning been so far? Mine's been—" He gave us a thumbs-up, winked, and clicked his tongue. "I ate pancakes for breakfast." He turned to Nari and repeated, *"Pancakes,"* enunciating carefully. She grinned into the plastic lid of her coffee cup, not meeting his eye. "Perfect, poofy, pillowy pancakes. Oh, and I had some juice. Green juice, in case you guys were wondering."

"And maybe some coffee?" I asked. "Other than that extra-syrup, extra-whip, extra-shot, extra-rapid-heartbeat mocha latte?"

"Why, yes, Reese! I did!" He looked himself up and down, patting his chest like he was searching for something. "Does it show?"

Bellamy and Nari giggled. I rolled my eyes.

Smiling, San shook his head. "You're vibrating, dude."

"Hey, if I'm going to be some hard-core getaway driver, the least I can do is give it my manic best, right?" He smiled too wide. *"Right?"*

"Right," Bellamy echoed. She eyed the blueprint spread out on the table, its corners held down with random junk: a bright red stapler, a Darth Vader bobblehead, an AP Physics book, and an actual paperweight, a glass sphere with a rendition of the solar system frozen inside. "Where do we start?"

Nari inhaled deeply through her nose and started talking.

An hour later, the blueprints were marked with notes, and the tabletop was strewn with papers. "Aannndddd . . ." Keagan raised his hand behind his back and swung his arm over and down toward the table. *"Break!"*

But no one even breathed a laugh. The mood was thundercloud gray, the kind that was tinged a little green and might turn into a tornado.

"It's so simple," Santiago said.

"Too simple," I agreed. Yeah, there were the radios and a fake identity for the bank account all that skimmed money would go into first. I'd helped Bells and Nari set it up by, well, watching them do it. And suggesting names, though Penelope McTittles shockingly didn't make the cut. There were also the fake IDs I'd designed, though they weren't part of the plan. And San's employee ID. But yeah. A wig, a bottle of fake blood, an employee ID, a malware-loaded flash drive, a wealth of knowledge about the inner workings of FI that we hoped we wouldn't have to use, ourselves, and . . . that was pretty much it. "No ropes? No glass cutters or industrial magnets or infrared? I mean, we deserve a grappling hook! Prosthetics! A voice distorter at least!"

Still no laughs, and Nari didn't even smile. "Simple is good," she said seriously. "The simpler it is, the fewer chances there'll be to screw it up."

"And if we do?" Keag asked, wearing that weirdly flat expression he practiced these days while performing his okayness. "Screw up?"

"Then"—Nari shrugged—"we improvise."

I glanced at Bellamy, waiting for her to fix the tension, even though Bells wasn't exactly an emotional fixer, or at least, I don't know, to say something, anything really. But she only frowned at the table, then abruptly stood up, walked back to her bedroom, and closed the door. Saying nothing, barely exchanging looks lest we twist that thundercloud into a funnel, the rest of us packed up the mess and left.

Classic clock wipe to twenty-odd minutes later at my house, where my mom and dad both were at the same time for the first time in . . . I don't even know. Weeks. At least three or four.

I walked through the back door into the kitchen to find them sitting at the counter, talking, voices low. When they saw me, they stopped.

"What are you doing here?" I asked my mom.

"Reese—" my dad started.

"I came by to see you. And to get a few more of my things."

"Like Dad's dignity and my sense of stability? You already have those."

She sighed. "No. But thank you, as always, for the hyperbole, Reese. I'm here for the rest of my clothes and to talk with your dad about taking some of the furniture. I found an apartment."

I slipped my boots off and started across the kitchen toward the hall and my room, giving her a thumbs-up as I passed. "Rad."

"Reese," my dad said. I stopped but didn't turn. He moved past me. Squeezing my shoulder, he said, "Talk to your mom. And try to remember that we raised you with manners," then left.

Another of the things I didn't get? His calm. I mean, my dad was almost always calm. A tranquil seafoam green. *Infuriatingly calm*, my mom had called it, screeched it, on several occasions. *Like a fucking brick wall!* Though I'm not sure if a brick wall is actually capable of being "calm." Reticent? Stoic? Impassive? Sure. But calm?

Maybe his guts were really an emotion pyre, a small, self-contained inferno devouring his anger and hurt, turning them to tiny piles of digestible ash. Or maybe he was mashing it all down inside and someday he'd snap.

I preferred a more direct approach: obscenities and pillow screaming.

"Reese," my mom said behind me. "Please."

Please. Except the way she said it didn't sound like an entreaty. More a demand.

I took a deep breath, stretched a semimaniacal smile across my face, and turned. "Yes, mother dearest?"

She sighed again. "Just how long are you planning to keep this up?"

"Keep what up? Hating you?"

She twisted on the stool to face me straight on, as I still stood halfway toward the hall. She'd curled her hair and pulled half back with a barrette I'd given her for Mother's Day when I was fourteen. *Subtle, Mom. Reeeal subtle.* "I understand why you feel like you need to hate me."

I clenched my teeth and took a deep breath. Looking at my mom was like staring into a pit of the deepest black. But not black like a void. Black like the dark beyond the edge of the world, a dark lurking with beasts and ghouls.

Okay, yeah, I like hyperbole.

"But you have to stop doing this," she said.

"Doing what, exactly?"

"Leaving whenever you feel like it, doing whatever you want. Acting as though you have no one to answer to and will suffer no consequences."

"I'm sorry, but this is beginning to sound like a lecture, and I'm not sure you're qualified. Not since your moral high ground vanished down that Huge Cheater sinkhole."

"*Hey.*"

"Are you denying it?"

"No. Reese. But you have to stop—"

"*I* have to stop?" I shook my head, disgusted, thinking of approximately 813 horrible things to say. Instead, I turned to go.

"You have a room," my mom called.

I paused.

"At my new apartment. You have a room there. I got you a bed. And a dresser. Something refurbished from a flea market, very colorful, mostly purple. I think you'll like—"

"No thanks," I interrupted, thinking *ice,* thinking *I'll show you a brick wall.* "Bye now. I have to pack."

KEAGAN

Sunday, March 24
5 Days

I pulled into a parking spot at Bellamy's apartment complex, killed the engine, collected our pizza from the passenger seat, and walked up the stairs to her apartment. Pepperoni, pineapple, and mushroom. Made wrong, clearly. Gross but also free. Perks of being a delivery boy. Is that PC? Pizza Delivery Young Man. Sexist? Pizza Delivery Young Person. Ageist? Pizza Delivery Human. There. Got it.

I knocked once and Bells opened the door.

"'Sup," I said.

"Hey."

She closed and locked the door behind me. It was elevenish. Her mom was still at work. I hadn't been home. Mostly because near the end of my shift my mom had texted me emojis of a key, a door, that guy with his arms crossed in front of his face and chest like "NO," and the couple side-kissing with the pink heart in between, which either meant "don't forget to lock the door to keep the kissing neighbors out" or "we're having special parent time," so yeah. . . . Ever washed a water bottle by pouring in a little hot water and dish soap and shaking it up till it foams all thick and spills out the top when you unscrew the cap? I needed that for the inside of my skull.

Anyway, this was a thing we did, Bellamy and me. She was alone a lot. I was third-wheeled by my parents a lot. So I'd come here, bring pizza, and we'd be less alone/third-wheeled together.

It was cool because as exceedingly cheesy as this sounds, she's family. Sister? First cousin? In-law? Sure, in-law. Since I got her when I got Nari. They'd been friends forever when I came along, and we melded. It was similar with Reese, and of course Santiago and I are super tight, but Bells and me . . . It's the latchkey kid/free-range parenting thing. The only child (Bellamy)/way older sibling (me, sister, age twenty-six) thing. We've both been on our own a lot of the time, so it just made sense for us to be on our own together for at least some of it.

I set the pizza on the coffee table. Bells already had a game of *Assassin's Creed* paused on the TV. "Going old-school?" I asked. She was playing the original. One we'd beat, I don't even know, a long-ass time ago.

She shrugged. "I like the world."

And that was Bells. *Here's what I think, the end.* No justifications. No qualifications. Just-this-is-it-ifications. Ha.

I sat on the couch next to her, opened the pizza box, and handed her a slice, then took one for myself. She saved her game and offered me the controller, but I waved it off.

"Pretty batshit, right? Feels extra real now."

Bellamy chewed a huge bite. Her brow creased. She swallowed. "'Feels real' is a misnomer. Unless you're referring to philosophy. Reality is reality regardless your perception of it. In fact, humanity's perception is so narrowed by the limitations of our mental and sensuous faculties that reality may be far more complex than our understanding of it."

That's Bells, too. Hyperliteral. "You know what I mean."

"I do."

"So? All obfuscation aside."

She grinned. "Six points."

"Aw, come on! That was *at least* eight."

"Hard six. Any more would be cronyism." She finished her slice, set her crust back in the box, and picked up another. "But yeah. Feels real. And a lot like anxiety."

I took a bite of pizza. I one-hundred-percent hated this idea. Start to finish, hated it. I thought it was pretty much the worst idea ever. Not worse than, like, taking that krokodil drug that basically makes its users' skin rot off, or getting a face tattoo or something. But still. This was . . . bad. This was *asking for it.*

And, for the record, I am *not* a shit friend to Bells for thinking that. It has been suggested that I "think it's okay for Bellamy to settle," or that I'm "just scared of doing something big." But, *for the record,* breaking umpteen laws with severity varying from misdemeanors to CLASS-A FELONIES LIKE GRAND THEFT WITH A SPRINKLING OF MAJOR CYBERCRIMES and ending up in PRISON is just a *smidge* worse than "settling," which wasn't at all what I suggested in the first place, *Nari.*

Whew.

Okay.

No, you know what? Not okay. Because I know *all* about loaded language. My parents are talkers, the sharing type, the *over*sharing type, and not just on subjects that'll make the average person's skin catch on fire with embarrassment. They talk about other stuff, too. Like the patriarchy. And everyday sexism. And how capitalism is basically a massive scheme for transferring wealth from the bottom up under the guise of consumer choice and emotional manipulation designed to make you crave shit you don't and will never need, meanwhile poisoning our populations with food stuffed with chemicals and polluting our planet to the brink of being unlivable.

Also, feelings.

I get it. I'm the only one of us without a plan. No art or space or diving or world domination for me. And I guess I've always been okay with that? Or haven't thought about it too much? At least, I've never thought of it as a flaw. I'm eighteen. I don't know what I want to do for the next fifty years of my life. Is that wrong?

But then Nari says stuff about settling. And that I'm afraid of big things. Which makes it sound like not having a passion like the rest of them means I don't get it. That I'm not qualified. To be a part of the conversation? To know what's right or wrong? Both? I'm not sure.

But anyway. Anxiety. Bells felt anxious, which was about five steps shy of the all-out dread I thought we should all be feeling. I took another bite of pizza. The "free" of it didn't cancel out the "gross" so much on the second mouthful. "Have you tried calling again?"

She sighed. "No." And slouched deeper into the couch. Her expression grew terribly, heartbreakingly sad, but it did not sway me. Could not sway me. I would not be swayed!

Okay, I swayed a little. Hey, I'd been there. I'd watched her face after the line went dead and she'd oh-so-slowly dropped her hand holding her phone into her lap. I am not heartless! I care! Very much, actually. But—

"Do you think he deserves it?" I asked.

Bellamy crossed her arms and rested her head on the couch's backrest, looking at the ceiling. Her glasses reflected the game menu on the TV. I waited, wondering what Bells's thought process looked like. Would it be one of those trippy artistic renderings of firing neurons? The black webbed with a network of glowing brain cells, a bunch of neon-lit thoughts racing about like they always did but, like, times a hundred?

Finally, she said, "Do you think I do?"

"Do I think you think he deserves it?"

"No. Do you think I deserve MIT?"

"Of course."

She looked at me. "Really?"

Ouch. "You know—" I stopped myself and took a deep breath. That hurt. That she'd even thought to ask a question like that. Like my answer would ever be no. But. I shook it off. Tried to shake it off. Because this wasn't about my hurt. "Yes, Bellamy. Of course you deserve MIT. But come on!" I dropped my half-eaten pizza slice back into the box. "I feel like I'm going crazy here. You're supposed to be logical! How am I the only one against this?"

"This *is* logical."

"It *so* is not."

She pursed her lips, and with her arms still crossed over her chest, tight and stiff, she seemed frigid. No, not frigid. The opposite. Like heat. Like compression. Something that gets hotter the tighter you squeeze it. "Yes," she said. "He deserves it. Not only to pay. But for us to take it."

I shook my head. "You sound like Nari."

She snorted. "*You* sound like that's a bad thing."

I shrugged, trying to seem all nonchalant, which meant I probably looked like I had an itch somewhere private. Especially since I was covering for what I really wanted to do, what I'd really wanted to do for weeks, which was to grab each one of my friends by the shoulders and give 'em a good shake. Or just scream in their faces, "WHAT THE HELL ARE WE THINKING?!"

Instead I said, "Yeah, well, maybe this time it is. Maybe she's wrong. Maybe we all are."

Bellamy stared ahead.

Bells isn't much for metaphors, but I'm fine with them. And this, her looking forward, determined to only see one thing, or to *not* see something, like, you know, *me*, was a metaphor. I'd been waiting. Biding my time. Which . . . whatever. I figured one of them would have to see sense and then I'd have backup. San, maybe. He's usually pretty reasonable, and I wasn't sure if his parents' refusing to support his Olympics plans was finally getting to him or if his being on board was more about his feelings for Bellamy, but I figured if he saw sense, then Bells would. Or vice versa. Then Reese might even, too. It wasn't like she'd do the thing anyway for shits and giggles and an adrenaline rush when Bells actively didn't want her to. Obviously, Bellamy was the linchpin. If she pulled out, the plan fell apart. Even Nari would have to respect that, wouldn't she?

But, well.

Bells leaned forward and picked up the controller off the coffee table. "Can we just . . ." When I didn't take it right away, she waved it around at me, not meeting my eye. "Please?"

I ignored it. Since that's what we did now, apparently. Ignore the things that didn't mesh with this grand idiot plan. Like reality. And consequences. And me. Until I couldn't stand it anymore, took the controller, and started a new game.

PART 3

NARI

Bon Voyage

The sun was shining! The birds were singing! It was Monday, four days till we did The Thing on Friday, and the clouds had parted and a beam of ethereal light had descended from the heavens upon Keagan's car, to the chorus of a perfectly harmonized hosanna!

Okay, no, that's not what happened. What really happened was a little bit of fog and overcast sky that'd hopefully clear off by midmorning and Keag and me standing in my driveway as my dad triple-checked that his car's tires had proper pressure, including the spare, and that the jack—as well as the windshield wipers, blinkers, headlights, taillights, door locks, seat adjusters, floor mats—worked properly.

Keagan watched as my dad unpacked all his carefully packed camping equipment so he could get into the compartment beneath the floor in the back. I stood close to him and grabbed his hand.

"Hey," I said.

"Hey."

When I squeezed, he squeezed back, even though things had been weird. Horrible weird. Tense weird. I knew he didn't approve (to make it a feather, a wisp, i.e., put it lightly) of all this, but I knew that was only because he didn't get it. Or didn't want to get it. I'm not calling Keagan naive. He isn't. Not with Paisley and Brent for parents. But he still expects the best from people. He still believed that if we waited it out, Bellamy'd get some magic and inevitable windfall, that it'd all just Work Out.

It was a symptom. That's how I thought of it. (Yes, *thought*, past tense.) Keagan's expectations of goodness and decency were a reflection of his goodness and decency and of his "distaste for confrontation." I'd say he hates it, but Keag doesn't like the word "hate," so.

For example, when that shitbag Barret says sexist and aphobic (yes, *aphobic*, because it still is regardless of his not knowing Reese is acearo) garbage to or about Reese, Keag's all "when they go low, we go high." Which, thanks to the White Allocishet Patriarchy, is pretty easy for him to say, right? I mean, bullshit stinks way less when it's being chucked at someone else instead of at you. But I'm more like, "Maybe I'll zip into my d0l0s skin and MAKE HIS LIFE A LIVING HELL." So, happy medium? I call him a fucker to his face.

More generally, Keagan legit believes that putting good out gets good back. That positivity and tolerance and optimism will each give you literal returns. Vibes, energy, whatever. That deserving will eventually equal receiving. Which is lovely! Delightful! And also not how life works! Sometimes you have to demand the goodness you deserve. Sometimes if you want something, you have to go and get it for yourself.

My dad, satisfied that Keag's car would not spontaneously disintegrate, started reloading the gear in back. Keagan walked over to help but ended up just handing my dad various items— sleeping bags, tent, camp stove, cooler—as he called for them, fitting it all together like a game of Dad Tetris. When he finished, he shut the hatchback and offered Keagan his hand for a firm shake, then came over to give me a hug. "Be safe and have a fabulous time, sweetheart."

He let go and stepped back, and I said, "We will. Enjoy your and Mom's test run at being empty nesters."

He gripped his heart dramatically. "Don't remind me!"

"Right, like I didn't see the tickets to the show you and Mom are going to in Portland Friday. They're taped to the fridge with a huge, rather obnoxiously detailed hand-drawn smiley face next to them."

"Not to mention what's written on the kitchen calendar," Keagan added. The front door opened behind us and my mom came down the porch steps, stopping beside me and looping her arm around my waist.

"Yeah. 'NARI GONE WE'RE FREE'? With *two* exclamation points? Little harsh, don't you think, Dad?"

"Hey, at least you didn't see the calendar in the home office," my mom said. "With the big red Xs counting down the days? Now *that* would've been uncomfortable."

"Har har har," I said. I squeezed her tight, then leaned down a little (Narioka Diane: 5'9"; Jillian Okada: 5'4" on a super good-posture day) to kiss her cheek. "Well, have an appropriate amount of fun in your depressingly quiet and lonely, not to mention boring, Nari-less house. I hope you miss me terribly."

My mom hugged Keagan. A real, genuinely affectionate hug

that he wholly reciprocated, as my mom really and genuinely loves Keagan, like a few shallow steps down from my brothers. It probably has something to do with all the politeness and respect and whatnot. And the fact that Keagan is one of those people. An enhancer of sorts. The kind of person who lifts you up, makes you better, happier, calmer. (That goodness and decency thing I was talking about.) The kind of person who makes you feel like you can do anything, be anyone, because no matter what, he'll be there, believing in me.

Round of hugs accomplished, Keag and I got in the car and headed off to pick up the others. I smiled at him from the passenger seat as we turned out onto the road. "I love you."

"I love you, too," he said. Not an endearment but a statement of fact.

We picked up Santiago, then Reese, then Bells, then stopped at Walmart for food and gas. Before we got out of the car, I held out my purse. "Okay, pretty people, commence The Fabulous Five Celebrate Life and Friendship and, wow, that's corny. Can someone please come up with a better title? But also, give me your phones. We're going off the grid."

"Why?" Reese asked, dropping hers into my bag. "To silence any potential snitches?" Santiago, Bells, and Keag followed suit. I kept my prepaid in my pocket. This wasn't all fun and games. It was also work.

"Course not." I shrugged. "I don't know. I just think it'll be fun to take a break."

"Exist only in the here and now," Santiago said.

"Yes! That. No distractions. No disconnect. Just us, together, right now. Think of Keagy's '94 Subie like a portal. A time machine."

"A schism in the space-time continuum," Bells said. "A time warp."

"Again, yes!"

"Except for letting our parents know we aren't missing or dead," San said.

"Yeah, except for that."

Inside, we split up. Keagan and Santiago went off in search of necessities like propane and dinner and chips and ice and things with nutrients while Reese, Bellamy, and I sought out all things essentially inessential. Like five pinwheels of varying colors, a neon-pink jump rope, a blank notebook and a pack of glitter-gel pens, cheap rain ponchos, a wand-esque toy that lit up to display rainbow stars on the walls. And candy. Lots of candy. Oh, and:

"Disposable cameras?" Reese asked. "I didn't even think they made these anymore."

"They're perfect!" I cheered, dumping ten (yes, ten) of them atop the adequately ridiculous contents of our cart. "No deleting, no editing. They're like tiny time capsules themselves."

"Ones we won't get to open until it's all over," Bells said.

Reese wrinkled her nose. "How ominous."

"No," I said. "She's right. Whatever happens, we'll have these on the other side."

"Again," Reese said. "Ominous."

"I prefer to think of it as premeditated nostalgia," I said, then surveyed our bounty. "Anything else?"

"Yeah, those unicorn ears and horn headbands we saw in the aisle with the light-wand thingy."

"Now that, my dearest Bluebells," I said, "is exactly the right type of thinking."

SANTIAGO

Feels Like Fire

Keagan looked through the contents of our cart, lips moving, talking quietly to himself, taking inventory. It was a good thing he'd elected us for this task, as leaving it up to Nari would probably have meant licorice and scratch-and-sniff stickers for dinner.

I followed him to the drinks aisle and helped him load a couple gallon jugs of drinking water onto the cart's bottom rack. He took over pushing the cart toward the checkouts, where we'd meet the girls, and said, "It's like riding in a car with no brakes."

I waited. He'd been reticent all morning—Keagan but with the dial turned down. Sometimes getting Keagan to talk about things he'd rather avoid is like trying to swat a fly that's flitting around your house. No matter how calmly and methodically you approach it, it can sense you coming. No matter how many times I'd skirted this conversation, for weeks, each time he saw it coming and darted away. Finally, I asked, "At full speed?"

He snorted. "Down a mountainside."

"Toward a cliff?"

"Above a pit filled with the vibrant green flames of wildfire."

We parked next to the wall of gift bags and greeting cards across the pathway from the checkouts. "So. Bail, tuck, and roll. Or?"

"Or . . ." He pantomimed an explosion.

"Okay, okay. But what if there's another option?"

"What," he said, cynical, "like Drogon will swoop in to save us at the last moment? Simultaneously setting our enemies aflame?"

"Aren't they already on fire in the pit?" I didn't think I needed to point out that in this scenario Nari was the "enemy." Or maybe she was the car. Maybe we all were, though of course it wasn't so simple as that. It never is. Keagan hating this plan but coming along to help us do it, my parents supporting my diving but not my goal of making it to the Olympics. People are complex and irrational and driven and idle and dedicated and changeful and loyal and prejudiced because people are full of contradictions and conflicting ideas and wants and needs and beliefs.

He shrugged a shoulder, pulled a greeting card from its slot, opened it, then—when a metallic version of "Happy Birthday" started to play—slammed it shut. "Setting them on double-fire, then."

I leaned down to rest my crossed arms on the cart's handle. "Or, you know, it could work."

Keagan pulled out another greeting card, this one covered in glitter with a picture of Chewbacca on the front. "Working or not working," he said quietly, almost to himself, "it all feels like fire to me."

BELLAMY

Experiments in Denial

"Sea Lion Caves!" Nari called from the passenger seat. We were thirty-three miles and counting west of home on Highway 101, heading down the coast. Nari listed off attractions from the map she'd bought at a gas station while the rest of us voted for which we'd like to see on a scale from one to ten.

I started the ratings with: "Eight!"

"One and a half," said Keagan. "Because of the cave part."

"*Fourteen!*" Reese bellowed.

"Rules, Reese!" Nari said. "Fourteen is outside the acceptable boundaries of the rating system."

"Don't care. Don't care. *Come on.* Sea. Lion. Caves. As in magical caves full of sea lions!"

"We went a few years ago," San said. "It's pretty cool."

"*No.*" Nari whipped around in the front seat, finger pointed back at Santiago. "No breaking the bubble, Santos! This is 1994. I mean, look at this map! It has folds! It is made of actual paper! You had not been to the Sea Lion Caves in 1994. You had not been born, nay, conceived or even *considered* in 1994."

"Right, right, of course," San said. "What was I thinking? I've never been to see the very-cool-for-a-short-period-of-time-before-the-barking-and-grunting-of-it-all-gets-slightly-boring-but-there's-an-awesome-statue-and-maybe-we'll-even-see-a-whale Sea Lion Caves. So, yes, that's where we should go."

"Seconded!" said Reese.

"Thirded," said me.

And that was that, majority achieved, despite Keag's groan.

While Keagan drove the fifty-plus remaining miles to the Sea Lion Caves, Nari studied her map, doodling on it with one of the glitter-gel pens we'd picked out at the store. Reese crocheted a skeletal creature of some sort for her Etsy store at my right, and San looked out the window at my left. He drummed his fingers on his leg in time with the song playing on the radio, smiled at me when he noticed me looking, and moved his hand to tap the beat against my thigh. I liked it. The casual way he touched me. His smile. My smile.

It'd been like this for a while. Extra smiles, extra touches, extra looks. Though I didn't know what it meant yet, what the equation looked like, or what I wanted the answer to be. All I knew was the constant: that we were both leaving for school in the fall. The variables were subjective and hard to define. How I felt. How he felt. How that fit with the other variables of our friendship and the constant of our leaving. But I liked it anyway. I liked San, his calm, his ambition, his hands and shoulders and face. I liked watching him dive, his incredible grace and proficiency. I also liked his combination of humility and confidence. He'd been the best diver on the high school team since freshman year, the best in the state since sophomore year, had been drawing scouts since junior year and secured his place at Stanford before most people in our class began applying for college. Yet when the local paper interviewed him this year before State, he talked more about the team than himself.

The song changed and Santiago shifted the rhythm of his knuckles against my leg to match the new beat. Considering the context, it felt almost wrong to enjoy this, both San's touch on my thigh and pretending that we'd stepped out of reality and were on a simple road trip. In social psychology this is called pluralistic ignorance. Except, of course, that in the true definition of pluralistic ignorance, an individual holds a private rejection of a norm they incorrectly assume the majority accepts. In our circumstance, we all agreed to accept a false reality while each knowing that that reality was a construct. All considered, it might've been more correct to call our situation an act of intentional collective denial or delusion. Here we all knew, privately, that the game was primarily a coping mechanism but accepted that the others were playing it in earnest, causing each of us to play along in a self-validating and self-perpetuating cycle of denial.

I'd gotten good at denial. Since I'd called and been hung up on by Robert Foster, since I'd talked with my mom all those nights ago, since I'd texted Nari that I was in, I'd cultivated a solid case of cognitive dissonance. I managed to believe that this was both a doomed idea and a plausible necessity. The likely consequences were dire. But framing it as a necessity let me justify them.

I'm not proud of that, but it's how I felt.

At the Sea Lion Caves we did everything: rode the three-hundred-foot elevator down into the cave to stare at the sea lions, stood at the overlooks to admire the view, watched successfully for whales, browsed the gift shop, bought some fudge, though we had at least four pounds of candy in the car already, and finally, posed at the sea lion statue. Nari flagged down another tourist and handed him one of our disposable cameras.

"Okay, everyone, look pretty!" she said, and we gathered around the statue, Santiago in the back, draped over the rear of the big bull sea lion, Nari and Keagan cuddled in the middle between the cow and the pup, Reese posed with her elbow propped on the bull's head while I sat on its back.

The tourist, a man in his mid-thirties, looked at the disposable camera and smiled. He wound the film with a *click-click-click*. "Ready?" he asked, holding the viewfinder up to his eye. "Smile!"

The camera flashed.

"Take a few more?" Nari asked. "Just in case. Thanks!"

Twice more, the man wound the film and took our picture. Then we all climbed down off the statue and he handed the camera back to Nari. "Thank you, sir," she said, and curtsied, holding out the hem of her oversized sweater when she dipped.

"Now what?" Keagan asked as we walked back to the car.

"Lunch," Reese said.

"Yes!" San and I agreed.

"Then driving," Nari said. "Lots of driving."

We continued south, waiting to find the strangest, "most intriguing without the threat of food poisoning," as Reese put it, lunch place. After more than two hours of snacking on Twizzlers and Oreos and chips in the car, Santiago spotted an acceptable option in Port Orford.

Keagan parked and we climbed out of the car, stretching, yawning. "Why do I still feel like I'm going sixty miles an hour?" he asked.

"You're velocitized."

"Veloci-what? Footnotes, Bells. Please."

"It just means that you were driving long enough to become accustomed to your velocity," I said. "Thereby altering your perception of your true speed."

"Delightful," Nari said, pulling out a disposable camera. She waved it around, urging us to pose in front of the little fish-and-chips shop. The coast dropped off behind it with the ocean stretching out in a gray mass beyond that. She snapped a few of the four of us making stupid faces, pointing to the restaurant's sign with exaggerated smiles, then stopped us as we made to disperse.

"Wait." She dropped the disposable into her purse and pulled out three of our phones.

Santiago frowned. "What are you—"

"Don't worry about it," Nari said, smiling. "We just need a few." She snapped candids and a few posed pictures, despite our lack of enthusiasm, with Reese's phone, then San's, then mine.

"For?" Keagan asked as she dropped one phone back into her purse and started up with another.

"Posterity! Nostalgia! Our parents!" she cheered, then shrugged. "And proof of our Totally Innocent Spring Break Redwoods Camping Trip aka our alibi."

KEAGAN

Love's Not a Changeling

The bubble had burst.

But it was a ridiculous bubble anyway, right? Except that it wasn't. It was a fun bubble. I *liked* it inside the bubble. It was simple in there, small and cozy without the need for alibis and that pesky threat of imminent doom.

We piled out of the restaurant and back into the car, stopped for gas, paid for from our crime-spree slush fund, and were on our way.

With a hundred and thirty miles left till we got to the campsite Nari had picked and reserved for us, we passed the time playing car games, making faces and posing for the disposable camera pics one of them always seemed to be taking, and trying to keep up pretending it was 1994, or now but without cell phones.

Reese was narrating some story, supplemented primarily by Bells and Nari, about the infrequently glimpsed fae world that had, just *had*, to live in the trees. Something about queens and lost princesses and dark magic and how they were probably watching us, keeping track of our progress down the road because Reese was really a changeling and her people were preparing to call her home.

"I could be a faerie," she said. "Check out my ears." I glanced in the rearview mirror at her as she gestured to the pointed shape of her ears, pulling her bright red hair back from the side that wasn't shaved to show off both.

"Absolutely," Bellamy said beside her. "And then there's your colorfulness."

"And your willowy-ness," San added. "Wait, is 'willowy' offensive? I just mean how it's like you started off normal and five foot something and then someone grabbed all your limbs and pulled."

"Hey!" Reese said, half laughing, and I heard her punch Santiago's shoulder followed by San responding, "*Ow.*"

"They're probably waiting for graduation," Nari said. "So they can free you publicly and make a truly epic scene."

"Now *that* is an idea I can get behind," Reese said. Then she said something else, followed by San saying something more, but I tuned them out and concentrated on the curves of the road, the gray light from the overcast sky, the intermittent views of the water, the bugs occasionally splatting on the windshield, the other cars filled with other people probably not on their way to commit multiple felonies, and how Nari had squeezed my hand in her driveway that morning and the way she'd said "I love you." We said it all the time. "Love you" when we hung up the phone, when we left each other's houses or at school or wherever, when we cuddled close on the couch in her basement watching bad movies and good movies and also when we breathed each other's breath beneath the blankets in my bed. *I love you.* It was always so easy, like saying "hi" or "bye" or "what's up, other weirdo who matches the inner weirdo of my heart and soul."

But this morning when she'd said it, it hadn't felt like any of those sorts of easy. It'd felt like she was saying it just to make sure I'd say it back.

REESE

Friendship the Color of Foreboding

Inarguable facts:

(1) Nature is beautiful.

(2) Nature must be respected and preserved.

(3) Nature is best experienced through a window or video screen within a climate-controlled room, because nature is also gross and dirty and, in late March, freaking cold.

Okay, that last one's less "fact" and more "opinion," but an opinion that is still entirely right because *I am an indoor girl, dammit!* I just happen to have outdoor-loving friends. Even Nari! Who will gleefully camp in leggings, ballet flats, and a chunky cable-knit sweater like a catalog model.

So, yeah, we were camping. In March. Despite my protests and reasoning that we could totally not and say we did since we were already planning to do that for the rest of the week anyway. But I was outvoted and overruled by the "best lies are based on truth" argument.

Keagan drove us around the dirt access road searching for the campsite Nari had reserved for us weeks ago. Not that that seemed necessary, seeing how we were one of maybe half a dozen groups batshit enough to want to go camping this time of year. When he finally spotted the right numbered marker, he parked and we climbed out.

Arms full of six-person tent, sleeping bags, backpacks, coolers, bags of food, blankets, and camp chairs, we waddled our way up a narrow trail through a stand of trees to the campsite, which sat on a sort of knoll? berm? whatever the hell you'd call it. A spot with a fire pit and a picnic table overlooking the beach and ocean below.

And, okay, inarguable fact number one? It was gorgeous. Frigid and wet in that way where it wasn't raining but the air was so heavy you could feel the water in it, like potential rain. Like, breathe it in and in and in and maybe drown a little, or at least feel your body's H_2O percentage rise. But gorgeous.

I dumped my armload of crap off to the side of the empty patch of ground where we were going to set up the tent and walked the few paces over to the top of the knoll to take in the view. It was a study in gray. Deep grays, thin grays, white grays, bluish grays, metal grays, even a few patches of sunlit grays, and on and on. You could do whole series of the ocean on overcast days. Not even stormy days, just overcast. This not-quite-tranquil, not-quite-turbulent in-between. Clouds of every colorless shade. Small whitecaps on small waves. The muted beige of the sand and the sea grasses blowing in a light wind.

"When is someone going to invent a self-assembling tent?" Keagan asked behind me.

I looked back to see San helping him put together the poles, the joints snapping where their elastic marrow pulled them taut. "Don't those exist already?" San asked.

"In a form that won't collapse and suffocate you in your sleep?" Bells said, looking up from where she tugged at the corners of the tent, laying it flat atop the tarp she'd already spread out on the ground. "Maybe."

I turned to help Nari dole out the sleeping bags and pads. After a minute, she looked up and said, "I'm going to make sure we didn't leave anything in the car," and headed off down the narrow trail.

I followed.

A pace behind, fighting that hiking-downhill feeling of wanting to run or trip gracelessly, I said, "We didn't leave anything in the car."

She glanced back. I could still hear Keag, San, and Bellamy putting up the tent behind us. "I need to check something."

"A nefarious-plan something?"

Nari stopped and turned to face me. "It's not nefarious." She looked offended, actually hurt.

I quirked an eyebrow. "Dubious, then?"

She turned and started walking again.

"Hey." I jogged a step to catch up. "It was a joke. We're on the same side. *Are* there even sides?" It was a stupid question, because of course there were sides. Nari's. Keagan's. But also, there weren't. Because he was here, too. And we were all in this together. Keag's voice of complicit dissent—disagreeing agreement? unified disunity?—notwithstanding.

At the car, Nari unlocked the driver's door and slid into the seat. I walked around to the passenger side, and after a pause so brief it might not have even been real hesitation, she reached over and unlocked my door. I got in and shut the door behind me. Even after most of the day with us in it, Keag's car still smelled faintly of pizza. Pizza essence. Eau de grease and old cheese. Like after the five of us got out, taking our scents with us, it oozed out of the seats.

Nari opened the glove box in front of me and pulled out her prepaid phone. She'd been using it from the beginning. Since before the plan was a plan, as far as I knew. Maybe she used it for other d0l0s stuff, too.

"What are you checking?"

"Emails mostly. Foster's." She flicked at the screen with a finger. "I want to keep track in case anything's canceled or changed." Her brow creased. After a minute she reached past me, chucked the phone back into the glove box, and slammed its door. "Service out here sucks."

"Shocker," I said.

"Yeah."

"Sorry about the nefarious thing. And the sides thing. You know I think this is awesome, right?"

She shrugged.

"Look." I angled toward her. "I know how much you want us to forget everything for now and have fun, but this isn't all on you, Narioka Diane. We're all doing it. You don't have to keep things secret. I mean, Kurt Cobain killed himself in '94. It's not like the year was *that* nice."

I searched the backseat and found the bag with the unicorn headbands and light-wand thing, and held it up like, *Here, this is what we came for.* "We got this. All of us. Even Keng," I said, opening the door; then, because I can't help myself, I added, "I mean, come on, what could go wrong?"

SANTIAGO

Five Years and the Future

The sun slid toward the horizon, a brilliant orb behind cloud cover that stretched and softened its light into a glowing halo. I stood atop the berm at the edge of our campsite and watched that light, the rays that pushed through like taut translucent ribbons and turned the choppy surface of the water to blinding shards of mirror where they fell. It was beautiful and immense, the kind of beauty that reminds me I'm so immeasurably small, the kind of smallness that makes some people feel expendable and alone but makes me feel integral, one of many, part of the human mechanism, giving and taking, creating and breaking, each of us a fragment of what came before and what'll come after.

The sun dipped below the horizon and I turned back to my friends.

Reese, looking over Keagan's shoulder into the pot he was stirring on one of the propane stove's two burners, said, "That looks like cud."

Keag scoffed. "How would you know what cud looks like?"

I added a log to the fire. We'd bought two bundles of dry wood at Walmart and scavenged what we could nearby, but that wasn't much. The fire wasn't likely to last long.

"It's regurgitated grass, Keagy. I think my imagination can handle the stretch."

"Whatever," he said, and grabbed a paper plate from the stack, ladling a pile of stewed kale onto it and adding a scoop of brown rice from the second pot before handing it to her. "You'll eat it, and you'll like it."

Reese saluted and took her plate over to sit by the fire. I stood to fill my own. "Think of it as a sponge. Soaking up some of the garbage we've been eating all day."

"Like donuts and coffee," Nari said. "Or bread and alcohol." She took a picture of Keagan at the stove with one of our phones, then accepted the plate he held out for her. She'd been doing that all evening, taking pictures with various phones, instructing us to pose and even change clothes a few times, saying she'd swap out time stamps to make one evening look like four after we got back. Between those and the random pictures we each took with the disposable cameras for fun, it was a strange mix, both real and fake, occasionally at the same time, and altogether a fitting parallel for this adventure as a whole.

Bellamy sat with her plate in the camp chair next to mine. "Or replenishing a deficit," she said. "Like watching an episode of *Nova* after bingeing three straight seasons of *Real Housewives* to salvage a few lingering brain cells and your sense of human decency."

We all laughed.

"Fine," Reese said. She held up a forkful of kale, wrinkling her nose at it before shoving it into her mouth and chewing and swallowing with her disgusted expression unchanged. "Yeah, super gross. But thanks for considering our health, Keag."

Keagan sat down in his chair, took a huge bite of greens, and gave us all a giant mush-filled grin. "You're welcome."

I laughed along with the girls, but after years of friendship I knew that Keagan's theatricality was directly correlated with his level of discomfort. And sure enough, the moment the others looked away, his expression fell.

"Okay," Reese said, displaying her empty plate before dropping it into the fire. "Nutrients replenished. Now I'm going to eat delicious hyper-processed animal parts." She got up and dug the package of hot dogs out of the cooler. "Anyone else?"

"That's horrifying," Nari said. "Also, yes."

Finishing our kale and rice, each of us save Keagan switched to hot dogs, holding our skewers over the fire.

"I want to play a game," I said.

"Something pig related?" Reese asked, waggling her eyebrows.

I shook my head. The fire was getting low. Bellamy handed me her skewer to hold while she added another log and stoked it with a stick. It was fully dark now. The sound of the water and the breeze, a steady hush, made everything feel both big and small, huge with the ocean and open air, but tight and close with the five of us huddled around the light of the flames. Opposite of what I'd felt watching the sunset, the dark made me feel like we were the only people in the world. "I want to know: Where are you five years from now? If everything goes exactly the way you want it to."

"Aw," Reese crooned. "Santiago the eternal optimist."

"You know me. Rainbows and kittens and glittery unicorn farts. Also, now you get to go first."

"Fair enough." She tested the temperature of her hot dog with her fingers, then held it up in the air to cool. The skin was crisp and one side split. Tapping her finger against her mouth and staring into the middle distance, she settled back into the bucket of her camp chair. "Let's see. Five years means I'll be twenty-three, so I'm sure my fae heritage will have made its full appearance by then."

"*Reese,*" Bellamy groaned. "Play along."

"Okay, okay." She took a bite of her hot dog, chewed, swallowed. "I'll be in art school. Chicago, maybe, or New York. A city, for sure. Somewhere stuffed full of weird and interesting people. Or just a more, um, eclectic assortment."

"Are you calling us allos *boring?*" Nari asked, feigning offense.

"Mmm . . . ," Reese said. "Yes." She grinned, showing all her teeth. "As I was *saying.* Somewhere that stinks of creative brilliance."

"And BO," Keag added.

"Yes, and body odor," Reese said. "Loads of it. Which will inspire my senior project and breakthrough series. It'll be my first semi-major gallery show, something to do with individuality versus the sheer masses of humanity, of flesh and fat and skin and body hair. That fascinating mix of our general disgustingness and our brilliance. Space travel and symphonies and syphilis.

"The show will be a massive hit, and I'll sell nearly all the pieces at the opening, including a few to the tastemakers. I'll build my career on it."

"What else?" I asked.

"Besides art?"

I nodded.

Reese shrugged. "Not sure. I'll still talk to you fools and visit everyone as often as we can, though I won't come back to Oregon much, since after my parents' divorce finalizes and I graduate, I doubt they'll both stick around. My mom will probably end up God knows where, and my dad might stay here for work, or maybe he'll transfer, or quit and start over. Meet the real love of his life. Have a few new-beginning kids." She shrugged again. "It'll be good."

I smiled at her, then looked at the others. "Who's next?"

Nari raised her hand. She talked about going to Berkeley, graduating at the head of her program in three years, counting summers, because she's a badass and because she'll have impressed and/or intimidated a good number of her professors into letting her test out of the basics, which I'm not sure is even a thing. "After graduation I'll have my pick of job offers from a few of the big ones. Google or Apple or somewhere. And from there I'll claw my way up the ranks. Basically I just want to do whatever I want with the most advanced computing technology in the world."

"That all?" I asked, smiling.

She grinned back, one eyebrow arched. "For now."

She'll also be happily either married to or cohabitating with Keagan, who took over the narrative after her to say that maybe he'll learn a trade. "Be an electrician or something. Maybe own my own construction company someday. Or just work for someone good. So, sure, five years?" He scrubbed his head with his beanie. Like mine, his hair had grown back past the obnoxious, itchy stage, so now the movement was more a tic, like cracking his knuckles. "Let's say I'll be working with a carpentry crew. Working with my hands. Building stuff. Living in the Bay Area with Nari as she works toward being the next CEO of Google—"

"Or my own company!"

"Right, or your own company. I don't know, maybe I'll do custom kitchens or restorations or something for all the rich people. I think I'd like that. Fixing things up. Making old stuff new again."

Nari, her chair pushed up close to his, leaned into his arm and gave him a look of total adoration. Keagan stared at the dying fire, brow tight. He reached for the stick we'd been using to stir it, then stood instead. "I'm gonna look for more wood," he said, and walked off into the dark toward the shore. Nari watched him go until his head ducked below the beach side of the berm, then got up to follow.

"Welp." Reese yawned, unfolding her limbs and pushing herself up out of her chair. "I'm tired. And freezing. And you guys don't seem like you need a third wheel. So I'm going to bed."

Bellamy blushed. "No, Reese, it's—"

Reese gave Bells a salute and a wink, then crossed between me and the fire.

"'Night, Reese," I said.

"'Night, kiddies," she said, and trekked over to the tent, zipping herself inside.

NARI

Phobias and Facades

I followed the roll of our campsite's berm down toward the beach. The sand was deep, and I was wearing impractical shoes. The wedge heels of my ankle boots sank with each step. I had to concentrate hard on not twisting an ankle. Keagan had walked down along the edge of the water to the other side of the small cove our site sat above and was sitting on the next knoll over, arms propped on his knees, staring out at the water. His fleece North Face jacket was flat black in the light from the few visible stars and the glow of the shrouded moon. I hugged my coat tighter around me and climbed the little hill to sit beside him.

He didn't look away from the water.

I've always hated the ocean at night. It's the hugeness of it. The cognitive dissonance, how even though dark water looks empty, even though you can gaze out at it and half convince yourself it's an enormous velvety carpet, you know instead it's teeming with fish and sharks and whales and plankton and probably at least one kraken.

I feel the same about space. Right then, above all that black ocean, small patches of stars showed through the clouds. And as I took in their majesty, their flickering brilliance that Bellamy wanted to someday shoot her body through at ungodly speeds on a vessel of her own design, I thought, *Ick*. And *Oh, sweet Jesus, why?* The emptiness, the silence, the unknown, the minuscule capsule of sustainability amidst an endless uninhabitable abyss. Like the water, space seemed oppressive in its utter indifference to you, in the very many ways it could kill you.

Bells tried to explain it (her space hard-on) to me once, likening it to another world, like d0l0s's, one where I had so much freedom, so much room for possibility, but one most people would never try to understand. And I was like, *Nope*. Crushing airless vacuum versus intangible strings of decipherable code that I could manipulate for my purposes? Yeah, I'll take the latter. To which she said something about string theory and universal fabric and similarities and I was still all *Nah*, because everything being constructed of the same infinitesimal fibers regardless, coding will never cause my corporeal liquids to effervesce inside my skin (low-pressure symptoms, look it up).

Keagan gets it because he's claustrophobic. And nothing exemplifies the terror of inescapable small spaces like a boat on deep water at night or a freaking spaceship or, say, a caving trip with your much older sister when you're seven and the flashlight decides to melodramatically flicker a few times in a "narrow rocky corridor of perpetual darkness and slow death," as Keag describes the moment he realized his phobia.

Which is a thing I know about him, which, actually, is a story I've heard at least half a dozen times from four points of view (Paisley's, Brent's, Keag's, and the aforementioned much older sister, Beth's), because we know things like that about each other. All the little things you learn about someone after two and a half years of them being your favorite person. Like how they like their coffee (as tea, sweet, since Brent's originally from Georgia and brought the tradition of that particular nectar northwest with him) or how they wear their socks inside out because they're weird about the feeling of the seams. You learn the big things, too. Like how being good and decent and unfailingly moral, to a strict and pretty unmeetable degree, is one of the most important things to them.

I slid my arm around Keagan's and set my head on his shoulder. The campsite behind us, the next one over from ours, was empty. The waves lapped at the shore. The breeze pushed through the dry beach grasses. And Keag was angry. I got it. He saw all this as moral failure. I thought he was wrong, but I got it. But when Keagan's angry, he gets quiet. And pestering him (as I was, per usual, *dying* to do) doesn't work, makes him angrier, which makes him quieter, a self-perpetuating system.

So, instead, I tucked my hand into the pocket of his coat. It was patched and worn, and my favorite. I crave hugs from Keagan when he's wearing that coat. "Carpentry?" I asked.

He cleared his throat. "Is that stupid?"

"Of course not." I snuggled up closer. "Will you restore our dream house?"

"If that's what you want."

I took a slow breath through my nose. "It is."

He didn't say anything, just leaned his head against mine, and we sat like that, the faint glow of our campfire growing fainter and fainter in the distance at my right, until I reached over with my other hand and slid it up under his jacket and shirt.

He jumped, laughing. "Cold! *Cold.*"

"For now," I said, and turned, leaning in to kiss him, making him move his arms so I could fit myself into them, pushing him back into the sand and dry grasses so I could lie on his chest, hand moving lower, lower, lower down the pane of his stomach. "My hand is cold *for now.*"

He smiled against my lips.

BELLAMY

3,100 Miles or Less Than an Inch

"I don't think they're coming back with firewood," Santiago said.

Not looking at him, I blushed. "Alone at the fire again."

He smiled at me, then glanced back at the tent. The inside had been lit by a flashlight moments before, but it was dark now. Santiago looked at me. "You never got your turn."

"You either."

"Very true."

"So," I said. "Five years."

"You first."

I shook my head. "Too many variables."

He got up and scooted his chair closer to mine. "Humor me."

"Well." With the fire burned down to coals, the cool night air heavy with moisture and our voices low, I felt encapsulated. "I guess I want to be started on my doctorate. Or maybe working on a master's? I'm not sure what the best path will be. I'll have double-majored in physics and mechanical engineering during undergrad and will probably continue with engineering for my doctorate. Though maybe something more specific like robotics. Or biomechanics. Plus biology and astronomy."

"And kinesiology and botany and geology?"

"And entomology and meteorology."

San breathed a laugh.

I smiled. "How do I choose? It's all fascinating."

He reached over, slid his hand down the length of the inside of my arm, and laced his fingers with mine. My gut twisted. My pulse sped, thanks to a flush of chemicals I couldn't remember the names of right then. I tried to stop smiling and feel calm, but I physically couldn't.

"What else?" he asked. He stared at our hands. "After you learn all the -ologies, that is."

"Um." My thoughts were muddled. Santiago played with my fingers like he was testing their feel, learning the shape and fit of my hand in his. "I can't really say. I hope by then my mom will have been able to quit one of her jobs. Or have found a better-paying one altogether. Her expenses will go down once I'm out of the house, so . . ." I shrugged. San settled his fingers back in the spaces between mine. I squeezed his hand. The light from the fire's coals faded further. I pulled the hood of my sweatshirt up over my head with my free hand and stared at the embers, letting my vision lose focus. "She thinks she's failed me."

"Your mom?"

I nodded. I'd never said that out loud before. Not since she'd told me so the night Nari proposed this plan. I was surprised by how much it hurt to say it. "And not just because of my dad and MIT." I cleared my throat. "Even though she's done everything for me my whole life."

We listened to the waves lapping at the shore for a few beats. Quietly, San asked, "Is that why you agreed to this?"

"Initially. Which is pretty illogical. Since if she knew what we were doing, she'd . . ."

"Kill you and the rest of us in a fit of rage?"

I laughed. "Probably something a little less violent. And permanent. But yes."

"She won't find out," he said. I looked over to find him already looking at me. "This is going to work, Bellamy. I can feel it."

"You can't actually—"

"Yes, I can," he insisted, smiling. "I don't care if it's unscientific and unprovable. I can."

I exhaled a deep breath and leaned my head against his shoulder. "Thank you." I don't usually like analogies. Say what you mean and spare the extra words. But I didn't have the right words for this. The tenuous joy of San's hand in mine. My anxiety about the next few days. Fear that we'd fail. Fear that we'd succeed. Guilt about lying to my mom. Guilt for crimes I'd already committed, like helping Nari set up the fake identity for the bank account for diverted funds. Shame that Foster had hung up on me. Excitement that this could be the answer to my problem. All while knowing that this one big risk would change the course of my life either way. My feelings were like puzzle pieces, each from a separate picture and with edges that didn't fit.

"What'll you tell her when this works?" San asked.

When, not *if*. "I don't know. Seems too early to worry about that."

"No vendas la piel antes de matar al oso."

"What?"

" 'Don't sell the skin before killing the bear.' Like, don't count your chickens before they hatch."

"Exactly." I pulled my knees up and snuggled deeper into my chair. "Your turn."

San hugged our linked hands to his chest. "I think you already know my answer."

"Tell me anyway."

"Olympics," he said, breathing it out like a sigh. "But."

"Your parents."

"It's not like they're wrong."

"Why do you say that?"

He was quiet for a moment. He changed his grip on my hand to trace circles on my palm with his thumb. "It's a long shot at best, right? And the extra training takes time and money. When I could be concentrating more on school and a career."

"True. But you'll dive for Stanford anyway, won't you?"

"Yeah."

"So . . ." I shook my head. "I don't understand."

"It's—I don't know. It's hard to explain. My parents love me. They support me. But they don't understand why I want to do this. They don't think I should risk failing to be extraordinary when I could easily succeed at being ordinary."

I frowned. "But you're already extraordinary."

He breathed a laugh and kept tracing my palm.

I sighed. I didn't know how to argue with something that made sense to his parents but seemed illogical to me. And calling his parents illogical didn't seem like a good idea either. I wasn't good at this. Moments like this were the ones when most people lied. They said things like "It'll be okay!" or "You can do it!" while lacking any evidence that either statement was true. Or "I believe in you," which isn't a lie but an unquantifiable opinion with no bearing on the actual outcome of considered events. Even though I did believe in him. But I think San needed to believe in himself, in spite of what his parents thought. Or because of it.

I should've said it anyway. I should've leaned over, put my hand on his cheek to turn his face toward mine, told him I believed in him, and kissed him. I didn't because I'm not a spontaneous person. I, quite clearly, have a tendency to overthink things. For example, in that moment I was thinking, *I want to kiss him. But what if he doesn't want to kiss me? It seems like he does, but we're also friends. Good friends. Which, if I'm wrong, would be awkward. Horribly awkward, the stomach-tightening sort that comes from a reaction within the right pregenual anterior cingulate cortex. Or if not awkward, then at least complicated. After all, it's late March of our senior year of high school. If all goes well, this fall we'll be more than 3,100 miles apart.* So instead I asked, "What else is happening in five years?"

San unzipped his coat halfway and tucked our cold hands inside it against his chest. The warmth, *his* warmth, was immediate. I felt his heartbeat through his T-shirt against the back of my hand. "Besides my Olympic fame and your having eight degrees?"

I grinned. "Yes."

"Ah, who knows. I guess I'll have gotten a degree by then, too. In physical education, maybe? I know I want to coach, so whatever ends up being best for that. And I'm sure I'll be back and forth from California to home to visit my parents and sisters. And you."

"If everything goes as planned, you and I will live on opposite sides of the country."

"I know. I'm not looking forward to that part."

"Me either."

He was quiet. I counted twelve of his heartbeats against the back of my hand. "I'll miss you more than the others," he said.

My lower stomach tightened, and I moved. Twisting toward him, bringing my right hand up to his cheek as I'd imagined doing a few minutes before. Tilting my face up as he angled his down and closing my eyes.

Our lips met.

For a beat, we stilled. Lips cold but warming. Soft, hesitant. Then San brought his free hand up between my face and the hood of my sweatshirt, chilled fingers pushing through my hair to grip the back of my neck. Our lips parted, our tongues touched, and we kissed.

And kissed.

REESE

Every Day's a New Dawn, Obviously

Tuesday morning. Or "morning," since it was still dark. And still cold. Because it was still March. I'd rolled against the tent wall in my sleep. Both it and my sleeping bag were wet with condensation. Everyone else was still out, Nari even snoring lightly beside me. Sleeping bag pulled up past my nose, hat yanked down over my eyebrows, I stared at a bead of water tracking down the wall of the tent. Choosing between getting up and going outside or staying in my bag inside what was basically a bubble of exhaled breath was like picking between going to the dentist or the gyno.

I unzipped my bag, pulled my shoes on, then crawled toward the tent's door, bringing my sleeping bag with me, draped around my neck like an enormous scarf. I let myself out and zipped the door closed behind me. No one else so much as twitched.

Some assortment of San/Bells/Nari/Keagan had cleaned the site up after I'd gone to bed: folding the camp chairs so their seats would stay dry, disappearing the food, probably back to the car, disposing of our trash in the bear-proof bins by the road.

I unfolded a chair, then stood in my sleeping bag, zipping myself back into it before curling up in the chair. If we were going to be doing too much of this, I'd need to invest in one of those wearable sleeping bag things, the ones with armholes and an open bottom.

Except, no. We wouldn't be doing too much of this. It was March. Yeah, yeah, okay. But March didn't only mean it was a ridiculous time for camping, it also meant there were only two months till graduation, and barely five till San, Bells, and Nari left for college, and Keagan left with Nari or wherever he ended up deciding to go. I'd already been pricing plane tickets, drafting my itinerary, sketching my plan into existence one line, one sale, one day at a time.

Because, yeah. Five months. Less, depending. Maybe Nari'll get an internship. Maybe San'll get a coach down at Stanford for the summer. Keagan'll follow Nari. Bells'll take summer classes or get into some genius program. As for me, maybe I'll leave early and skip the death throes of my parents' union. The embalming. The preparing of the corpse. Corpse, divorce. Divorce, corpse. How appropriate that that rhymes, right?

I leaned my head back and watched the sky lighten. It was full of puffy outcroppings of clouds, the cotton-ball kind, the perfect-daydream kind, the kind I used to build whole imaginary worlds in when I was little and stuck in the car on some trip or sitting out in the backyard staring at the sky. They were houses. Not house, singular. But houses like Dr. Seuss drawings. The ones with all the stairs and doors and windows to rooms inhabited by furry, body-sock-wearing creatures. Except my cloud colonies were home to beings of a darker sort. Ethereal. Beautiful. But also with, like, pointy teeth. For biting.

I wondered what the dresser looked like. The one my mom'd bought for "my room" at her new apartment that was apparently "purple" and also "very colorful" and she thought I'd "like."

It probably had daisies or some shit painted on it. The seller probably called it "country chic."

The sound of the tent unzipping made me turn. Santiago crawled out, blinking. Inside, Nari sat up in her bag, running her fingers through her long hair. Keag was already stuffing his sleeping bag into its sack. Bellamy crawled out after Santiago, hood of her sweatshirt up over her head and eyes puffy behind her glasses.

"Good morning, beautiful people," I said.

Yawns, a groan, San's tired smile.

He unfolded the rest of the chairs while Bellamy grabbed the keys from Keagan and headed to the car to retrieve the box of donuts we'd bought to eat this morning. Keag, Nari, and San joined me around the fireless fire pit, staring glassy-eyed out at the ocean or down at the dirt, as one does the morning after sleeping on the ground outside.

Bells came back and passed the box of donuts around. I let everyone eat for a minute before asking Nari, "What's on the itinerary for today? More 1994?"

From her seat across the circle, she gave me a narrow-eyed look, then licked the chocolate from the corners of her mouth. "Nope. At T-minus eighty-odd hours and dwindling till we do the thing, today is solidly a present-moment day."

SANTIAGO

A Perfect Point in Space and Time

The mood changed.

The closer we got to the city, the harder it was to pretend. The realness of what we were planning to do here grew like a balloon inflating in my chest, making my breath tighter, my thoughts thicker, my tongue heavy in my mouth. By the time we reached the hotel, the only voice we'd heard for the past hour was that of the lady giving directions on Keag's maps app.

When we finally found a parking spot outside the hotel, Nari climbed out before Keagan cut the engine and shut the passenger door behind her without a word. Reese jumped out and hurried after her toward the office's doors. Keagan, Bells, and I continued the silence, watching the traffic on the road and sidewalk outside. Sitting in the rear middle seat beside me, with Keag staring blankly out the windshield, Bellamy slipped her hand into mine and I felt the balloon deflate.

"This changes things," she'd said the night before, pulling back from our kiss, her lips stretched in a wide, infectious smile.

With the coals burned low and the air cold, our breath had

fogged between us. "Good changes," I'd said, and leaned in for another kiss. It was the momentum of chance-taking. Doing this epic, risky thing made the barrier between us evaporate, made me wonder why I'd been so sure of its existence at all. I'd known I was done negotiating that nervousness, that uncertainty, before Reese even went to bed. I'd known that tonight I'd kiss Bellamy. She'd simply beaten me to it.

When we'd parted again, Bells had rested her head on my shoulder. I'd still gripped her hand against my chest within the warmth of my coat. She'd reached over and tucked her other hand between my right arm and side. "And complicated changes," she'd said.

"Like?"

"Time."

I'd taken a slow breath through my nose. The cold made it sting. "Yeah." I hadn't said more because I hadn't wanted to. We were seniors in high school, March of our last semester, and we both knew it was only months before everything began to change. But it hadn't felt like a moment for pragmatism. It had felt like one for possibility.

"You know how Einstein developed his theories based on Minkowski's hypothesis that time is the fourth dimension?" she'd asked.

I'd breathed a laugh. "No, I don't." Only Bellamy would know that, right there on the tip of her tongue. Like how she could watch me practice a dive, calculate my angles and force and trajectory in her head, then tell me how far to shift forward or back, how much harder or softer to push off the board, to perfect an imperfect dive; or like how one afternoon when my Harry Potter–loving sisters had come with Keag, Bells, and me to the beach, she'd described the possible quantum physics behind Apparition. "Explain it to me."

"Okay." She'd snuggled even closer. "Minkowski space combines space and time into a single manifold, meaning, basically, that events occupy unique positions in spacetime, or spacetime points, that exist continuously and concurrently, rather than vanishing into nonexistence once they're past. Past and present and future, therefore, coexist in the spacetime manifold, regardless our sequential experience of the 'passing' of time. Meaning that if time travel were possible, you could visit the spacetime points, the coordinates of 'past' events as they exist in the manifold. But because time is both continual and punctuated, even if you could go back and retry the different options, make different decisions, each time you would irrevocably change who you'd been when you traveled in the first place. Which could negate the reason you went back at all.

"But that isn't my point. My point is that we can't go back and try out different decisions, so." She'd shrugged.

"So . . . unlike working out a math problem or practicing a dive, you don't get to try again and again until you get it right." She'd nodded. "Exactly."

The breeze had picked up, blowing in the sea-soaked air from the water. "What would've happened if you hadn't kissed me?" I'd asked. "If you'd made one of the other decisions."

She'd taken a deep breath. "I'd have left for college in the fall regretting not being brave enough to kiss you."

I'd smiled, though she couldn't see me. There was no version of any future in which I would've let Bellamy leave for MIT without telling her how I felt, even if it was a risk to our friendship, even if she hadn't felt the same. I knew that now. And maybe she'd have argued that having it happen was what made me know, that every choice is the result of the series of choices made before it, but I believe that some things are inevitable, no matter the path that leads there. I believed that we were inevitable. "Then what?"

"Then, I don't know. The same as before?"

"Except maybe in that future, five years from now, I'd come home for a visit at the same time as you. And I'd call you or send you a brain ping using the minicomputer embedded in my cerebral cortex"—she'd laughed and squeezed my hand inside my coat—"so we could meet up. I'd come to your door, five years older."

"And weighted down with Olympic medals."

I'd smiled. "Of course. Because I'll wear them everywhere I go."

"I mean, why wouldn't you?"

"And you'd open the door to your mom's apartment, wearing an MIT sweatshirt, hair up in a knot, five years more amazing, five years more brilliant, and say something like 'Santiago! Why the hunchback?'"

She'd giggled. "No, I'd say, 'Hi, San, I missed you most.'" Then she'd turned her face to mine and, voice low, little more than a whisper, said, "But I won't have to say that. We made the other choice."

Packing away the food and dousing the remaining coals before tucking ourselves into our sleeping bags in the tent, we'd decided to keep our night to ourselves, let it settle before we told the others, maybe till after Friday, maybe longer. It felt nice to keep this feeling, this change, only ours.

In the car, she squeezed my hand and let go. Before my fingers lost the feel of hers, the front passenger door opened and Nari said, "Okay, team. We're all checked in."

NARI

Practice Makes Perfect

"Um," Reese said, stepping into the hotel room aka Heist Headquarters and our home for the next three days.

"I'll second that um," Santiago said. He dumped his armload of cooler and garment bag onto the nearer of the two beds before slinging his backpack off onto the pile. The beds' thin polyester comforters wore a faded floral print to match the walls' faded wallpaper and the floor's faded carpet, like the whole room was a picture with the saturation setting turned down low.

"Welcome to two stars," I said. I admit! I concede! The room was shit. Like, don't go barefoot on the carpet, and sleep in your clothes shit. But, damn, do you have any idea how flipping expensive San Fran is? And my first-class, suave-criminal fantasy of a high-rise suite–slash–command center would've required a larger slip of morality than I figured Keag could handle, so. "At least I sprang for a private bathroom."

"Thanks?" Reese said. "Sure, I'll go with 'thanks.'"

I elbowed her in the ribs. "Ingrate."

Bells and Keagan followed San into the room and dropped

the rest of our gear onto the second bed. Its frame squeaked under the weight, less because it was a lot of weight and more because it was a shitty frame. Though also we had a lot of crap. Especially since, after finding an elusive nonmetered twenty-four-hour parking spot many blocks away, we'd vowed to make the trek back exactly once and hauled everything we needed plus some in from the car.

"Good location," Bells said, ever pragmatic.

"Yep," I said. "Walking distance to FI. Plus they didn't make me leave a credit card to reserve the room. No extra fraud and/or identity theft needed."

"Perks," Keag said. Well, *muttered.* He muttered it. The distinction felt important.

"Well." Reese closed the door, nose wrinkled against the room's admittedly twisty smell. "Now what?"

I opened my mouth to answer, but San beat me to it. "Practice," he said. "No one does a perfect dive on the first try."

"Precisely, Santos." I held my hand up for a high five. He obliged. And we got to work. Reese organized the rest of our food into the ancient mini-fridge and atop the equally ancient microwave stacked on it. Bellamy arranged everyone's bags into the tiny closet next to the bathroom. Keag and Santiago went searching for fresh food at a shop down the block. And I set up my computer and files of research on the room's small desk, pulling it away from the wall so we could all crowd around. I did my thing, settling into my d0l0s skin, triple-checking that my IP was masked, and worming my way into Foster Innovations' surveillance system. By the time the boys came back, I'd cracked it and had three video windows (main lobby, FI executive floor lobby, and one angle of the exec floor itself) open on my screen.

"Gather round, gather round," I said as San shut and locked the door behind him, "and let Operation Hole Up and Obsessively Prepare commence."

Turned out, after about four hours watching people walk through the lobby and halls of FI's building while contemplating eventualities ranging from the plausible (Bellamy: "What if they lock the main doors to the Foster Innovations executive floor and San can't even get inside?" To which San answered, "We'll have to time it just right, so almost but not everyone is gone") to the absurd (Reese: "What if one of the security guards hits a silent alarm and SWAT comes pouring into the lobby, aiming the sights of their weapons at me all at once like neon polka dots, and I have to do a triple backflip over their heads and out a shattered window to escape?" To which the rest of us groaned), we were all deliriously bored.

By 6:42, when the last of the FI executives exited the twelfth-floor office suite (leaving the main doors, thankfully, unlocked behind her), a solid twenty-two minutes after Robert Foster left, the room and everything in it felt stale. Maybe it was the lingering campfire smoke in our hair, on our clothes. Or maybe it was the musty blankets on the beds, the dingy carpet, or the fact that the room's windows didn't open and the air conditioner set into the exterior wall pumped out what smelled like pre-breathed air. But everything felt dank.

I stood up and moved away from the table to stretch. Keagan, who'd been sitting cross-legged on the bed to watch the screen over my shoulder, took my place in the room's only chair. Bellamy and Santiago (San and Bells! Santiallamy! Belltiago! Please oh please, let it be for real! I mean, I didn't *know* know. But there was closeness! And capital-L Looks!), sitting side by side on the other bed, watched him switch between windows. Reese, who'd been studying blueprints as we plotted San's best possible route alongside the video feed, stood from her perch on one of the bedside tables we'd cleared off and dragged over. She cracked her neck and turned to kick the air-conditioning unit. Again. It hiccupped once, then continued its arrhythmic chugging. "Do you think they'll charge us if I break a window? Isn't this a fire hazard? Against some code or something?"

"Yes, yes, and probably," I answered, stretching up onto my toes with my arms above my head. I could smell campfire in my hair and was about to escape into the bathroom for a shower when Keagan huffed and shoved away from his seat in front of my computer.

"What?" I asked.

He shook his head and pretended to study our stockpile of food.

"No. Say it."

"It's just—" He shrugged, but it was fake. All pretense, no actual apathy. "They're people. We keep saying 'Foster Innovations.' FI, FI, FI. But watching that—" He waved a hand at my computer. "They're people. Employees. And not just Bells's dad or the other execs. They're interns and guards and that guy at the front desk."

The four of us watched him. Well, three, since Bells was looking at the floor. "Meaning?" I asked.

"We keep acting like this is a victimless crime. Or, well, one victim? Justice or whatever. I don't even know. But then there's Joe Whoever in accounting and Jane Whatsit at the bank. Real people. Who might get blamed or fired or . . ." He trailed off with another affected shrug.

"Only if we get caught," Reese said.

"No. If the *discrepancy* gets caught," I said. "Which it won't. Because I know what I'm doing."

I waited for Keagan to challenge me. I almost wanted him to. Rip off the Band-Aid. Get this over with. But he didn't. Instead he took a deep breath and smoothed the anger from his face, leaving a blankness where it'd been, then brushed past me into the bathroom, where a second later the fan came on and the shower started.

Coward, I thought. Yeah, I know, real mature, Narioka Diane. But seriously. Like we were pushing an old lady over in the grocery store parking lot to take the money out of her purse while she cried. Like we were stealing Christmas gifts from an orphanage, then lighting their tree on fire. Okay, that was a tad over the top. But it wasn't so freaking black-and-white!

"Anyone hungry?" San asked. "I'm hungry."

Reese turned away from the air conditioner. "Smooth segue, Santiago. Also, yes."

"I'll go look for ice," I said, and ducked out into the hall.

The hallway was dimly lit. The floorboards creaked, old wood beneath thin carpet. I walked toward the stairwell, then leaned against one of the floral-papered walls. I didn't even know if this place had an ice machine. That, and I hadn't brought the ice bucket. Was there an ice bucket? I probably should've just said, "Keag's shit makes this room feel impossibly small, so I'm gonna check out the hall for a bit," instead of the ice thing. That would've been more in keeping with Reese's we're-all-in-this-together, full-disclosure request.

Except. Well. Were we?

Keagan was like dead weight. Here, but not here. With

us but against us. And because we're a We, it felt like he was mostly my weight. Slack arms thrown over my shoulders. Limp body draped on my back. Waiting for me to drag him along. And I was getting tired of dragging.

Because you know what? I'm amazing. (Yes, confidence is one of my strong suits.) All of this was. The whole Thing. And I'd done it. I wrote the codes. I did the phishing. I hacked into FI's security system. And I was proud. Was it weird to feel proud about swimming deftly, *elegantly,* through this sea of moral grayness? Maybe. I guess I didn't know. I knew the thing with Keagan sucked. But I also knew I didn't feel guilty about the things he thought I should feel guilty about.

The door to our room opened. Bellamy came out and walked toward me down the hall. Saying nothing, she leaned against the wall beside me, slid her arm around mine, and set her head on my shoulder. I rested my head against hers.

And that was—*is*—why. Why I was proud instead of guilty. Why the reward so outweighed the risk. Robert Foster had stolen the opportunity of a lifetime from Bellamy, and I had zero qualms stealing it back.

KEAGAN

How Many Wrongs Does It Take to Make a Right?

So there's this thing called Kohlberg's Stages of Moral Development. Lawrence Kohlberg was a psychologist who basically furthered this other, earlier psychologist's theory of cognitive development by saying that moral reasoning, as in how you decide what's right and wrong, has six stages of development. Or, really, three levels with two stages each. He did a bunch of studies and whatnot to prove and clarify his theory, but the nitty-gritty of it is that as you grow from a child to an adult, you (should) progress from the first, preconventional stages, the cause and effect, action and consequence, obedience and punishment stages, to the "I'll do this for you, you do this for me" smaller group stage, to the conventional stages that consider things like society and laws and norms and the general consensus about right and wrong we all must (again, *should*) accept, semiregardless of consequences, because that's how we all manage to semipeacefully and semiproductively coexist.

Whew. Inhale.

Anyway!

All that mess is really just a buildup for this: I care. I care about being ethical and moral and *right*. Not right as in "I'm right, you're wrong," but as in Right versus Wrong. As in Good versus Evil. As in I want to be a six, six being the highest stage, where you move beyond the duality of right and wrong as society defines them and into a more abstract sort of reasoning. There's debate about whether more than a few people are even capable of reaching stage six. But goodness is important to me. Like, really important. And not just in a don't-go-to-jail way, but in a be-the-change way.

Which I realize is complicated, right? Because helping Bellamy, I mean, breaking laws to help Bellamy, not myself or even Nari or my parents or something, could've been that exact sort of morality. But, then, that wasn't taking into consideration *everything else*.

For hours we watched everyday people doing their everyday things on those FI security camera feeds. And, like, they were all just people. As much as Nari or San or Reese or Bellamy or me. Each one of them—a pair coming back from lunch, some lady in workout clothes headed to the in-building gym, another rubbing her creased forehead while she paced the lobby alternately listening to and talking into her phone—was in the middle of their own universe.

And say Nari was wrong. Say she made some mistake and the "discrepancy" *was* found out. Not even the how. Not even that we did it. Just that it was there. What if one of those people we watched going about their own business, totally unaware, ended up being seen as responsible? What if they lost their job? What if it looked like they did it? Not just that they were negligent but *culpable*. What if they were *charged*?

It was so self-centered to forget that, so selfish to not care.

And that was only when we cast the net wide. But what about a little net? What about just, like, the five of us? What about the very real possibility that this could completely ruin all of our lives, right? RIGHT?

But nope. Couldn't talk about that, could we? Couldn't even brush up against it. Because then it was all "Keagan doesn't think Bells is worth it!" and "Keag's too naive to see the *nuance*." The freaking *nuance*. Like this wasn't all some batshit Machiavellian ends-justify-the-means, narrow-minded, wish-fulfillment disaster waiting to happen but rather an adventure! The *right thing to do*. And I was just a wah-wah wet-blanket whatever.

Okay. Deep breath.

But really. *Of course* Bellamy's worth it! But I also thought, nay *believed*, way deep down inside my squishy pink heart, that there was. Another. Damn. Way.

There was. There were.

Ways like calling Robert Foster again. Or Bells deferring for a year and trying again after she's eighteen and on her own. Or disowning Foster or him disowning her or something, cutting each and every legal tie. Or, like, freaking *contacting MIT* and, I don't know, explaining the extenuating circumstances? Life is messy! Shit happens! People understand!

But, they kept telling me, none of that was the *point*.

To which I should've said, When does the point stop being justice and start being revenge?

Ugh.

Wholeheartedly, *ugh*. I even said it out loud in the shower. Some days, like today and yesterday and the day before and, okay, yeah, most of the days between today and that day at Bellamy's when Nari introduced us to this grand scheme, I felt like the odd man out. And not because I was the solitary "Um, how about no?" among four emphatic yeses. But because I was the only one who, apparently, didn't get it. Because I was the only one who didn't have some epic Thing I'd do anything for.

Until all of this, I hadn't really felt it. But now it was like I was missing the extra limb all my friends had. San had his diving appendage. Bellamy her astronaut one. Reese her art. Nari's was coding and ruling the universe. While there was me, Keagan, with the average number of protuberances (seven points), the standard number of bodily accessories. Bodily accessories? Yeah, that's totally on the brink of gross.

Anyway. There I was, feeling like an acceptably average, reasonably complete person, albeit one with rather extraordinary friends, friends I'm so wildly proud of by the way, when here came this Thing drawing a line between us. On one side were the special people, the ones with goals and hopes and plans, with dreams they'd claw and scratch and write illegal code for. While on the other side was me. Basic, undecided me. Me, who thinks about a life spent working for someone ordinary, doing something ordinary, and feels . . . honestly? Pretty okay with it. But even feeling "pretty okay" started to feel "less than okay." Like I should want more even though I really don't. Like not wanting more meant there was something wrong with me. Like I was deficient.

Which, again, *ugh*, because I know my friends don't think that about me. At least, I didn't think they did. But knowing that didn't make me feel it less.

Wow, I mouthed, and turned off the shower. Enough of

that. I grabbed a towel from the stack, dried off, and re-dressed in my camping clothes because in my hurry to avoid finishing the conversation I'd started with Nari, I'd forgotten to grab new ones.

Out in the room, San and Reese were making sandwiches for dinner. Bellamy and Nari weren't there. Santiago, spreading mayo on slices of bread, looked up and asked, "Mustard?"

"As in 'did the shower cut the—'?"

He rolled his eyes and went back to spreading. "That one's too inane even for me to appreciate."

"Cutting the mustard?" Reese asked.

He nodded.

"Like a seed? Or the spread?" She cocked her head to the side. "Can you cut either of those things?"

"Is there really more than one way to skin a cat?" I asked.

"Probably," they both said. Then Reese shook her head and, peeling slices of cheddar out of a package to put on each sandwich, said, "This is pointless. One of you, talk about something else."

"Okay," I said, and talked about how many different kinds of mustard there are until Reese pretended to die of boredom. Then Nari and Bellamy came back, and we all ate sandwiches and continued on continuing on. By which I mean Nari opened her computer and the security cam feeds again, but it being eight then eight-thirty then nine and so on, there wasn't much to see. Meanwhile the others took turns in the shower, and by ten even Nari'd agreed there was really nothing left to look at so closed it down and opened Netflix looking for the best-worst B horror movie we somehow hadn't already seen.

San and I shoved the beds together to make one Superbed.

Reese picked a movie about a yeti. We ate snacks, brushed teeth, cuddled up, and fell asleep to the sounds of yeti mayhem and the street outside. Then it was morning again, Wednesday morning, two days to go, which meant more of the same. Eat. Watch security feeds. Argue routes: Stairway? Elevator? Side entrance? Front? Argue specifics: How early should Reese go in? How long would it actually take San to get to Foster's office, install the malware on his computer, and get out again? How long into that would Reese's distraction need to last? Argue scenarios: What if someone spotted San on the FI executives' floor? Could he fake it? Would his ID hold up? Should he just turn and run?

"No way—I can do it," San said. "Just wait." And he closed himself in the bathroom with his garment bag, throwing the door open a few minutes later and striking a pose.

"Daaaammn." That was Reese. Bellamy blushed. Nari whistled. And I said, "Call him Bond, Santiago Bond," in a British-ish accent. I mean, I'd seen the suit before since I went with him to buy it a couple weeks back, but still. Wearing it—gray with a white shirt, matching narrow gray tie and brown leather shoes—San could've passed for twenty-two, twenty-three, easy. Even brimming with my epic misgivings, I didn't think anyone would give him a second glance. At least, not the kind we were worried about.

He struck a few more poses while we cheered him on, then said, "Okay, okay, now it's weird," and ducked back into the bathroom. When he came out dressed as regular Santiago again, we agreed; yes, he could fake it. It'd be enough.

Then there was more watching and eating and sitting and arguing and deciding and eating and deciding and sitting and watching until I was sure even I could recite the name, job description, and favorite color to go with every senior *and* junior executive's face and probably all of the associates and interns from the other floors, too, and it wasn't even my job to be in the building Friday.

But it wasn't me who finally snapped and kicked the air-conditioning unit for the third time, screaming, "IF I DON'T GET OUT OF THIS ROOM SOON, I'M GOING TO RIP THIS THING OUT OF THE WALL WITH MY BARE HANDS AND THROW IT THROUGH A WINDOW!" It was Reese.

"Need a break, Reese?" San asked.

"Yes," she panted. "Please."

BELLAMY

Slow Fuses Still Burn

Reese was bouncing. Literally, not figuratively. Bobbing up and down on her toes where we stood on the sidewalk in front of our hotel.

"Okay." San clapped his hands, like a coach bringing his team to attention. I smiled at him. He smiled back. "What's the plan?"

"Dinner!" cheered Nari.

"And drinks!" Reese added, and pulled five fake IDs from her pocket. "See, see, see?" she said, continuing to bounce as she passed them out to us. "Aren't they great?"

They were. Mine had a picture of me, my first name with a different last, and my birth date with only the year changed to make me twenty-one. She'd done the same with the others', only varying birth years a bit. San's said he was twenty-three; Keagan and Reese, twenty-two; and Nari, twenty-one like me. "Because you two look the youngest," Reese explained.

"I still don't look twenty-one." I don't wear makeup and my regular attire of jeans and a T-shirt didn't tend to age me up much.

"That's okay," San said. "You don't have to use it if you don't want. Or if you do, I'm sure you'll blend in with the group."

I nodded and decided not to worry about it. The IDs did look really good. Reese had been thorough, even including our signatures in different handwriting styles and missing only the holograms some licenses had.

The story was that we were college students from Wyoming— because, according to Reese, "Who the hell's from Wyoming and knows what their driver's licenses look like?"—in the city for spring break.

"So," Keagan began, still examining his ID, and I tensed. He'd been quiet all day, and my first thought was that the fake IDs crossed his line. My second was annoyance. But less with whatever objection I assumed he'd voice and more because he was a walking reminder of all the things I'd spent the last days and weeks choosing to ignore. But he only tucked his ID into his wallet and asked, "Where to?"

We wandered toward Union Square, following Nari and Reese as they looked up places to go on Nari's phone. Keagan walked behind them, with Santiago and me at the back. Navigating the other foot traffic, San moved closer to me. I reached for his hand and interlinked his fingers with mine. He squeezed. Then Reese pointed her finger toward the sky, announced that she'd picked a place, and we let go.

The place was a bar and grill, moderately busy at seven-thirty on a Wednesday night. "Decent reviews, a full bar, and two dollar signs," Reese said. "Sound good?" We nodded, and Keagan held open the door for the rest of us to file through.

The hostess sat us in a booth in the back corner. The waiter didn't blink at our IDs as we ordered a round of drinks. "Brava, Reese," Nari said once he was out of earshot.

Ten minutes later, drinks in hand and orders placed, we sat listening to the general din of the restaurant. Our silence was awkward. Silence had never been awkward between us before. I took a sip of my drink, an eleven-dollar cocktail that was supposed to taste like lemonade but mostly tasted like vodka. "Nearly useless superpowers. San, go."

Santiago swallowed a mouthful of his beer, brow creased in thought. "Okay." He set his glass down. "Magnetism. But not like Magneto. I can't control metal, I'm just, you know, magnetic."

"You'd never lose your keys," said Reese.

"True. You could just stick them and your phone to yourself," I said. "No need for pockets."

"Perfect," San said, smiling, and tapped his glass against mine.

Nari decided on speaking with animals but only cats, "Because they wouldn't give two ripe shits about me. With dogs you could make, like, a dog army. But cats?" She shrugged. "They'd probably still ignore me most of the time."

"Yeah." Reese stirred her blended cocktail with her straw. "Or resent your ability to speak their language and pee on your bed."

I settled on levitation, but only a few inches above the ground. "At least you'd never trip," San said.

Nari nodded. "Or step in anything gross."

Reese went with X-ray vision.

"But X-ray vision is awesome!" Santiago argued. "It's a staple. Freaking *canon*."

"No way," she said. "X-ray vision *plus* something is awesome. Plus superstrength or shooting laser beams from your eyes or whatever. Just being able to see inside shit would be totally purposeless. And kind of inconvenient. I don't want to see people's guts. And if I did find something rad hidden somewhere, how would I get to it with my wimpy noodle arms?" She wiggled one thin arm around for emphasis.

"Fair enough." San turned to Keagan. "Keag?"

Rolling his already empty beer glass between his hands, Keagan looked up. "What?" He hadn't been listening. To any of it.

Santiago frowned. "Mostly pointless superpower."

Keag opened his mouth to say something, but his eyes flicked to mine and he closed it again. "Dewrinkling," he said, and tipped the last drops of his beer into his mouth. "My clothes would always look fresh even without an iron or a trip through the dryer."

"Nice," San said. "Now you get to pick the next—"

"I'm gonna get another drink," Keagan interrupted, and pushed out of the booth, empty glass in hand.

San watched him walk to the bar. "Well."

"Whatever," Nari said. She scooted out the booth's other side and went in the opposite direction from the bar toward the bathroom. Reese gave Santiago and me a toothy grimace and followed her.

I groaned and set my forehead on the table.

San slid his arm around my waist. "Don't." I looked up. The feeling, the casual frequency with which he'd started to touch me, was still so new. It was all so new. Knowing that those touches meant what I'd hoped they did. Knowing that they were the promise of more. While still knowing that, with college and complications and time constraints, they were mismatched puzzle pieces, with pictures and shapes that didn't fit.

But I wanted the pieces anyway.

"It's not your fault," he said.

"Except it is."

"You're the reason we're doing this. But Keagan's crap isn't your fault. They're different things."

The waiter, laden with a massive tray of food, approached our table, so I didn't say it, but I wondered, *Are they?*

Keagan didn't come back until we were nearly done with dinner. Reese, Nari, San, and I ate quietly, joylessly, while he stayed at the bar nursing another beer, his plate sitting next to Nari's, untouched. By the time the bill came and we'd had his meal put in a to-go box, San was ready to drag him back over. Instead, Keag walked up to the table with a wide smile and his hands full.

"Shots!" he cheered.

"Keagan . . . ," San said.

He set five shot glasses of brown liquor down on the table, spilling a few drops from two of them, then slid one to each of us. "Come on," he said. "Cheers!"

No one moved. "What? Aren't we having fun or celebrating or some shit?" He lifted his shot glass from the table. "No takers? Really?" He took the shot in one quick swallow, then reached for the one in front of Nari. "More for me, I guess." And he swallowed that one, too.

He reached across Nari for Reese's, but she threw it back with a gasp and a shiver before he could grab it. "There," she snapped. "Happy?"

"Not even remotely," he answered, and turned to San and

me. San, hand on his shot glass, sat rigid between Keagan—still standing at the end of the table—and me in the corner of the booth. But it was me Keag focused on. "Bells?"

I could already feel the alcohol from my lemonade-vodka drink dilating the blood vessels in my face and hands, making me feel hot and puffy, interfering with my neurotransmitters, giving me a sense of separation and looseness. I held his eye and swallowed the shot in one rough go, coughing on the fire of it as I set the empty glass back down.

"Cheers, Bellamy," he said. "Glad to see you're still a sucker for peer pressure."

"*Jesus*," Nari hissed. "Quit being such a dick, Keagan."

He turned on her. "A dick? Really?"

"All right." San took his shot in one quick motion and stood from the booth, forcing Keagan to step back and let him out. "We're done. Let's go." With a hand on Keag's shoulder, he aimed him toward the door.

I stared at the remnants of liquor in the bottom of my shot glass, feeling the heat of it in my gut, burning me from the inside out.

SANTIAGO

Okay Okay Okay

I walked Keagan through the restaurant and out the door, keeping my hand on his arm, not because I thought he'd do something stupid but because I honestly didn't know what to think.

Out on the sidewalk Keagan paused, scrubbing his hands through his short hair, smearing them down his face; then he tipped his head back and stared at the sky until the girls walked out the door behind us.

Keagan didn't turn, but he must've heard them, because he said, "Sorry," before starting in the direction of the hotel. I jogged to catch up with him, looking back once to see the girls following a short distance behind.

"You okay?" I asked him, though of course I knew he wasn't. The other questions that'd filtered through my head had seemed too loaded, too leading. Maybe I was avoiding them, refusing to poke the bear, stir the pot, yank the tiger's tail.

He stopped, arms crossed, in the middle of the sidewalk. I paused beside him and he turned to face me, expression cutting. "Are *you* okay?"

I opened my mouth, but whatever he saw on my face made him scoff. "You're really just *okay* with all of this?" He didn't wait for me to answer, only shook his head and strode off down the sidewalk.

I caught up. "Yes."

He barked a laugh. "Yes," he mimicked.

"I'm serious." I dodged a couple walking toward us. Keag stomped straight through them, making them drop their linked hands. Their posture made me think of Bellamy, and I looked back for the girls, now more than half a block behind us. "I'm okay with it."

Keagan glanced at me, disgusted. "Just like that." He snapped his fingers. "From the beginning."

"It's not that—"

"What? Simple? It's not that simple?" He stopped, shaking his head. "Well, you've fooled me. Which is just so fucking *fitting*, right? Keagan's the fool! Keagan's the one who *doesn't get it.*"

"Keagan. No one thinks—"

He turned to me and spread his arms wide in an irate gesture. "This isn't a game, Santiago! We don't get to make up our own rules! How do none of you *get that?*"

"I—" I didn't know what I was going to say, but Keagan didn't want to hear my answer either way. He crossed his arms, furious, and resumed walking. We didn't talk the rest of the way.

REESE

Light the Match, Pull the Pin

Nari, Bells, and I followed half a block behind Keagan and Santiago all the way back to the hotel. Nari walked with her arms crossed, brow tight, and eyes on her feet while Bellamy and I looked between her and each other. The mood was iron, rust, the color of corrosion and a smell like blood.

Back in the room we arranged ourselves on the chair, bedside table, and Superbed, and the mood shifted, cinching tight, tight, tighter. I knew this feeling. This sick anticipation. The twist in my guts. The air stretched and twanging while I waited, already wincing, for the rubber band to snap.

So, I decided, *screw it!* The night was already shit, right? Might as well light it on fire.

"Split Pig," I said.

Sitting on the other mattress next to Nari, Bells shook her head. "Reese, *no.*"

She was probably right. Bad idea. But I felt my skin crawl. I have a total love-hate relationship with confrontation. It's the child-of-a-dysfunctional-marriage thing. And maybe a little bit the no-regrets thing, too, since confrontation's a tightrope of dos and don'ts and shoulds and shouldn't-haves. I hate the damage of confrontation. I hate hurtfulness for the sake of hurting. I hate bickering. Hate it. Shit like arguing about the "right" way to load a dishwasher or mow the lawn or pack luggage into the car. I hate how bickering over whether the mugs should go topside up or down in the cabinet leads to State of the Union, *I hate everything you are and everything you do* fighting. But I love—love? need?—the other kind. I need to light the match when the room is filling with fumes.

Example:

"Reese," she'd said. Over and over. *ReeseReeseReese.* Chasing me, still tying her robe around her waist, bare feet thumping down the hall and into the kitchen as I ran for the back door. I was fire. The hottest blue. The color when copper burns. *Reese-ReeseReese.*

She'd caught me right as I reached the door. Grip so hard my arm bruised the next day.

"Reese," she'd said. "You can't tell him. Please. Give me a few days. I'll—"

There'd been a thud down the hall. In my parents' room. Because they'd been in my parents' bed.

I'd yanked my arm out of her grip, said, "Fuck you," slammed the door so hard behind me the window cracked. And told him. My dad. Not that minute or hour or day, but I told him. Because I wasn't sure she would. And because I'd rather light the match and burn to death than suffocate as the gas slowly replaces all the breathable air.

But before I could take it back, diffuse, open a metaphorical window, Keag lit his own match.

"Great!" he said. "I won last time, so it's my turn. And I've got a good one." He laughed. Darkly. Really, super darkly. "Five teenagers, each with their own special skill set—except, well, whatever—plan the heist of all heists. The Big One. The Epic Thing. Or whatever the hell we're calling it. To rob an innocent-ish albeit shitbag of a man for their own means, like they're all in some fucking movie instead of real, go-to-jail, have-no-superpowers life. And . . . go!"

"Keag . . . ," San said.

"Nope. Not this time, Santiago. You all want to play pretend and make up your own rules about what's right and wrong? Sweet! Let's play!" Keagan stood up off the chair, his eyes a little glassy, his expression almost manic. "Like, best-case scenario? We commit a shitload of crimes, but you know, for a good reason. Two or ten or twenty wrongs make a right, *right*? Worst case?" He shrugged. "Jail? But, hey, I bet someone can think of something better! An armed security guard? Come on, people! Start the thread! Who's gonna go out first? San? Reese? My bet's on Ree—"

"*Keagan*," Santiago said. "Bad. Idea."

Keag turned toward him, and we were off. Fuse less lit than *skipped*. Straight to the flash and bang. "I'm sorry. Did you say this is a bad idea? *This*? The *game*?"

San looked up at Keagan from his seat straddling the bedside table. Shoulders relaxed. Hands loosely clasped. Long legs dangling on either side of the little table. Defusing, *deferential*. "You know what I mean, Keag. This. Now. It's not the right—"

"It's *exactly* the right time. Actually, no. It's *way fucking late*."

"Keagan," I hissed. "Keep your voice down."

He turned to me. "Why? Reese the adventurer. Reese the

freaking *enabler*." I felt a flush of angry heat. Up my spine. Across my forehead. Settling in my cheeks. "You worried someone'll call the front desk to complain and, what? They'll come up and bust us for being underage? Figure out we've got more people staying here than we paid for? Or should I be more specific and start shouting about THE FELONY YOU ALL APPARENTLY CAN'T WAIT TO COMMIT?"

San and I were a chorus, both of us whisper-shouting for him to *shut the fuck up*. Bells was silent, pale. Nari's jaw clenched.

He started in on "Right, tell me to shut up. Tell me to get over it. Tell me I'm ridiculous. That I don't get it. That—"

"You don't."

The four of us turned to Bellamy.

"What?" Keagan asked.

She frowned at him. "You don't get it."

Keag's jaw worked. "What don't I 'get'?"

I knew that tone. My mom and dad had both used it a thousand times in a thousand fights. It was smug expectation. Not a rhetorical question, exactly, but one they assumed they knew the answer to. An answer they already knew was bullshit.

But then Bells said, "My mom doesn't sleep. She doesn't have days off. We've never been on a vacation. And she's worked the last four Christmases in a row. Every month, we're on the brink. There's never any extra. If the car breaks down, we either have no car or pay to fix it, then have no way to pay rent.

"It's a cycle. One she's been in her entire adult life. For me. *Because* of me." Her expression broke my heart. I mean it. It was the deepest wine color. Less angry than the red-black of blood, less solid. A windowpane the hue of merlot. The rich color of sadness and emptiness and hurt. "She dropped out of high school and got her GED, because of me. Didn't go to college and works low-paying jobs, because of me. And because of him.

"Because Robert Foster abandoned us and never looked back."

She coughed a devastated sort of laugh. "He has five houses, Keag. *Five fucking houses,* while my mom and I can barely pay rent. And you know me well enough to know I don't feel like I'm owed much of anything, that it's about earning, not being entitled. But dammit, he *owes* me this. And not just because of the financial aid. For everything. My whole life. He *owes me.*"

We were quiet.

Traffic droned down on the street. A car honked. Someone yelled. Someone else yelled back. A group of people started laughing.

Nari stood up. "Well," she said to Keagan, furious, "is that enough yet?"

"Nari," Santiago snapped, glaring. "Let it freaking *go!*"

But it was like he hadn't spoken, like Bells, San, and I weren't even in the room.

"Come on, Keagan! Tell me! Does that finally pass your test?"

Keag crossed his arms and stared at the floor. "Life isn't fair."

"Life isn't fair," Nari repeated. Incredulous. "What do you even mean? 'Life isn't fair.' So, what, we do *nothing?*" Her expression, her tone, grew mocking. "Well, damn, life gave me a shit sandwich. Guess I'll just *eat it anyway?* What a fucking cop-out."

Keag looked up. "That's not what I meant."

"Then what did you mean? Or are you still not getting it? That big goals sometimes take big risks."

His expression said *hurt*. In his twisted brow and open mouth. H-U-R-T.

Nari breathed a livid laugh and shook her head. "You know what, then why are you here?"

It coated us like grease. The malice of it. When my parents fought, I always thought of grease. A thin, transparent sheen covering the walls, furniture, appliances, picture frames. A slick on everything you touched.

Nari took a half step toward him. "If doing something like this, wrong as you think it is, to help Bellamy do something *great*, isn't enough. If her *whole life* still isn't enough. Then why. Are. You. Here."

A gut shot. I could see it on Keag's face. She knew exactly where to slip the knife. His expression dropped into one so vulnerable, I almost looked away.

"Because of you," he said, quiet. Then, louder, "You know this isn't the only way. *You* know this is a shit idea. *You* know this is dangerous and illegal." Louder still, "*You* knew I'd do it anyway! For *you*! And you act like that's some sort of *strength*. Like being arrogant and manipulative makes you powerful! Like not caring about consequences and taking your precious 'risks' all because you have some big selfish dream makes you *better* than me. Smarter. Stronger. When really, you're just self-righteous. And self-important. And more than willing to take *all of us down with you.*"

This was . . .

Horrible.

Yep, horrible. But I couldn't move. None of us did. Though the room had shrunk to a pinpoint. No colors, just a scribbly mess. I sat, still like furniture.

Nari's jaw clenched. "That's not fair."

"Not fair?" Keagan scoffed and shook his head. "*Now* it's okay to talk about what's fair?"

"Yeah, Keagan. It is. Because that's not *fucking fair.* You have spent *weeks* saying yes. We've all said yes! Over and over and over. But you're going to put that on *me*? I'm not responsible for your decisions, Keagan. *You* are. You didn't want to do this? You think I'm freaking 'arrogant' and 'self-righteous'? Then *say no.* Freaking speak up! I don't need a goddamned babysitter."

Nari's eyes were wet. So were Keagan's. Bellamy looked like she'd evaporate if she were able. The muscles in Santiago's jaw flexed, clenching and unclenching as he looked from Bells to his knotted hands.

Nari took a heavy breath. Her shoulders slackened. "I refuse to be terrified of possibility," she said quietly. "And I refuse to look the other way. Looking the other way is easy. Ignoring injustice is *easy.* Staring it straight in the face and *doing something* is what's hard."

"Is that what you think?" Keagan's bottom lip trembled. He squeezed his eyes shut for a beat before looking at her again. "That I'm a coward?"

Silence.

And more silence.

He whispered, "I'm not a coward. And just because Bells's dad is wrong doesn't mean what we're doing is right." And left the room.

KEAGAN

Aftermath

That was awful. I was awful.

I'd say I didn't recognize myself or wasn't acting like myself or whatever myself. But that was me. That was all me. Like a can of soda I'd been shaking periodically for the past however many weeks, culminating in an evening of throwing that same can at the wall a few times before choosing to just crack it open. And let it explode. All over me and my friends and the room, the carpet and walls and furniture; onto the ceilings and floorboards, into the crevices and corners; coating the place in a cloud of sticky emotive mess.

I went down to the street and sat on the curb. There was a metaphor in that. Trash. Curb. Taking it out.

I didn't know what time it was. Dark, not too late. The street and sidewalk were still busy with people going places and doing things that probably didn't involve planning multiple felonies. Though, who knew, right? Different strokes for different folks. Ha. I'm guessing that phrase isn't meant to sound dirty. I just mean that everyone has their own stuff. The million things, big and small, that make them *them,* the web of their life. Job, family, friends. Wants, needs, opinions, goals.

Goals.

I dropped my head into my hands and stared at the gutter.

Back when he was mostly painting, before the pottery thing he does now, my dad did a series of paintings of crowds. Not crowds like at a concert or event or something, but like this. Maybe "crowds" isn't the right word. More like street scenes, park scenes, stuff like people going in and out of a grocery store. All strangers. All minding their own business. He'd focus on one still figure in the middle of it with the rest of the painting's occupants and goings-on slightly blurred. In the muddle, that figure would be stark emotion. In their body language, their face, they'd embody grief or fear or anxiety or desire or elation. As a nine- or ten-year-old, I found that even the happy ones made me feel inexplicably sad. Inexplicably because I was nine or ten and couldn't name the terrible, muggy loneliness those scenes made me feel.

Dark, huh?

But I felt dark. I felt, I didn't even know. It was the overlap. Those scenes so much like the one I was sitting in now, with me the solitary focused figure. My isolation. My, I don't know, left-out-ness. The Totally Illegal Shit's Cool as Long as It's in Pursuit of Some Kick-Ass Goal That Keagan Doesn't Have Club, population four. And me.

And, apparently, not having some huge goal made me in-capable of understanding what that drive felt like. And not understanding that drive made me incapable of understanding why anyone would take risks for it. Which made me a coward.

I shook my head.

Coward, coward, coward.

Jesus, and Bellamy's face. He'd abandoned her. I knew that. I'd always known that. In theory. But I'd somehow never really thought about what it meant. How do you do that? Know someone as well as I thought I knew Bellamy yet still feel like you know nothing. Or at least not enough. It was like taking for granted that summer turns into fall turns into winter. Or no, more like that Christmas means Santa Claus. And not just the idea of Santa Claus, but him as a fat white guy with the big white beard and red suit. It was normal. The shape of things. Until you made yourself remember that that version of Santa became *the* idea of Santa thanks in part to Coke ads starting in the 1930s and that he's not *the* idea of Santa to everyone.

I exhaled a thick, barrel-chested sigh. Robert Foster had abandoned her. And abandoning her had shaped her and her mom's entire life. Which was so far from being fair.

But was that enough? I just . . . I didn't know.

My brain was still sloshy; echoes of *coward* and *abandoned me* and *enough* repeated in a round in my head. Plus the gutter between my feet had started to spin. So I called it and went inside, where everyone was either asleep or pretending to be, and lay on the grimy floor. In my clothes. Not even taking my shoes off. As punishment, I guess. It seemed appropriate to be uncomfortable. Because while I felt guilty for exploding, while I felt horrible for Bells, I also felt relieved. And then guilty for that relief. Because, sure, the way I'd said it all was wrong. So very wrong. But what I'd said? That was still right.

I woke up the next morning to the sound of the shower in the bathroom. Someone else rolled over on Superbed, making the springs and frame squeak. I was on my back on the floor at the foot of the side closer to the door. The carpet smelled. Or I smelled. Probably both. I sat up.

The mattress beside me creaked and feet swung over the end at my back. "Hey," Bells whispered.

"Hey," I whispered back.

She trod over to the food pile and grabbed a half-empty box of powdered donuts before opening the door and gesturing for me to follow her into the hall. I did, glancing back to see Reese and Santiago still sprawled out asleep. The shower turned off.

Bells leaned against the wall beside our door and slid down to sit, the box of donuts in her lap. "So, last night," she said, and took a bite of one.

I joined her and she handed me another. It was both dry and greasy. A paradox. Or just stale.

I chewed the sad, old donut. "Yeah, last night."

"You were an asshole."

I chewed, and chewed, and chewed my bite of donut into a paste until I finally managed to swallow. *Gross.* I dropped the rest of it back into the box, wiped the powdered sugar from my fingers onto my jeans, and pressed my palms over my eyes. They hurt. My eyes. My eyeballs. The strings holding them in my skull. A hangover? Sure. That's probably what this was. "I'm sorry," I said, eyes still covered.

She sort of grunted. "Yeah, me too. But not like how you're sorry."

I got that. Sorry for the situation. Sorry for realities within and beyond her control, even if they didn't need apologizing for. I pushed the heels of my hands into my eye sockets. It felt . . . less bad. "But you still think we should do this."

Bellamy chewed quietly. I could hear her jaw and teeth and

mouth muscles moving. Finally, I heard her swallow and she said, "Yes."

I kept mashing until dots of light pinpricked the dark inside my eyelids. At least her answer was definitive? Though that made me feel better, like definitively knowing my sore throat was actually strep made me feel better.

"And you obviously still don't," Nari said.

I lifted my head. The light was weird. Too bright or lacking contrast or something, thanks to my eye smashing. Nari stood in the doorway to the room, already dressed, looking gorgeous and prepared to take no shit. Even from me. Especially from me. My gut dropped into my ankles, an unpleasant trip since I was pretzeled up on the hallway floor.

"Can we talk?" she asked me.

I nodded and moved to stand, but Bellamy got up instead, giving Nari a tight smile before ducking back into the room and closing the door behind her.

Nari sat cross-legged in the spot Bellamy'd just left.

"Sorry," I said, because I was, that slice of relief regardless. Or because of it. Because I still felt guilty for feeling relieved, which felt a little like shame, which made me feel a little angry, which made me want a glass of water and a long hot shower because now I was hungover *and* confused. "I'm just . . . sorry."

She didn't look at me. The space between us, an oh-so-intentional couple of inches, felt gelatinous. "But you meant it. All that stuff you said."

"Maybe. Partially."

"So you think I'm arrogant and self-righteous."

I swallowed. God, my mouth tasted horrible. The donut hadn't helped. "I think this plan is arrogant. And I think calling it 'justice' is a good way to let yourself off the hook." Not gonna lie, I was proud of myself for that line. It came out so calm and solid! And I hadn't even practiced it in my head all morning first. "And you think I'm a coward."

Staring at the opposite side of the hallway, dimly lit with yellowing floral wallpaper, Nari chewed the inside of her cheek. She hated that habit. And it always got worse when she was thinking hard.

This wasn't like us. We didn't fight. We didn't even bicker. We were . . . easy.

"You're going to take me out."

Those were the first words she ever spoke to me, two minutes into our shared biology class the first day of fall semester sophomore year. She made the girl sitting next to me swap seats, then plopped down, said, "You're going to take me out," and held out her hand for my phone. She put her name and number into my contacts, then texted *How about Friday?* to herself. When her phone dinged two seconds later, she pulled it out, smiled widely, and proclaimed, "Friday sounds great!"

When I finally recovered enough to breathe, I laughed; then she laughed and blushed, like, super beautifully; then our teacher told us to shut up please and the rest of the class laughed, too.

And that's how it'd been for the more than two and a half years since. Nari leading, me following. Which maybe sounds emasculating but only if your masculinity is painfully fragile. Plus that's who Nari is. A leader. While I'm less a follower and more undecided. Not about Nari—just about, I don't know, me? Life? Nari's like an arrow. A freaking laser beam of focus on her Bright Future, while I could sit in this hallway meditating about life goals and passions for a year and still not know.

Before this, I'd always been okay with that, with all of that. My place. My uncertainty. My being the one who follows. Nari's the one with grand plans, and I was happy to figure my stuff out along the way.

Was.

Because this was different. This wasn't easy. It was premeditated disaster, a trash fire waiting to be lit.

"You're not a coward," Nari finally said, still staring away from me. "But just because you're scared of the consequences of doing something big doesn't mean you shouldn't take a chance."

I ran a hand over my hair. It was still short enough that it felt super soft, like those velour-ish blankets that get all staticky. "Okay," I said. "But just because you *can* take a chance, even on something big, doesn't mean you get to act like the consequences don't matter."

NARI

Irl

The day was mild. The sun was bright. The birds were singing, the bicyclists cycling, the Starbucks customers customering, and five bright-eyed teens assumed their positions around the Foster Innovations building to commence the day's agenda: case the joint.

In person, I mean. Up close and person-all. (Puns, I know. But I was a teensy bit stressed out. Just a tad. Like blowing a giant bubble with your gum till it got all transparent and windowpane thin. I was that bubble. Two seconds before it popped and permanently adhered itself to your hair.) We were hitting the pavement, doing some good old recon. The plan was to quadruple-check everything we'd already triple-checked during the last two days of staring at the security feeds. Plus, I know I'm all d0l0s the Deliverer of Digital Destruction Muwahahaha, but we needed to experience this for real. Or at least for real by proxy, since San and Reese needed to keep their beautiful mugs anonymous for tomorrow.

Yes, tomorrow. Because this was it. Thursday. One day to go.

Oooooh, ominous, right? Or, exciting! This. Was. It. Time for lens flares! Voice-overs! A crackling, quick-cut montage to the tune of the movie score's most kick-ass track!

We started out at a Starbucks around the corner from FI, for coffee (obviously), because no one could stand the room anymore, and so that five teens huddled in a group, discussing Something of Importance with decidedly suspicious vibes, weren't, you know, suspicious.

Though maybe that was ridiculous? Lens flares and voice-overs, right? Maybe that was just me being arrogant. Me being self-important and the reason we can't have nice things or whatever.

"San and Reese," I said, clutching my latte close, "you're on outdoor duty because anonymity. Bellamy, Keagan." I couldn't meet his eye. I was brave enough to infiltrate the digital recesses of a major company, but I couldn't look my boyfriend in the eye after a fight. "We'll do what we can to scope out the inside."

"What are we, you know, looking *for*?" Reese asked.

Good question. We weren't robbing some super-vault in a casino or lifting a priceless piece of art from a wall in the Louvre. We were having a faux employee walk into an office building, into an office, to plug a flash drive into a USB port and download a malicious program onto a computer. That's it. Ta-da. No vault to crack. No sack of cash to pilfer. Just a puncture, a drip. A digital trickle to carve a canyon over time.

"Just . . ." I shrugged, which was probably not super confidence inspiring. But hey, call me flustered. Consider me Taken Down a Peg. Half a peg. A quarter peg. "What normal feels like." I shrugged. AGAIN. Ugh. Like even my regular Nari skin didn't fit quite right that morning. "I don't know. Practice walking to the building like you do it every day, or something. Look for the security cameras on the street. Check for exits we might've missed on the security feed. We want San to be as ignorable as possible tomorrow. And for both of you to know all your outs."

Reese took a sip of her coffee. "Gotcha." No smile. No wink. If this was getting even to her? I was down a third of a peg. At least.

"And us?" Bellamy asked.

I smiled. "We get to do the fun part."

REESE

Sun Flares and Satellites

"B squad," I said.

San laughed. "Today."

"True, true. Tomorrow will be our time to shine."

"Like a sun flare," he said.

"And its shadow."

"Do sun flares have shadows?" He shrugged. "I'll ask Bells." He pulled out his phone to text her. Half a minute later, his phone buzzed with her reply. "No," he read. "Charged particles at the poles can cause auroras, though. And they can disrupt wireless communications."

"Huh. Still cool. And still sorta works. I'll be the flare—"

"And the aurora."

"—and you're the disruption."

He laughed a little, still looking at his phone, texting Bellamy back. Something between them had shifted. Their will they/won't they dynamic brightening from a pale salmon pink to fuchsia. Which made me think the shift was from "will they" to "they did." Plus I totally eavesdropped when we were camping. Rude, sure, but come on. Who doesn't like to eaves-drop on occasion? It's better with strangers, but still. I didn't hear much, considering the tent was set back a few yards from the fire and I was cocooned deep in my sleeping bag with my hat pulled down over my ears, but there was definitely sweet laughter and cozy murmuring and a lengthy quiet during which I fell asleep.

"She okay?" I asked him. I hadn't had a chance to talk to Bells alone yet, but I had thought about what if my mom had peaced out instead of trying, rather relentlessly, to prove she loved me despite the broken home, and the feeling was the color of punching a wall. Blood orange, but rotten and tinged black. I was taking a leap—a baby step?—that based on the above observation, San *had* talked to her alone.

He exhaled a heavy breath. "I think so." And we shared a look. I may be aromantic, meaning I've never been romanti-cally attracted to someone, I've never had a crush, but I know what it's like to care deeply. All of us, couples and attraction aside, we care deeply, wholly, enough to hurt with and be hurt by and to hurt for each other. And that's what was in our look. A quiet acknowledgment. Because quiet was all we needed.

We meandered down the sidewalk along the side of the FI building. I'd tell you what side, but I have no sense of direc-tion. Like, none. I knew the ocean was west, but I couldn't see the ocean, so. It was not the front side, which was Nari, Keag, and Bells's problem. Or the back side, since that was an alley. Or the other side, which was attached to the neighbor-ing building.

Our job was small. While the others got a feel for FI's actual goings-on, San and I were to basically stay out of the way. I'd have offered to stay out of the way while window-shopping and browsing art galleries, but I think the unspoken other item was *provide moral support*, the "hurt with" part. And I felt a little guilty already. Not that last night's shitstorm was my fault. Keagan threw his own grenade. Suggesting Split Pig hadn't helped, but we were already primed and, yeah, thanks to my contribution of the fake IDs, lubricated. What I mean is, guilt or none, when the ice's this thin, you scooch across the surface with caution, with hands joined in a human chain in case one of you breaks through and falls in. You don't stomp across the frozen lake alone.

I stopped and looked around. The traffic was steady. People walked the sidewalks minding their own business. Some of those people walked in and out of the Foster Innovations building's side doors. I tried to decide if they looked very innovative, but it was mostly folks in suits, who were maybe innovators and maybe accountants and human resources managers and interns and whatnot. Maybe they didn't even work for Bells's dad at all.

San glanced back down the block. "Well. Now what?"

"Uh . . . we lean against that wall over there"—I gestured across the street—"and try to look inconspicuous?"

San nodded. I waited for the inevitable joke about me never being inconspicuous, but then I remembered I was talking to San and not some rando or even Keag. Santiago didn't tease people. Ever. He wasn't the sort. Took people at face value, while somehow silently encouraging them to give him their best face. It was a skill. Skill? Character trait? I don't know. Charisma or something. He'll make a great coach someday. Because he believes in people when they need it most. Example:

The week after I came out as acearo to them late sophomore year, he gave all of us pins of the ace pride flag and told me that if I ever wanted them all to wear them, for whatever reason, to say the word.

We walked to the end of the block and crossed the street like normal, ignorable people, then made our normal, ignorable way down to loiter against an empty space of wall.

The brick was warm, soaked through with delicious sunshine. I leaned my head back against it and felt the heat sink through my hair to my scalp.

"You think they'll work it out?" I asked. A truck drove past in the bus lane, a huge ad for office supplies on its side.

"Nari and Keagan?"

I rolled my eyes at him like *obviously*, and he said, "Yes."

"Just 'yes'?"

He shrugged. "Unless Keag's right, and we get caught and go to jail."

His face was totally expressionless, but when I sighed a laugh, he smiled.

Through the slow-moving traffic I watched a man walk out one of FI's doors and head down the street. He was totally banal. White and middle-aged with brown hair and a black suit. Seriously, a clone. But I had to wonder, *Is that him?* Him, Robert Foster. Nari had shown us pictures: a current professional portrait, one from when he was in a frat in college, a few from vacations he'd taken with his wife and kids. All from Facebook and Instagram. You know, the low-level, socially acceptable brand of stalking. And damn if I could remember what he looked like. He was *that* bland. That *boring*. If a much richer and cleaner and better-dressed sort than average. But it made me work to remember that yes, all people are their very own special people living their very own special ohmygod I couldn't even finish the thought it's so freaking dull.

Instead, I looked Santiago straight on. "Why are you doing this?"

He glanced at me, then back at the doors to FI, all forest-green politeness and calm. "Because I care about Bellamy."

"Sure, but also?"

"Because I want to see if I can do it."

I frowned. "Do it, meaning walk into a building and plug a rectangular thing into a suitably rectangular slot and double-click a mouse?"

He shifted his shoulders against the wall and said, in all seriousness, "I want to know I'm worth betting on."

My eyebrows rose. "For real? State Champion Santiago?"

"Is that so weird?" he asked.

"Yes."

He laughed a little. "How about: because my parents don't support me trying something they can't be sure I won't fail at, so I want to prove to myself I can do something extraordinary and not fail. Better?"

I nodded. "Yeah, better."

"Why are you doing it?"

"Um, because as Keag so loudly pointed out last night, I am the 'adventurous' one?"

"Public disturbance and possible criminal trespassing, not to mention aiding and abetting, are a tad more adventurous than dyeing your hair."

I put a hand to my chest, covering an imaginary wound. "Damn, San! That *stings*."

"Hey"—smiling, he held his hands up in surrender—"I told you mine. 'For real.'"

"True." I slouched against the wall. "But that is my 'for real.' Mostly. I just don't ever want to be one of those people who say no to something out of fear."

"Fear seems like an okay reason to say no to something."

"Fear of regret, then. Not, like, fear of dismemberment or serial killers."

"So . . . base jumping?"

"Do it."

"Swimming with sharks?"

"Really? They put you in a freaking cage under the water. How is that even scary?"

"Okay, okay. Sail around the world alone."

"*Yesss.* That. That is a perfect example," I said. "Storms, equipment failure, communication issues. You could die. People have, right? But that's life-changing. In the best way. Even if you don't meet Poseidon or make friends with a pod of dolphins."

He smiled. San has a good smile. Like sunlight. Not a color, really, just light. Warmth and brightness. More a feeling than anything else. Well, and nice teeth. "But you wouldn't be risking what we're risking tomorrow," he said. "Sailing doesn't tend to end with life in jail."

"No." A cloud passed over the sun. I pressed my palms to the wall, absorbing the heat still trapped there.

San's phone buzzed. He pulled it out of his pocket, looked at the screen, and smiled to himself before tucking it back into his pocket. From his grin, I'd bet a thousand glitter pixie wishes it was Bellamy again. "But," he said, "if we can pull this off, the success might feel the same."

I met his eyes. *"Exactly."* San got it. Honestly, I was a little surprised.

We went back to standing quietly and watching all the individual people with their individual lives filled with individual hopes and dreams and tastes in music filter past, equally uninterested in us as I was in them, until I said, "I can't do this anymore. I'm becoming one with the wall, with the pavement. Let's go count cameras again or something, then find those guys for lunch."

Paternity Isn't Parenting

Emotions are chemistry: stimuli and chemical reactions in your brain and body that result in what we call fear, lust, anger, sadness, and so on. Dopamine, or 3,4-dihydroxyphenethylamine, produced primarily in the midbrain, is a "feel-good" chemical, playing a major role in reward-motivated behavior, motor control, arousal, reinforcement, and pleasure. Another "feel-good" chemical is serotonin, the vast majority of which can be found in the body's enterochromaffin cells in the gastrointestinal tract, where it regulates intestinal movements. Then there's norepinephrine, which is synthesized and supplied by the central nervous system but can also be released directly into the bloodstream from the adrenal glands located above the kidneys. Related to the "fight-or-flight" response, norepinephrine increases alertness, enhances memory and focus, and promotes vigilance in the brain while increasing heart rate and blood pressure in the body. Shifts in brain and body chemistry can contribute to everything from a sense of wellness to debilitating depression to diseases like Parkinson's. But for me, in that moment, they were making me feel in danger of shifting clean out of my skin.

My father was in that building.

My father, the contributor of half my DNA and an unknown assortment of genetic traits ranging from predispositions to various diseases to certain of my mannerisms, not to mention the color of my eyes and the shape of my thumbs.

Last night I'd filtered through memory after memory; absences and almosts. All the times my mom and I had come up short or missed out. The new laptop she wanted to buy me but couldn't afford. The trip to see her favorite aunt that we'd never gotten to take. Jobs she couldn't get without the education she could never afford. Holidays spent with Nari's family because my mom was at work. Her dyeing her hair out of a box because she couldn't afford the salon. Our secondhand clothes, shoes, kitchen table, couch. My friends buying me dinner, never asking me to chip in for gas, and now . . . this. A hundred opportunities sitting out of reach. The thousand little indignities that come with being poor. And finally, the biggest ones, MIT and the sound of Robert Foster hearing who I was and hanging up.

He wasn't my father. He was our mark.

Nari, Keagan, and I loitered across the street from the main entrance to the Foster Innovations building and watched the comings and goings of the people with business there for most of the morning. We matched faces to the pictures Nari had saved to her phone from Foster Innovations' HR files, searching the continuous stream of people entering and exiting for those we knew had meetings scheduled with FI's executives, if only to check that those meetings were kept. Around eleven, Keagan split off to see what he could of the lobby.

Nari and I watched him walk down the block toward the streetlight. At the corner, he waited patiently for the light to change and the walk sign to flick on. Nari scoffed and shook her head. "He won't even jaywalk. I don't know why I ever thought he'd be okay with this."

I pushed my glasses back up my nose, more out of habit than because they'd slipped, and rocked back and forth from my heels to my toes. I couldn't make myself still. When I tried, crossing my arms and concentrating on keeping my feet flat, my attention to myself was distracting. The light changed and Keagan crossed the street. Nari stared at the sidewalk, chewing the inside of her cheek.

Nari and I are devoted. I don't have siblings, so I can't liken our friendship to that sort of bond, but we've been one of the most important people to each other for more than half our lives. I'll stand beside Nari through anything. I'll defend her even when she's wrong. I'll choose her, every time. She makes me stronger, brighter, more daring. But she's still the strongest, the brightest, the most daring. For us, for the most part, that's okay. It works.

But sometimes the brightest stars make the others appear duller if only because the dimmer stars are farther away. Nari shines so brightly now. But maybe Keagan will shine just as brightly later.

"Maybe," I said, "this doesn't have to be something he's okay with."

She frowned.

"You're—*I'm* asking a lot of him. Of everyone."

She looked up and met my eye. "We. *We* asked. But also? We *asked*. As in, past tense. He could've said no."

"You know he'd never do that."

"Well. Maybe he should have."

"That isn't fair." Nari's brow creased. She looked at the sidewalk again. "He hates this idea," I said. "But he's here anyway. For you. For me. For Reese and San. He's here for us. That's admirable, Nari."

"*God*," she groaned, and let her head roll back so she was looking at the sky. "I know. I *know*. Which is just so *obnoxious*."

I laughed.

She laughed, too, and met my eye again. "Right? Mr. Moral Nobility making me feel all . . ." She wiggled her shoulders, squirming like her shirt itched.

"Imperfect?" I offered. "Fallible? Vulner—"

She knocked me with her elbow. "Thanks, Bells. Point made."

We watched the traffic for a minute; then, quietly, she said, "It isn't your fault. Keag's . . . whatever. The whatever between him and me."

I stared up at the windows of FI's higher floors, still rocking back and forth from toe to heel, heel to toe. "I know."

"Also, your dad? And that whole abandonment thing? Not your fault either."

I snorted a laugh and looked back at Nari. She was trying and mostly succeeding at keeping a straight face. "Oh yeah?"

"Yeah. Totally."

And we both burst out laughing. She wrapped her arms around my shoulders and squeezed.

Across the street, Keagan came out of FI's front doors, waited for traffic to clear, then jogged across the street. I poked Nari. She dropped her arms, looked to where I pointed at Keag jaywalking toward us, and rolled her eyes.

"You're going to be shocked," he said when he stopped between us. "But it looks exactly the same as it did in the eighteen-plus hours of security footage we watched."

"Well, that's good news," I said. "What now?" Nari glanced at me, chewing the inside of her cheek again. Then her gaze shifted down the sidewalk behind me to where Reese and Santiago approached.

Reese smiled at Nari and asked, "Phase two?"

Nari narrowed her eyes at FI's main entrance.

"Phase two," Keagan repeated, a question without the inflection.

"Yup," Nari said. "I'm going inside."

KEAGAN

If You're Not Paranoid, You're Not Paying Attention

"It's no big deal," she said, adjusting the pin she'd stuck to the collar of her blouse. An owl, which was . . . ironic? The whole wisdom/night-watching thing? Or maybe it was just fitting. I don't know. I could look up the definition of "ironic" eight thousand times and still not be exactly sure what it means. But set in the owl's belly, looking like a polished oval of decorative glass, was a camera. A camera linked to an app on her prepay. Because, well, this was really happening and I should've known Nari'd go full on spy. "I added this appointment to Foster's schedule weeks ago."

"What appointment?"

She rolled her eyes at me but, like, good-naturedly at least? "The one with Rowan Malik of Malik's Motifs' hyper-eager teenage cousin who happens to have an interest in fashion *and* complex cybersecurity."

"And he, Super-Important Billionaire and CEO Robert Foster, just . . . agreed to that?"

She tipped her head to one side coquettishly (seven points!)

and said, "He didn't *disagree*. Meaning I added the appointment to his calendar, then fabricated and archived a short email exchange between him and Rowan with him agreeing to it. I'm banking that he'll feel too guilty about 'forgetting' the favor he promised to the creator of his highest-performing fashion brand to turn me away."

"Diabolical, Dr. Okada."

She grinned, not like a "happy" or "this is funny" grin, but an "I'm humoring you" or "at least I'm trying" one. Then shrugged. "If it gets weird, I'll leave."

I glanced across the street, looking for Bells, who leaned against a cylindrical billboard thing pretending to stare at her phone by, well, staring at her phone. San and Reese were around the corner, or down the block or who knew where, since Reese had seemed less than enthused to return to staring at a wall for the afternoon. Which, granted, seemed a little ridiculous, the spying and splitting up and acting nonchalant. And I'd have called it balls-out batshit, except that it didn't *feel* ridiculous. It felt like a thousand all-knowing eyes were watching us and some grotesque ultrasecurity guard with, like, six arms of steroid-popping body-building muscle was waiting around every corner.

Or maybe I was just paranoid.

Ha ha. Sure. *Just paranoid.*

Arms crossed, Nari looked past me, through me, around me, despite me? Does that one work? Nah, not a preposition no matter how "in spite of" I felt right then. I knew she was expecting me to argue or try to stop her or reiterate how amazingly stupid this all was. But I was feeling pretty over it by that point. I was sick of being the ignored voice of reason, so I said, "Which wins, Pop-Tarts or Toaster Strudel?"

Her eyes flicked to mine. "Toaster Strudel, hands down."

"What? No way. Pop-Tarts, no contest!"

She arched a perfectly sculpted eyebrow. "Really?"

I held up fingers to count off my reasons. "Uh, portability? Built-in frosting? They are not frozen?"

"Okay, except they also taste like cardboard and Toaster Strudels are basically donuts you get to cook, all hot and gooey and frosting-drizzled, at home."

"That's only one to my *three*."

"Eatability counts for at least five."

"Pop-Tarts may be cardboard-like, but they are no less eatable."

She rolled her eyes, lips curved in a reluctant smile, and turned toward the entrance.

"Okay, who am I kidding?" I said to her back. "Pop-Tarts are gross. Their only salvation is that they can go in a vending machine."

"Damn right," she called, pulled open one of the doors, and stepped inside.

Through the windows, I watched her cross the lobby in a few long strides and stop at the information/security desk inside. The two men working behind it turned their attention to her, at first unsmiling; then she tipped her head—long hair swishing a bit to the side, hands up on the countertop, one knee bent with her hips off-kilter—and a few seconds later, both men smiled warmly, obligingly, while the bald one with strikingly white teeth moved from behind the desk to show her the way.

NARI

Violets Are My Favorite Flower

Security Personnel Winston led me across the lobby toward the row of turnstiles at the rear, soft-soled shoes softly stepping while I, in my favorite pair of brown suede booties with stacked three-inch heels, snapped along behind him. At the turnstiles Winston swiped his ID card across the scanner, the light flashed green, and the clear plastic barriers retracted. He motioned me through first, then repeated the process for himself.

"This for a school project or something?" he asked as we continued down the wide hall to the elevators. I did a slow spin, taking in the (honestly, not all that) grand world of Venture Capitalism, i.e., capturing the hallway with its high ceiling and oversized pendant lighting and the placement of, count 'em, one, two, three security cameras on my handy Owl Cam.

"Nah, just exercising a little light nepotism, you know? Angling for a letter of rec."

He chuckled. A deep, rumbling, honest-to-god chuckle. I'd stopped at the desk, feigning ignorance about the location of FI's executive floor (with a touch of ineptitude since that info was online as well as, you know, literally printed on the wall) because both of those guys were scheduled for tomorrow and why not introduce myself to a possible hurdle in the flesh?

He smiled back at me. "A go-getter?"

"You know it. Gotta be competitive these days."

"Yeah, that's what my niece is always telling me." He pushed the button to call the elevator, and we waited. "She's a junior in high school, too"—(I'd changed the faux cousin's age. And name. And where she was from. Obviously)—"and hoping to get a scholarship to study music. I think she's brilliant. But she's always saying, 'Winston, *everyone's* brilliant.' You can't just be good anymore. You can't just be smart."

The elevator dinged and we stepped inside. He hit the button for the twelfth floor. After the lobby, floors two through nine, per my research, were home to the offices of various businesses both unaffiliated (including a restaurant and a gym) and affiliated with Foster Innovations, while FI itself used only the top three floors.

"She's right," I said, both because she was and because that's what Winston wanted me to say. "Which is why I'm so grateful for your help! This letter will be super impressive with my applications. If I can get it."

"Well, I wish you luck," he said, and smiled his thousand-kilowatt smile at me again. "You want to be the next Robert Foster?"

I grinned back. "That. Or rule the world."

He laughed, hearty and full.

When the doors opened on the twelfth floor, I made sure to catch as much of the lobby as I could on the Owl Cam. This was the way we'd decided Santiago should come tomorrow (why crawl through a window if the front door's unlocked, so to speak), and since the security so far had seemed pretty minimal, this was where he'd face his first real threat of being caught.

The room was smaller than it seemed on the camera feeds, less a lobby and more like a vestibule or antechamber. Everything was a shade of gray or white or natural wood, and it all screamed, *Expensive and trendy and maybe even* futuristic *business is done here!* Which was not altogether true since it wasn't as if any of the businesses FI funded—such as, say, 2550 Robotics, a company that's pretty self-explanatory, being that they design and build, you know, robots—were actually doing anything on these three floors. Specifically, 2550 Robotics had a lab across the bay, but they sourced their materials and bulk parts from places like Indonesia, China, Mexico.

FI's assistant office manager, Patrick Buckman, was at the reception desk. Age twenty-eight, formerly of Akron, Ohio, with degrees in business and interior design from NYU, Patrick had plans to meet up with his boyfriend and a few friends at a new restaurant they'd all been waiting to try after work on Friday. Now he stood behind the bar-height wood and brushed-nickel desk wearing a crisp, white button-down shirt, super-skinny tie, and narrow leather suspenders beneath his fitted and currently unbuttoned suit jacket. Which, I mean, did he *try* to match the room? Though, also, he looked dapper as hell. We could've posed together for some hipster photo shoot. Him with his perfectly trimmed hair and beard. Me in my blouse printed with tiny black bird silhouettes, pleated leather midi-skirt, wool tights, booties, and Owl Cam.

Winston walked over to the desk and introduced "me."

"Patrick, this is Violet Murakami, here for her appointment with Mr. Foster."

Patrick's eyes met mine, and I gave him a warm, Violet-y smile. (Violet Murakami was sweetly intimidating. Like one of Reese's big-eyed creatures, all cute and soft and hiding a set of razor teeth. She also had a fondness for cats. Because, hello, Murakami.) I offered him my hand across the desk. "It's a pleasure, Patrick."

Patrick arched an eyebrow and gave my hand a pert shake. "Thank you, Winston," he said to Winston, and to me, "I'll let Mr. Foster know you're here."

Winston turned to go, smiling at me as he went. Patrick reached for his phone and informed Foster that his next appointment was here.

"Yes, sir, I'll ask," he said, then covered the mouthpiece to speak to me. "He says his assistant doesn't recall scheduling the meeting."

Of course she didn't. Because she hadn't. I put on a Moments Away from Crushing Disappointment expression and said, "I'm Ms. Malik's cousin? She said she confirmed a few weeks ago?"

Patrick nodded and held up a finger for me to wait. "Yes, sir? She says Rowan confirmed some time ago." He nodded again. "Okay, certainly." Covered the mouthpiece again. "What did you want to discuss with him?"

"FI's role in the diversification of the cybersecurity market with regard to his partnership with CyTech and the accessibility and transliteration of SIM-ex653."

Patrick's eyes widened.

"Oh, and how he managed to build all of this, of course! Freaking amazing, *right?*"

197

He uncovered the phone's mouthpiece. "Sorry, sir. Ms. Murakami would like to speak with you about your success story. And she has a special interest in cybersecurity." There was a final pause during which Patrick listened and nodded and I did a slow rotation, focusing my Owl Cam on the frosted-glass doors to the right of Patrick's desk, the security camera above it, and the other one mounted on the ceiling by the elevators, then back on Patrick himself.

He hung up. "All right, Ms. Mur—"

"Violet, please."

He half smiled. "All right, Violet. Mr. Foster agreed to give you ten minutes. But only ten. He has a conference call at one." (Yeah, with the founders of a company pioneering the use of 3-D printers with organic material that he was hoping to invest in. I'd read the confirmation email Bells's dad had received that morning.)

I smiled back with Violet's charming mix of delight and conceit, as though I was both grateful for getting what I wanted and unsurprised that I had. Which I guess was pretty much a Nari smile, too.

Patrick led me through the frosted-glass doors into Foster Innovations proper. As this was the executives' floor, the mood was subdued. No manic ringing of phones. No pit of intern desks filled with eager interns. No overworked junior associates darting around as though ropes of tangible deadlines were tightening around their necks. Just a wide and ridiculously beautiful common area (atrium-like, complete with an assortment of fancy and immaculately maintained flora alongside fine white furniture plus loads of natural light from the giant skylight centered in the ceiling above it) flanked on either side by offices and conference rooms and so on.

I took a moment, soaking it in, turning my body in a slow arc from left to right, catching it all on the Owl Cam and letting the reality overlap with my mental image of the video feed and the floor's blueprints.

Patrick waited, his expression patient with a touch of smug, then said, "This way," and motioned for me to follow him around the common space to the right.

We passed a series of offices, some with doors open, some closed, all with nameplates on the walls and large windows that could frost for privacy with the flip of a switch. Each office had exterior windows overlooking the city and bay. Robert Foster's office—the largest, of course—was located in the northeast corner.

Patrick knocked on the open door. I stood back a pace to catch the door itself on the camera and noticed a problem: an electronic keypad lock above the handle. *Shit.* Seated deep inside the huge space at an imposing dark-wood desk, Robert Foster looked up. "Ms. Murakami," my guide announced, and Foster rose from his chair. Patrick moved aside. I took a steadying breath and strode into the office without deigning to look back.

"Mr. Foster," I said, walking toward him. "Thank you for giving me a few minutes of your time."

He breathed a small laugh. Amused. He was amused by me. Which, I suppose, was what I'd wanted. To seem innocent and eager. But he looked at me as if I were a puppy. A toddler. Something small and cute and needing to be (a bit grudgingly) entertained.

"Ms. Murakami," he said, coming out from behind his desk to shake my hand.

"Violet, please."

He gave me a curt nod and gestured to an arrangement of furniture off to the right of his desk. I sat on one side of the stiff gray love seat, my back to the coast and the bay out the over-sized windows behind me. He chose the matching gray chair across from me.

I shifted, crossing my legs, aiming my shoulders toward his desk. There were two computers set up on it, a Mac desktop and a MacBook, open, the apple lit. I imagined he carried the laptop home with him evenings and weekends, but I also knew they were linked, mirrored. So even if the laptop was gone to-morrow when San got here, he could load the malware onto the desktop and it would be equally effective.

"So, Violet, cousin of Rowan Malik," he said, grinning, "what can I do for you?"

You can tell me why you abandoned your daughter and never looked back.

You can tell me why, when that daughter summoned all of her courage and held back an entire life's worth of emotional hurt to call you, you hung up.

You can go over to that grand desk of yours and write me a check for seventy, no, screw it, let's make it a full two hundred and fifty thousand dollars and save us all a load of trouble.

You can stop looking at me with that smug fucking expression.

This was why criminals return to the scenes of their crimes, this *power.* Pure adrenaline coursed through me. It was like knowing All the Secrets. Being about a hundred steps ahead. This man thought I was Violet Murakami, teenage cousin of one of his first and most successful partners. Violet Murakami, high school junior with a naive sense of entitlement. At best, I was a blip in his day worth grinning at, and at worst a minor nuisance. He thought he was the mighty one here, bestowing a few precious moments of his time upon me. Like charity. A good deed.

He had *no clue* how far and deep and wide my d0l0s fingers stretched. How strong my grip was. How, with a few keystrokes, I could burn his whole life down.

But hey!

Lucky for him, that's not my style.

"Well!" I said, and I launched into a fawning diatribe about my respect and interest and blah blah blah.

Fourteen minutes later Robert Foster was at his desk offering me his personal business card, "In case you're staying in the Bay Area for college, or even afterward, and are interested in an internship." When he called for Patrick to escort me out, he said, "Give Rowan my best."

I dipped my head and replied, "Of course."

Five minutes after that I was waving to Winston as I crossed the lobby, striding out the door, meeting Keagan where he waited impatiently outside, and folding into an elegant and triumphant curtsy.

SANTIAGO

Think It, Believe It, Do It

The office's door lock was a snag, but one Nari assured us could be smoothed out. "San'll just need the code, right? Easy-peasy." And it was easy enough. We gathered back at the hotel room and Nari immediately pulled up the security camera feed for the executive floor, zooming in as much as she could on Foster's office door. Then we watched. All afternoon. In shifts. Waiting for Foster to leave and lock his office, then return and key in the numbers on the pad, which he did only twice, typing in a five-digit code, the camera feed too blurry for us to do much more than follow his finger's positions on the pad, but that with a double-check the next morning would have to be enough.

After Foster left for the day, closing the door and checking the handle to make sure it had locked behind him, we watched the footage from Nari's owl pin camera at least six times together and I watched it alone another three after that. It was simple, straightforward, but I wanted to memorize every moment; how many steps, the look of every pathway and turn. I wanted to be able to do it with my eyes closed.

I figured it was like learning a new dive, as much in my head as it was in my body, so I visualized:

Wait for Reese to start her performance, walk through the lobby, head up, steps even. No glance at the security desk. No nods at anyone else lingering in the lobby. No need. I'm normality. I'm there every day. I belong.

To the turnstiles. ID and flash drive in my pocket, listen for Reese, wait for solitude, quick glance around, jump the plexiglass partition.

At the elevator, hover till I can catch an empty car.

Up the elevator to floor twelve. Cross the antechamber and go through the double doors. Listen for Nari in my ear, watching the cameras, acting as my eyes a few steps ahead. Follow the right-hand pathway to the rear corner office.

Key in the code: 17985.

Open the door.

Go inside.

Wake up the computer, enter the password provided by Nari's keystroke spyware.

Plug the flash drive into the USB port.

Download.

Repeat all steps in reverse.

Done.

Blinking open my eyes, I let out a full-lung sigh. The others were asleep, but I'd stayed awake, lying flat on my back on the window-side edge of the bed. The room was dark and overly warm, causing the already low ceiling to feel even lower. It seemed to hover a few short feet above me, making me feel trapped and heavy.

I rubbed my eyes. My elbows were stiff from lying with my

arms motionless at my sides for so long. I stood up, rolling off the bed as carefully as I could, and stretched my back, reaching for my toes, listening to the evenness of the others' breathing, wondering if anyone's sleep was faked. I wondered how Bellamy was feeling and fought the urge to wake her where she slept less than an arm's length away. But I stayed where I was. Because as much as I wanted to talk to her, touch her, kiss her, despite all of this being for her, what I was feeling right then wasn't. It was for me.

As close as we all were and whether we voiced it or not, each of us was here for our own reasons, beyond Bellamy. Reese because she refused to live a life of missed opportunity and avoided adventure; Nari because she truly believed this was justice and because she pushed herself to do big things if only to know that she could; Keagan because he was the fixer, the voice of reason, the one who kept us all from slipping over the cliff's edge; me because I wanted to prove to myself that my wanting was a good enough reason for me to try.

I lay back down.

"Es muy poco práctico, Santiago," my mom had said, or maybe it'd been my dad. In my memory it was my mom, but I'm certain they've each said those words to me at least half a dozen times. *Es muy poco práctico, muy poco práctico, impractical.* "Tú te irás a la universidad a estudiar."

"Of course I'm going to college to study," I'd argued back, "but I earned my scholarship *because* of my diving."

"Exactly," my mom said, arguing our perpetual argument in the kitchen after my sisters had gone to bed. "Ya tendrás suficiente trabajo con las obligaciones del equipo. Si te comprometes con algo más, no tendrás tiempo para los estudios." She was convinced that with classes and diving for a college team, I would already have enough work, enough obligations, it was all enough, enough, enough. Anything else would be a detriment, would jeopardize my education because "It will be *too much, Santiago*."

"It won't!" I kept my voice an angry whisper. "I can do it. The team, the extra training, school. I know it will be hard, but I also know I can do it." Standing in the kitchen, looking between my mom and dad with my arms crossed and brow tight, I'd asked, "Si me creo en mí, ¿por qué no quiere creerme en mí también?"

If I believe in me, why won't you believe in me?

And my dad had answered, "No puedes saber lo que podrás hacer."

You can't know what you'll be able to do.

That was the argument. That was always the argument. I'd heard it too many times to count.

I know there are parents who celebrate, worship even, their kids' lofty ambitions, parents like Nari's, and Bellamy's mom, and Reese's, current dramas notwithstanding. Keag's would, too, I'm sure, if he knew his specific ambition. But not mine. Mine want me to respect their wishes and their choices and their sacrifices. And it isn't that they aren't proud. They are. And it isn't that they've discouraged me from reaching the place where I am now. They haven't. But earning an athletic scholarship to a top-tier school where I will get a top-tier education that will help secure me a steady future of steady, life-supporting work, hopefully close to home, is a far stretch from chasing an unlikely dream down a road paved with extra expenses, time, and uncertainty. Which I understand. Their argument has its logic. It is safe. My dream *is* impractical.

But if our story is proof of anything, it's that impracticality is less a reason not to do something and more a reason to try harder.

I took a heavy breath, closed my eyes, and started again:

Wait for Reese to draw attention, cross the lobby like I do it every day. Eyes forward, attention focused yet nonchalant. Head to the turnstiles . . .

PART 4

KEAGAN

Loiter, linger, skulk, loaf, lounge, idle, laze.
Wait.

"Hot chocolate?" I stood inside the door, grocery sack in hand,
doling out the junk food I'd blown the rest of our slush fund
on after keeping back just enough to pay for gas to get home.
Though we'd be blowing this Popsicle stand, aka the scene of
our crime, one swift minute after the deed was done, Nari'd reserved the room through the night. Which meant no checkout
time. Which meant we'd kill pretty much the whole day here
before our scheduled programming, watching crap cable while
at least one of us kept an eye on the FI security feeds, waiting to
triple-check Foster's door code and generally making sure the
place didn't burn down before our planned pillaging. Really, I
was gonna miss the place. The room. Heist Headquarters. Cha-
teau de Shit. It'd really grown on me. Like fondness. Or some
kind of fungus.

"Me!" Bellamy called, hand raised. I threw her the box.

"Cool Ranch Doritos?"

"Here," Nari said, and I tossed them to her on the far mattress.

"Seasonal fruit bowl?"

"Yes!" Reese said, then, "Wait. Does 'seasonal' mean canta-loupe, honeydew, and three mushy grapes? Because I take issue with that."

"Maybe some of us *like* honeydew, Reese," San said. He stood from his seat in the room's lonely chair and held his hand out for the fruit bowl. "Maybe some of us happen to be craving those three mushy grapes."

Reese rolled her eyes. "Fine, but if there's non-mushy straw-berries, dibs."

I handed out the rest of my stash, from every kind of Skittles they'd had to a bunch of bananas, then settled in with my own picks: a cup of microwaveable oatmeal, two apples, deli sand-wich, bag of peanut butter M&M's, and a liter of diet Dr Pepper.

The others sorted through their respective snack piles while Nari flipped through the channels looking for a movie. "*Ocean's Eleven!*" she cheered. "Hello, serendipity!"

I shook my head, but whatever. I was done fighting it. Not because I'd had some grand and convenient change of heart, but because . . . I dunno. A few things, I guess. Part of it was Bells's stuff the other night, which had made me like her dad even less, and I already liked him a negative amount. Part of it was the one-versus-four thing, the momentum of it. Nari, San, Bells, and Reese, they were the train, speeding down the track with lonely little me clinging to the caboose, heels dug in, try-ing to stop all few thousand tons of it with my pathetic human muscles. So rather than get dragged along the ground being shredded into pulpy ribbons, I jumped on the train. I know that seems too simple. Why not just leave? Well, because contrary to the events of the other night, I am not a selfish asshole. At least, not usually. Maybe three percent. Yeah, I'd say I'm three percent selfish asshole and ninety-seven percent not the kind of person who would bail on my friends when they need me, even if they need me for something illegal and supremely reckless.

Another thing was the video. That footage from Nari's Owl Cam? It swayed me. The fancy-ass lobby up on the twelfth floor, Patrick all tailored and trendy like he'd come out of a 3-D hipster printer, the office space itself with all that glass and light and the awesome plants and impossibly white furniture. Then, por supuesto, Robert freaking Foster himself. And not even that he was kind of a dick, talking to "Violet Murakami" with that steady condescension, but how I could see Bells in the shape of his eyes. It'd felt so *real* then. And I don't mean the impending crime, I mean the abandonment.

So, was I a convert? Meh. But I was on board, even if more as a reluctant stowaway than a co-conductor.

Two-thirds through the movie, I grabbed a stack of plastic cups and poured a bit of my diet Dr Pepper into five of them, passing them out as I did.

"Time for a toast," I said, standing and holding my cup up.

San looked into his cup, lip curled. "With diet Dr Pepper?"

"You'll drink it and you'll like it!" Nari snapped, then giggled.

I grinned at her. She held my eye a few seconds longer than she needed to, and I let my smile turn genuine and warm. We'd barely talked after she'd done her thing yesterday, but I'd slept next to her in Superbed, and when I'd looped my arms around her in the night, she'd scooted her back up flush with my chest.

"Hey," Reese said, snapping her fingers at me. "The toast. Or are we all holding up our cups of chemical-laced sugar water for fun?"

"It's diet, Reese," Bells said. "Sugar-free."

"Fine. Chemical-laced chemical water, then. Also, *toooooaasst.*"

"Okay, okay. Ahem," I said, "throat-clearing, the tapping of flatware on glass."

"Thanks, Keag," said San. "I think I would've been confused about what you were doing if you hadn't described a few pre-speech sound effects."

"You're welcome." I tipped my head to him. "Now, we're gathered here today in the name of the Family We Choose, to cement this union with the most lasting and strongest of glues, shared guilt and criminal activity."

Groans.

"Also! *Also.* Before that, before today. Before all of this. You guys are . . ." I looked up at the ceiling, thinking. "You're my Mutant Ninja Turtles. My Avengers *and* Justice League. You're—

"San." I gestured to him with my cup. "I swear if you wanted to, you could make yourself grow literal wings. You can do *anything.* And I cannot wait to scream my guts out for you, to a truly embarrassing degree, from the stands at the Olympics someday.

"Reese, you are such a brilliant weirdo. Our *ace* in the hole." Laugh-boos all around. "Truly, though, you're so creative and original, and my life would be very beige without you in it."

Reese lifted her cup and said, "Buff. Oatmeal. *Ooh!* Khaki."

"Thanks," I said flatly, and turned to Bellamy, seated at the desk on security-feed-babysitting duty. "Bells, my bestest latchkey pal. You're right. You deserve this. Whatever crap I've pulled and said and I don't know. Just, you deserve the best and a puppy that barks rainbows, too.

"And Narioka." I looked at her, sitting next to San on the window-side half of Superbed. She was so freaking beautiful. I mean, she *is* so beautiful. Like, I know how all this conflict and discord probably makes us seem. But that's a sliver, a narrow wedge, in the pie chart of Us. "Nari, d0l0s, Dr. Okada. I love you. Like in a totally obnoxious and irritating-to-our-friends way. In a follow-you-to-hell—or, you know, the Financial District of San Francisco—and-back way. Partly because I figure you'll rule the universe someday and I want to stay on your good side. But mostly because you're incredible. And brilliant. And driven. And generous and passionate and kind. And I can't wait to spend my life finding out how amazing you are.

"All of you. You are my favorite people." I raised my cup, smiling wide. "And if we get caught and have to go to jail, I'll miss you so damn much."

SANTIAGO

Fresco como una lechuga.
Cool as a cucumber.

Keagan parked in a metered spot a few blocks down and around the corner from FI's main entrance, far enough away that if Reese or I were caught, the police might not think to track us all the way back to his car.

"Remember," Nari said as I adjusted my earpiece for the fifteenth time. "I've only swapped the feed for the cameras on FI's executive floor, since if they checked the lobby and didn't see Reese, it'd be, you know." She shrugged.

"A flaming red flag?" Reese offered.

"Yeah. That." Sitting in the passenger seat with her computer on her lap, Nari scanned through the camera views, opening new windows, navigating her way through it all and preparing to swap the feeds with a scary sort of competency. It was like watching a professional pianist compose an elaborate new piece on the fly, her movements so purposeful and efficient, where if I sat and stared at the same arrangement of notes and keys, I wouldn't know where to start. "But the rest of it—" She waved at the array of windows piled atop each other on her screen, views of the street and sidewalk from FI's external security cams, three different angles of the lobby, even the traffic camera at the corner. "You'll have to just keep your head down."

While I watched her screen, Nari pulled the window showing the executive floor's antechamber forward. Patrick stood at the reception desk talking on the landline. He gestured with his left hand as he spoke, waving it in the air, sandwiching the receiver between his head and shoulder to grab his bag and pack his laptop and travel mug. Finally, he hung up, looped the strap of his satchel over his shoulder, and pulled out his phone, scrolling through whatever he was looking at with an occasional flick of his finger.

"Has my father left yet?" Bellamy asked. She sat next to me, perched on the edge of the middle seat. She said the word "father" stiffly, like the shape of it felt foreign in her mouth. On her other side, Reese rummaged through her canvas messenger bag, dumping out the stuff she didn't need onto the floor and pulling out her wig, black and sleek with blunt bangs. She worked on tying up her own vermilion hair to stuff beneath it.

Nari swapped Patrick's video feed for the only camera with a view of Robert Foster's office and shook her head. The door was closed. The privacy glass was switched on, making the windows opaque. "No. Unless I missed him leaving early."

Bells slouched back in her seat and looked up at me, unsmiling. I looked back, trying to silently communicate everything I felt: how I wanted to pull her close and kiss her; how I wanted to fix this with a flick of a switch; how I was nervous and uncertain; how my parents' words circled my thoughts, slathering my wall of doubt with thick layers of fresh paint; how I'd face that doubt down for her, and for me. In lieu of all that, I squared my shoulders, mimed straightening my tie, and gave her my best impression of a debonair smile. She smiled back. And that was enough.

When I looked back at Nari's computer, she had Patrick's window pulled to the forefront again, showing him walking out from behind his desk, crossing the antechamber, and passing below the camera mounted above the elevator. It was 5:47.

Nari turned around in the front seat and offered me the second of two small radios. The first she had in her lap, a headset already plugged into it. I took the other, plugged my clear earpiece-and-mic set into it. "The channel's already set," she said. "Get out so we can test it again."

I tapped Bellamy's thigh with my knuckles, gave her a final grin, and climbed out of Keag's car onto the sidewalk, closing the door behind me. The radio, small as it was, was too obvious tucked into the pocket of my slim-fit suit pants and too obnoxious in the interior pocket of my jacket, so I clipped it to my belt at my right hip and checked to make sure the bottom of my jacket covered it. The mic I'd clipped to the back of my tie, under the knot, with its wire run behind my shoulder and down my back, hidden beneath my jacket. I reached for the button on it, watching my reflection in the car window, and said, voice low, "Nari?" It was awkward to hold the button while I spoke, but unless someone focused too long on me, they'd only see me adjusting my tie.

"*Works*," Nari's voice sounded in my ear. "*A little muffled, but it works.*"

I buttoned my suit jacket, smoothed my hands down my sleeves, rocked up onto the toes of my stiff new shoes, and checked for the flash drive and fake ID badge in my pocket, imagining myself becoming him, Ethan Marques, Foster Innovations employee.

The street-side rear door opened and closed. I looked over the Subaru's roof at Reese. She wore her black wig and bright, blood-red lipstick, her messenger bag slung over one shoulder. I tipped my head at her. She winked, then rounded the back of the car to join me on the sidewalk as Nari, still watching her computer, rolled the manual passenger window down.

Finally, Nari exhaled a long, deep breath, turned to us, and said, "Time to go."

REESE

Green. The color of sunlight through spring leaves. Bright and eager and anxious and vibrating.

I went inside first. Santiago followed a few paces behind.

The lobby was mildly busy. Like a school hallway five minutes after the last bell. People loitered, chatting, while others breezed through on their way out the doors. I strode through them toward the center of the room, projecting don't-fuck-with-me confidence while my guts puckered like I'd eaten something sour. Out of the corner of my eye I saw San skirt the outer edge of the crowd.

I dropped my bag on the marble floor.

And began.

"LEECHES!" I shouted.

My voice echoed deliciously.

People turned.

"BLOODSUCKERS! SELLOUTS!" I bent to my bag to pull out the sign I'd made and slung it around my neck. *Foster Inequality*, it read in letters finger-painted in fake blood. "WORSHIPERS OF PROFIT! SYCOPHANTS TO THE ALMIGHTY DOLLAR!"

Everyone was watching now. The guards stood behind their desk. Frowning. Waiting.

I let my eyes sweep the crowd, looking for San, but he was already gone.

"SEE ME!" I yelled. I had everyone's full attention now, so I brought it down a notch. From "shrieking zealot" to "impassioned exhibitionist." "*You, the shills of capitalism! You, the carriers of the contagion Affluenza! You! Death Eaters feeding on consumers' corrupted souls!*"

One of the guards stepped out from behind the desk.

I swung the sign around my neck to hang across my back and slammed a fist into one of the blood packets I'd taped to my chest beneath my shirt.

Fake blood splattered across my shirt. It dripped down my stomach, staining my hand.

People screamed.

"*I bleed for Mother Nature! For the lesions you carve in her forests! Her oceans! Her plains! I ache for the workers you have made ache! I scream for the voiceless!*"

I hit my chest again, popping the second packet. Their attention, their screams, felt *amazing*. A pulsing electric purple.

"*You who would rape Mother Earth for a dollar! You who have shattered and auctioned off the pieces of your soul!*"

The guard who'd come out from behind the desk took another step toward me, hand on his hip. Radio, not gun, thankfully. The second one stood there, struck dumb.

I popped the third and largest sack of blood with both hands. Taped to my stomach and filled with maybe a pint of blood, the effect was *mwah!* Choice.

Shouts. Gasps. For real, I'm pretty sure someone fainted.

"I am your heart," I growled, lifting my blood-soaked hands to my face. *"I am your future."* Smearing my cheeks with it. *"I am your conscience. Your shame. Your guilt."*

Finally, the guards came for me. And instead of running right away, which, yeah, I probably should've done, I stood my ground, threw my red-stained hands in the air, and shrieked. Like a siren. A *banshee*. A pure and incredible wail.

Haven't you ever wanted to do that? Just scream total, bloody murder in public? No? Well, I had.

So, I did.

No regrets.

SANTIAGO

El hábito no hace al monje.
The clothes don't make the man.

I heard Reese scream, *"Leeches!"* and made my move, skirting the rear of the gathering crowd, aiming for the turnstiles and wide hallway beyond. Behind me, Reese's voice echoed, "Bloodsuckers!" I glanced back, keeping my face aimed away from the camera I knew was mounted on the wall to my right as Reese yelled, "Sellouts!" The hallway was empty around me, the crowd in the lobby rapt, and a second later Nari's voice confirmed in my ear, *"It's clear."*

Without missing a beat, I braced my hands on either side of the turnstile and jumped the retractable plexiglass barrier.

"Worshipers of profit!" Reese yelled behind me, voice ringing off the lobby's marble floor and walls.

I strode down the hall.

"Sycophants to the almighty dollar!"

Hit the button for the elevator.

"See me!"

Waiting, my anxiety felt like carbonation, a million bubbles pulsing through my blood, making my heart rate speed up and

221

my nerve endings vibrate. I rolled my shoulders, straightened my spine, and took three deep breaths. I was Ethan Marques. And Ethan Marques belonged.

From the lobby came Reese's yell again, but I couldn't understand what she was saying anymore. Then the settling of mechanics, of pulleys and winches and cables holding all that weight, followed by a ding, and the elevator doors opened onto a half-full car. I waited as the passengers filed out, each with their attention aimed toward the lobby, two with their phones already out, one saying, "Some sort of demonstrator? Not sure. Mitch texted that . . . ," to another as they hurried past, and zero sparing a glance at me. Once the car was empty, I stepped inside.

I pushed the button for the twelfth floor and checked in with Nari. "In the elevator," I said, pressing the mic's button and ducking my head to bring my mouth closer to my tie. I let go of the button and waited for her reply.

"Good," she said. "Reese is rocking it. I don't think anyone even noticed you."

I exhaled, long and slow, sank my hands into my pockets, and watched myself in the elevator's stainless steel doors. Soft around the edges, a little indistinct, my reflection looked like a man people would listen to, a man who'd walk into a room knowing he could command it, knowing attention wouldn't need to be asked for because it'd be immediately given. The breadth of my shoulders, tapered width of my waist, cut of my slacks, and shine on my shoes made me look not only older but also confident, not only confident but also ready, not only ready but certain.

My heart rate slowed in time with the elevator. It settled, the doors opened, and I stepped out.

"*Hang on.*" Nari's voice was a tiny vibration in my ear, a breath, a whisper at full volume. I fought an urge to rub my ear and waited a step outside the elevator, its doors closing behind me. From Nari's video and our research, I knew the camera that watched this room was mounted on the wall above my head and a little to the right, but by now she should've swapped the current feed, the one she still watched on her laptop, with a twenty-minute stretch she'd copied from yesterday evening's recording.

"*Sorry,*" Nari finally said. "*I thought I— Never mind. Go, San. Go now.*"

So I went, crossing the small lobby, pulling open one of the frosted-glass doors, stepping through with confidence and starting right because that was the plan, a straight shot past the other offices along the corridor to Robert Foster's back in the corner.

REESE

Flickering between electric purple and blue. Happy panic.

I screamed. And screamed. Because this was total bucket-list material, like one step below flinging a gallon of milk as high as I could in a grocery store just to watch it fall and explode on the floor. I shrieked until my voice cracked. Until the first guard got within arm's reach.

Then I ran.

Twirled on my toe and bolted. Straight for the doors. Where I reached for the handles with my bloodied hands, leaving magnificent prints. One lovely one smeared in an arc across the glass. Another wrapped around the brass-plated handle. Like the last brushstrokes on a painting. A swish here. A swipe there. A quick splatter and *Masterpiece*. Then the guard, the one who wasn't supposed to chase me because I was nothing but a spectacle, a nuisance, here and gone, caught up to me and grabbed me around the waist.

I fought. I squirmed.

I *writhed*.

Arms and legs pumping. Twisting, bucking, flailing.

He lifted me off the floor and carried my thrashing self across the lobby.

SANTIAGO

Entre la espada y la pared.
Between a rock and a hard place.

"Stop!"

I stopped.

"Left." Nari's voice was thin, strained, calm over panic, silk over fire. *"Go left."*

I spun on my heel and went left. A few seconds later, half a breath after I'd shifted course, circumnavigating the airy common space, I heard voices, two of them, a man and a woman speaking casually, then laughing as they passed through the glass doors to the lobby. I took a deep, calming breath.

The light in the common space was bright like daylight, clean like sunshine, making the plants strung about the central atrium, a living art installation, pulse with an almost preternatural green. I focused on that color, glancing between it and the blond wood floor in front of me as I followed the path past offices closed up for the weekend toward Robert Foster's in the opposite corner. The green, the light, the furniture so white it nearly glowed, was calming, like the gurgling of pool drains, the creak of the board bending beneath my weight, the shush of the air moving past my ears as I performed my approach and pushed off into a dive.

Then, in my ear: *"Fuck."*

Slowing as I rounded the last corner, I lifted my hand to my tie, ready to push the button, when I saw what she meant. At the end of the hall, the door to Robert Foster's office, being the very place I was headed to commence deeply illegal activity, opened.

"Fuck, fuckfuckfuckfuck."

I stopped.

The seconds stretched. A bead of water growing heavier, heavier, heavier, waiting to drop.

I pushed the mic's button and whispered, "Not helping."

Robert Foster paused in his doorway, holding open the door with one hand and looking at his phone in his other.

"Shit. Okay," Nari said in my ear.

He tucked his phone into his pocket.

"Two doors up. Conference room next to his office."

Looked down the hall in front of him.

"San!"

Turned toward me.

"GO!"

And I moved.

Three smooth paces forward to the door, and I grabbed the handle, slipped inside, and closed it behind me. Heart in my throat, I huddled against the wall in the corner beside the door, away from the room's huge windows looking out onto the common space.

"Hang tight, Santiago," Nari said. "Foster didn't see you. He went back into his office. I'll keep watch and let you know. But for now, just—" A pause. "Just . . . wait."

I know when a dive is going to go wrong. Long before I hit the water, before an ill-executed approach, before an unbalanced takeoff, before I over- or underrotate, I can feel it, deep in my gut. Bells would tell me that feeling is a consequence of brain signals and body chemistry, that we call it a "gut feeling" because of whatever cocktail of hormones and neurological twitches makes us feel unease in our abdomen.

But this is bone-deep, marrow-deep, intuition, not thought.

Maybe they're the same thing told differently, but in that instant, when I know I won't make my revolutions, that I'm going to smack the water so hard it'll feel like solid ground or that my head is going to pass far too closely to the end of the board, I know it in more than my hormones and nerve endings. I know it in my self, my soul.

Back pressed against the conference room's wall, watching for a figure in the window or the depression of the door's handle, I searched myself for that feeling, waiting for the exact moment I'd know this had gone too wrong to correct. I felt for the fake employee ID and the flash drive in my pocket, then brought my hand to the mic at the back of my tie. "Nari," I whispered, "what should I . . ."

There was a slight click in my ear.

A click, then silence.

BELLAMY

Epinephrine (adrenaline).
Molecular formula: $C_9H_{13}NO_3$.
Effects: increases heart rate and blood pressure, expands air passages of the lungs, enlarges pupils, redistributes blood to the muscles to maximize blood glucose levels.

Nari clicked off her headset, and Keagan asked, "Why hasn't he left yet?" He was kinetic, shifting in the driver's seat, drumming his fingers on the wheel, eyes darting between Nari's computer screen and the rearview mirror. *"Why didn't we make sure he was gone?"*

"I don't know!" Nari shouted. Frantic, she switched between two windows on her laptop's screen: the first the view of the lobby, now empty of everyone but a few reeling observers, and the second Foster's closed office door. "He has dinner across the bay at seven. An email from his wife at four confirmed it. He should be gone by now."

I leaned back. I was going to be sick.

They were going to be caught. Both of them. All of us.

Because of me.

Why hadn't I tried calling again? I could've begged and yelled. I could've, should've—I'd been impatient. And selfish. I'd wanted to hurt Robert Foster for hurting me, for ignoring me. I'd wanted revenge. So I'd sat back and looked the other way while the wrongness of this stared me straight in the face, all while letting Nari and Keag and Reese and San risk everything. *Everything.*

I'd done this.

I'd done it.

I'd—

I blinked and focused back on Nari's computer screen. I'd swear it had been minutes. Whole minutes since the guard hauled Reese, kicking and flailing, across the lobby, since San ducked into the conference room. But when I glanced at the clock in the screen's header, the time hadn't changed.

Nari scanned through the other camera angles, watching in real time while the false loops she'd spliced into FI's security footage still played on their feed. But she couldn't find one that showed Santiago or even a better view of the room he'd hidden in. She looked at Keagan, then back at me, eyes wide. "What do we do?"

We both stared back, silent.

For one beat . . . two . . . three.

I reached for the door handle. "Get San out," I said. "I'll go get Reese." And before Nari or Keagan could protest, I'd climbed from the car and was walking down the sidewalk toward the main doors to FI.

I didn't know what I was going to do, what I was going to

say. With each step, I grew incrementally and inevitably closer, yet I still didn't know.

What I did know was that I wanted to travel to other planets someday. I wanted to float through the silent weightlessness of space. I wanted to walk on Mars, watch the rings of Saturn through the window of a spacecraft I'd helped design. And I knew that all that was possible. In the incredible expanse of human ingenuity there were answers to questions we hadn't even thought to ask yet.

And if I meant to summon the bravery to leave my planet behind someday, I could damn well save my friend from the consequences of a risk she'd taken to help me eventually do that.

SANTIAGO

La necesidad agudiza el ingenio.
Necessity is the mother of invention.

Silence.

Nari was gone. I was alone.

I pulled the earpiece out of my ear, letting it dangle from my shirt collar, and rested my head back against the wall. The conference room's exterior windows looked out on the neighboring buildings, the angle of the sun low and casting their shadows in stark relief. The long conference table reflected the view like a mirror on its polished black surface. The temperature of the room was perfect, completely ignorable and kept that way by the gentle whir of air flowing out of a large vent in the ceiling in an easy, artificial breeze.

I tried to rationalize. I hadn't done anything yet. Was I even technically trespassing? I hadn't broken in, only slipped past the building's rather lax security. Couldn't I, simply, leave? Walk out right now? But then, what about Bells?

What about me?

Giving up now, this close, literally down the hall from the last step in this grand scheme, this plan I'd decided was a metaphor for my own ambitions, was too much metaphor even for me.

I stared at the ceiling, waiting for the door to open or not, sifting through my existential crisis, deciding whether to stay or bail, when my attention settled back on the air-conditioning vent.

"*San?*" Nari's voice asked, small in the earpiece still hanging down by my collarbone.

I tucked it back in my ear, held the mic's button, and answered, "I'm here."

"*Thank God.*"

I held the button again. "Foster?"

"*He's gone.*"

"Great," I said, looking through the conference room's window to make sure I was alone. "See anyone?"

Nari answered, "*No. It's clear.*"

I inhaled deeply, let go a long, controlled breath, and left the room.

Standing at Foster's door, tapping the code into the keypad, I was a filament. Bright and hot, buzzing and visible. I typed the code in: 1-7-9-8-5. A light in the pad's top right corner blinked red once. I tried the handle.

Nothing.

I keyed the number in a second time.

Another red blink, and the door stayed locked.

This was the number Foster had used yesterday. I was sure of it. I'd watched him key it in once myself. Bellamy had checked it again this morning.

Yet.

I stood there, staring at it, for one second, two, three. Did I try it again and risk hitting my limit, like messing up your pass code too many times and getting locked out of your phone? Would it sound an alarm? Send an alert to an app on Foster's phone?

What did we miss?

"Uh," I said into my mic, taking quick strides back to the conference room, "we have a problem. The door code is wrong."

A pause. Then Nari's voice, inflectionless: *"What do you mean, 'wrong.'"*

"'Wrong' as in *wrong*." I closed the conference room's door and leaned back against it. "Or it was right; then he changed it. Doesn't matter. 'Cause the code I have won't unlock the door, and I'm not going to stand out there trying it till I get caught."

"Um," Nari said, and I pictured her sitting in Keag's car, slack-jawed and stumped. *"I don't—"*

"Wait." My eyes rested on the air-conditioning vent in the ceiling. The rather large air-conditioning vent. Maybe even large enough to fit my shoulders. "I have an idea."

REESE

Maroon. No, mauve. Because I hate mauve. Stupid, dread-filled, muddied, might-get-arrested mauve.

The security guard hauled me bodily around the corner behind the info desk, following the other one into a small room. I stopped fighting the moment the guard carrying me stepped inside. "You good?" he asked.

I answered, "Yep," and he set me down. I sat in one of two chairs arranged in front of the room's only other furniture, a desk with an out-of-date PC on it. For real, that was it. No wall of state-of-the-art surveillance screens, no "Hang in there!" kitten poster, just . . . nothing. A fuzzy void with the three of us floating in the middle. Taupe incarnate.

The two of them stood behind the desk, apparently totally unsure what to do.

Finally, the one Nari had charmed the day before—Walton? Weston? He didn't wear a name tag—shook his head and asked, *"What the hell?"*

I shrugged.

"Are you *high?*"

I lifted my chin. I could feel the fake blood drying on my

face, neck, hands, chest, stomach. "I am the voice of the mis-used masses!" I shouted. "I am your conscience personif—"

"*Okay!*" the other one barked. "Enough of that. We don't care and there's no one else listening."

"Cool, sure," I said, and settled back into the chair, all calm and casual while inside I was freaking the fuck out. Because

(1) Office, guards, door shut tight behind me. You know, *the obvious.*

(2) If I was in here, *where was San?*

(3) What the hell was I doing all this for anyway? To help Bells? Sure. For my own excitement-loving self? Okay. But oh my God if I didn't get out of here, this one stupid decision could rob me of everything—*everything*—that I wanted out of the next few years, the next decade? Two decades? My entire *life?*

(4) HOW WAS I GOING TO GET OUT?!

Seriously. SERIOUSLY. All that planning? It'd been San, San, SanSanSanSanSan. How to get *San* in. How to get *San* out. How to deal if *San* got caught. But what about *me?* What about *Reese?* "Run," Nari had said. Run and "hope they don't chase you."

Except, well, funny thing? HE HAD.

I took a slow breath through my nose, held it, and exhaled, trying and failing to slow the iridescent hummingbird pace of my heartbeat.

The guard from Nari's Owl Cam—I'll go with Waldo—sat in the desk chair across from me, hands folded on the desktop. "So, Miss . . . ," he started.

"Voldemorta."

The other one—let's say . . . Garth—arched an eyebrow. "Voldemorta?"

"If you prefer, you may call me She Who Must Not Be Named."

Garth rolled his eyes and sighed.

Waldo took his hands off the desktop and put them in his lap. The gesture made him look softer, shoulders more rounded, stance informal. "Help me out here," he said, eyeing me up and down. I imagined what a macabre sight I must be and, for the span of a good spine-length shiver, felt a glittering Super Pegasus's worth of proud. "What is all this? Protest? A cry for attention?"

I was at a loss. I got why I hadn't gotten one of those cool Secret Service earpieces, since I was supposed to stay in character, and if I was caught, explaining why a performance artist protester was wearing a freaking earpiece and radio would be sorta tough, not to mention incriminating. But also, *What if I got caught?*

I was thinking, racking my brain for the easiest, most direct, most expedient lie, anything I could force out of my throat as it constricted with panic, when there was a knock on the door.

Waldo and Garth looked at each other. Garth moved to see who was there. The door was behind me and to my right a little, so I couldn't see who Garth was talking to when he cracked the door and asked, "Yeah?"

"I'm here for my friend." Bells's voice was low and steady. Garth opened the door a little wider and I saw her, standing there in all her sweatshirted, blue-jeaned, ponytailed glory. She looked at me, covered in fake blood, and didn't so much as flinch.

"Voldemorta is your friend?" Garth asked.

Waldo snorted.

Bells pushed into the room, and in that instant I quit

237

lamenting that she was my rescuer. I'm not proud of it, but yeah, I'd wanted Nari. Nari, so quick on her feet. Nari, so charming and flirtatious. Nari, who'd met Waldo the day before. "*Voldemorta* is a minor," Bellamy said. Not true. I'd been a full-blown legal adult for almost four months. But they didn't know that. She took a wide step past Garth and gestured for me to stand up. I did. "A *minor* whom you unlawfully restrained. Whom you laid hands on for exercising her right to free speech and freedom of expression."

I wanted to cheer. Apparently, Nari wasn't the only one quick on her feet.

"Hey," Waldo said, standing behind the desk. "She's trespassing. *You're* trespassing!"

Bellamy arched an eyebrow. "Physically occupying the common area of a commercial building during business hours is not trespassing. Maybe loitering, but unless otherwise posted, my friend was entirely within her rights."

"Within her rights to go completely crazy?"

"Crazy?" If a voice could do things like "drip with disdain," Bells's would've been doing just that. Salivating with it, *drooling*. "Using performance art to express her disgust with the iniquities of globalism and unfettered oligarchical capitalism is 'crazy'?"

Both men raised their eyebrows. Garth opened his mouth to speak, but Bellamy took half a step forward and cut him off with a steady stream of ad-libbed awesome. "Are you aware that the clothing for Rowan Malik's department store line is manufactured in factories in Southeast Asia where employees, young women mostly, work sixteen-hour days and live twelve to a dorm room? And that that clothing, not including the impact of the refinery of the raw materials needed to make it, is then boxed up and loaded onto enormous barges that not only pollute the air with massive emissions of greenhouse gases but also cause oil and acoustic pollution of the oceans? And that once those boxes are delivered, they're trucked all over the country to be peddled by workers who primarily make minimum wage, meaning they can't afford things like health care or college or, at times, basic necessities like housing, which contributes to the cyclical nature of impoverishment among the working poor?

"And that is only one fraction of one aspect of one of Foster Innovations' affiliated businesses. I can continue. Or, perhaps, we could instead agree that acting upon a passion about the shape of our world, a shape that will doubtlessly affect my friend's and my future, not to mention the vast majority of the world at large, has little if *anything* to do with an individual's state of mental health."

There was a beat of silence. The most incredibly satisfying beat of silence I have experienced in my life so far.

"Jesus," Garth muttered.

Waldo pressed the heels of his hands into his eyes. "It's Friday," he said to Garth. "She didn't hurt anybody."

"Agreed." Garth turned to us. "Get out."

We did.

SANTIAGO

Llevar las riendas.
Take the reins.

An eternity later, which Nari assured me was closer to five minutes, after she'd described the venting schematics she'd managed to find and checked all the floor's cameras to ensure that it was finally and completely empty, I stood on one of the conference room's rolling chairs and did a ridiculous thing. After all, apart from my ability to wear a suit while looking a passable twenty-two or -three, this was why I was here. Not to stand on a rolling chair, using the corners of my faux ID to unscrew a vent cover from the ceiling, specifically, but in the event that something demanding the physicality of, say, squirming through a vent or maybe sprinting down eleven flights of stairs in a mad chase occurred.

With the adjustable rolling chair elevated as high as it would go, balancing a foot on each of its armrests, I reached above my head and unscrewed the twelve small screws securing the air-conditioning vent's cover to the ceiling, putting each screw in an interior pocket of my suit jacket as I went. Next, I wedged my ID under one side of the cover and gently pried it from its encasement, hopping down from the chair to set it on the floor once it was free.

The vent itself was maybe eighteen inches square and rose at least a foot straight up into the space above the drop ceiling before the shaft leveled out and, per Nari's research, ran parallel to the outer wall of the building until it took a ninety-degree turn above Foster's office to run along the other exterior wall.

"*Well?*" I heard Nari in my ear, impatient. There were no cameras in this room, and I imagined her not being able to see me drove her nuts. As for me, my hands were slick and my heart had grown to fill the entirety of my torso.

Staring up into the duct, I answered, "I can do it."

I took off my suit jacket and draped it carefully on the conference room table, then tucked my tie inside my shirt between two buttons so it wouldn't flap around in my way. The radio I unclipped from my belt and put in my front shirt pocket.

"Here goes," I said into the mic. "Aunque la mona se vista de seda, mona se queda."

"*What?*"

"'Although the monkey's dressed in silk, she remains a monkey.'"

Nari laughed a little in my ear. I listened hard but didn't hear Bells in the background. "*Again, what?*"

I smiled and pressed the button to speak again. "Just thought the moment needed a little something extra, you know?"

"*Sure, San, extra,*" she said, but I could tell she was smiling. "*Maybe go now?*"

"Okay."

I closed my eyes, took one deep breath, then climbed back onto the armrests of the chair. With my arms outstretched, the ledge where the duct leveled out was at least six inches above my fingertips. I held my arms straight above me, bent my knees, and jumped.

I made it. Fingers curled over the flat edge of the vent, the metal slick with a fine layer of dust, legs dangling, chair pushed out from underneath me from the force of my jump, I pulled myself up, careful to keep my elbows tucked in tight at my sides. My shoulders brushed either side of the narrow space. Once I got my chest level with my hands, I stretched first one arm out, then the other, bracing my hands on the duct's sides, squirming up and forward with muscles straining until, finally, my whole body was in the duct.

The interior was dark, lit only by what light came up through the vent. I lay on my stomach, propped on my elbows, to catch my breath. The steel was cool. I kept my head down to keep from brushing the top. According to the plans Nari'd found, the ductwork ran from the conference room to Foster's office through his private bathroom, my exit point. I took as deep a breath as the narrow space allowed and moved, army-crawling forward through the duct.

It was not quiet or graceful. I sincerely hoped Nari was right that no one was here.

After ten or fifteen feet of that, I came to the next vent, constructed the same as the other and looking down into Foster's bathroom. *Shit.* How was I supposed to get *out?* The screws needed to be unscrewed from the *outside,* and breaking the vent would, well, leave a broken vent.

Beyond the foot-and-a-half gap above the bathroom vent, the duct continued on through Foster's office, the space quickly growing too dark to see where it turned to follow the offices along the building's eastern side. Lying on my stomach with my arms folded beneath my chest, I stared down the dimly lit vent shaft at the view of the bathroom floor below, then squirmed forward, bending at my waist over the edge of the opening to reach down and shove at the cover with my hand. It was solid.

I pulled myself up into the duct again and moved forward across the gap until I could get my feet down to the vent cover, which I kicked, gently, trying to get the screws to give. *"San?"* Nari asked in my ear. I ignored her. Over and over, at each of the four corners and along the sides where I knew the screws were from the other vent, I kicked and pushed at it with my toes. One or two at a time, the screw holes stripped, and the cover loosened and finally, *finally*, clattered to the ground.

Carefully, I lowered myself down the shaft and dropped to the tiled floor, pitching myself slightly to the side to avoid hitting the vent cover.

I stretched my back and wiped my dusty hands on the thighs of my slacks, then reached for the mic at the back of my tie knot. "I'm in." In Robert Foster's private bathroom, a billionaire's private office bathroom that looked exactly as I'd imagined it might: huge, immaculately clean, nicer than anyone could ever need, with an oversized steam shower, built-in closet unit with frosted-glass doors, one of those state-of-the-art electronic toilets, and black marble everywhere. I took it all in as my heart rate slowed; then I retrieved the vent cover from the floor.

"Awesome," Nari answered.

I leaned the vent cover, thankfully only slightly marred, against the vanity and searched the floor until I found all twelve screws. Cupping them in my palm, checking the count again, I held the mic's button with my other hand and asked, "How's Reese?"

Silence as I stood on the counter next to the sink, balancing carefully near the edge, fake employee ID in one hand and cover held up with the other, refitting it into its slot. Silence as I fit the first few of the small screws back into the corners. They hadn't fared too well, but I managed to force enough of them into their stripped screw holes that the vent seemed solid enough. Those that wouldn't stay I tucked into my pocket.

"Nari?"

I took a hand towel and wiped down all the surfaces I remembered touching and a few I didn't, just in case, then threw the towel over my shoulder to wipe down the desk and computer.

"She's fine."

I paused. Nari's tone was flat and hesitant, but if she was lying, there was nothing I could do. I opened the bathroom door.

While Foster's bathroom screamed tech-obsessed point-oh-one-percenter, his office was a little more demure. I'd seen it on Nari's Owl Cam, but compared to that narrow, slightly fish-eye version, the real thing was, well, *real*. The hardwood was a darker color than the floors outside. The air smelled slightly of lavender, maybe eucalyptus, something subtly floral and fresh. From inside the bathroom doorway, I scanned the windows, desk, walls, and was about to step out into the space when I saw it, a single security camera above the office's door.

"Nari," I whispered into the mic, eye on the camera. "Are you watching Foster's office camera feed?"

"What camera?" She paused. *"Shit."*

"So that's a 'no'?"

"It's not— Hang on."

I waited, feeling for my heart rate, trying to keep it slow. If I had to bail and go back through the vent, I'd never get the cover on and—

"Found it. Private feed. I can't— Dammit." I heard her frantic typing in the background. "I can't swap the feed—all I can do is pause it."

"Can it see the bathroom doorway?" I sank farther back into the bathroom.

Her hesitation was damning. "Yes."

"Can you see me?"

"No."

"So we just have to hope he doesn't notice. That he won't have a reason, say seventy thousand reasons, to check the footage."

"The program's good, Santiago," she said, defensive. "It'll work."

What had Keagan said? Working or not working, it all feels like fire to me. I clenched my jaw, fingers on the flash drive in my pocket, thinking of Bellamy, my parents and sisters, then myself and that feeling when I know I've done a dive right.

"Okay. Pause it." I took a deep breath, and as I finished exhaling, she said, "Okay. Go."

I crossed the open floor to the desk in six wide strides, pulling the virus-loaded flash drive from my pocket. I clicked the mouse to wake the computer up. The lock screen flashed on, and I typed in the password Nari had learned from the keystroke spyware she'd delivered to Foster weeks ago in an email. Once the home screen opened, I plugged the flash drive into one of the USB ports on the back of the computer, waited the few heartbeats it took for the folder, labeled *HAHAMOFOS* in true Nari style, to appear, opened it, downloaded it, and . . .

That was it.

I ejected the flash drive and shoved it back in my pocket, closed out of the computer, wiped everything down with the hand towel and returned it to its rack in the bathroom, unbuttoned my cuff to use my sleeve to close the bathroom's door and open the office's, then stepped out into the hall.

The door closed on its own behind me. The lock on the handle clicked as it shut.

I pressed the mic's button and said, "Done."

REESE

I am a rainbow.
Freaking incandescence personified.

"Holy shit—I can't believe you pulled that off," I said, three inches out of FI's main doors. The air was fresh! The sky was blue! The sidewalk glittered in the setting sun! Well, no, it didn't. It was a sidewalk. Concrete and black gum stains and bird shit. But we were free, *free, FREE!*

"Oh God," Bells said, "same."

"What!" I spun on her, smacking her shoulder, still feeling like I was a thousand feet above the ground. My messenger bag, which I'd scooped up off the floor on our way through the lobby, bounced against my hip, heavy with the half-empty jug of fake blood I'd taken in, you know, just in case. The mess of it on my face cracked and flaked around my mouth as I smiled. My shirt was sticky with it. The empty packets were still taped to my stomach. "You just . . . *winged* it?"

Bellamy giggle-snorted. "Yup."

I let out a mad laugh. "I gotta tell ya, Bells. I wouldn't have thought you had it in you."

Bellamy, four or five inches shorter than me, jogged a step to keep up. "Me either," she said.

We charged toward Keagan's car, basically skipping down the sidewalk, freaking *flying*. For real, a sinkhole could've opened up in front of me and I'd have either leapt across it in one weightless bound or cackled the whole way down.

The fear was still there, whispering, *You almost got totally screwed. If it weren't for Bells* . . . But success was a cheering stadium, drowning it out. And I knew I'd chase this feeling my whole life.

Which made me think, even as we walked, with traffic passing and people giving me the strangest looks, *I get it.*

My mom.

I got it.

Not the flaming garbage fire of *what* she'd done. But why. I could see it. I could comprehend. Her problem wasn't wanting this feeling. This electricity. Like my blood was a current buzzing about beneath my skin. Her problem was refusing it, beating it back if ever she got a taste. Spending her life pounding on that brick wall. Not my dad, but a wall of her own design, one she'd slammed down around herself to keep practicality in and dreams out. Or maybe it was the other way around. The wall trapped whoever it was she really wanted to be inside, and the only way for that true self to survive was to smash through that wall in the worst, most destructive way. Leaving my dad and me coughing and hacking and trying to breathe despite the dust of her rubble.

Bells and I crossed the street and walked up behind Keagan's car. Nari must've seen us in the side-view mirror, because she burst, surged, *bounded* out of the passenger side, tossing her headset on the seat behind her. She held her hands up, fingers splayed, dropped her jaw, and silent screamed.

Bellamy laughed.

I hurried forward and ducked into the backseat. Bells and Nari followed.

Keagan looked back at me from the driver's seat and said, "You need a hose."

Bellamy focused on Nari, all intense, and asked the question I hadn't bothered to even think yet: "San?"

SANTIAGO

Las palabras se las lleva el viento.
Actions speak louder than words.

Walking out of the FI building, after wiping my prints off Foster's office door handle with my sleeve, after reattaching the vent cover in the conference room, checking the sleek black table for smudges, and returning the chair to its place, after fixing my tie and slipping back into my suit jacket, after striding, confident, down the hallway around the atrium, through the doors into the antechamber, after riding the elevator and crossing the lobby unnoticed, I pushed through the main doors thinking *impractical, illogical, risk.*

Words.

Only words.

Words that were so quiet, forgettable, lost in the wind beside the anchored reality of my actions.

I walked the sidewalk back to Keagan's car, hands in my pockets, gripping the flash drive in one and the ID in the other, looking nearly the same as when I'd gone in, save some scuffs on my new shoes and the smudges of dust on my slacks, and felt my smile spread like a thing not entirely owned by me, wide and bright and not altogether under my control. I felt vivid. I felt invincible.

Because I'd done it.

I was a damned good bet.

NARI

If only I knew then what I know now.

We did it.

We. Did. It.

We were rock stars! Robin Hoods! Five Batmans righting wrongs and slaying villains in the night! Or, you know, in the evening. And less slaying than reappropriating funds from. Oooh, The Revengers! Okay, fine, still no luck on the cool title front. But who cared! We'd done it. And (insert awkward grimace while fidgeting here) yeah, there were a few moments when I wasn't sure we would.

But we did.

The mood in the car was loose with it. Yes, loose. Like muscles after a workout, like we'd all just finished running a race. Exhausted, introspective, relieved. Same as when we'd pulled into the city a few short days before, the only voice in the car was that of the maps app, calmly directing Keagan where to go. An hour and a half later, we stopped for gas. Santiago and Reese went inside to change. Bells went for snacks. Keag filled the tank. And I checked the still-nonexistent balance of our fake person's bank account and the current cost of Bit-coin, guesstimating how long it'd take for Foster to activate my malware on each of his accounts, how long it'd take to siphon enough money after that to buy each Bitcoin.

I hoped we'd make Bells's first payment deadline in August.

I hoped it wouldn't be too tight.

PART 5

KEAGAN

$0.00

"Can I call you later?" Nari asks, leaning down to look in through the open passenger door, laptop hugged to her chest.

I rub my eyes. They feel like wax. Or sand. Sandy wax. Waxy sand? I just need to sleep. It's early. Seven-ish. And I literally drove all night. Actually literally, not even the fake, I-really-mean-figuratively kind. "Of course," I say, and she looks relieved. Like I'd say no? But I get it. Things are still weird. Like when you get out of a super-intense movie and feel like part of you is still living in it. Sometimes it's awesome. Especially after some epic sci-fi or a superhero flick where afterward I feel like maybe, if I really wanted to, I could up and fly.

This is not like that. "Or just come over," I say.

She nods and closes the car door, then takes a wide step back, and through the window I watch her raise her arm and blow me an emphatic kiss. A proper Swim Fast Salute.

I give her a tired smile and drive away. Halfway home my car's fuel light flicks on and I pull into a gas station. Leaning against the back door as the pump chugs, I cross my arms and close my eyes. I keep seeing Reese and Bellamy striding down the sidewalk, Reese still in her wig and covered in fake blood dried a red so dark it looked black in places, Bellamy full-on *beaming*, like she'd swallowed a tiny star. She seemed taller, like after doing all this she took up a little more space. Next, Santiago. He'd glowed just as bright. They all had. Even Nari. And me?

The pump clicks and I turn to put the nozzle away, then screw my gas cap back on. Seen through the rear window, the backseat looks like one of those confetti poppers has gone off, except instead of colored paper bits, it's filled with junk food wrappers and empty coffee cups, a goo-covered black wig, and San's discarded tie.

I pull up to the curb in front of my house, eyelids drooping. The mess and camping gear can wait. I'm at least twenty-five percent asleep, maybe even thirty, as I walk up the path and shove open our moisture-warped front door. I figured the house would be quiet, but my dad's in the kitchen eating what looks like leftover fried rice. His hands still wear dried smears of clay from a predawn pottery session.

"Hey, kid," he says, chewing.

"Hey."

"You're back early."

"Yeah." I feel dizzy. Delirious. Either the room's swaying or I am. "You're up early."

"When inspiration strikes, right?"

"Sure, whatever."

He frowns. "Hungry?"

I'm not. At least, I don't think I am. I don't know. But I sit across the rickety little kitchen table from him anyway. He passes me his bowl and fork. After the first bite, I shovel the rest into my mouth, barely chewing.

"Guess that answers my question," he says.

I shrug.

"Mr. Noncommittal this beautiful a.m., huh?"

"Guess so."

I finish the rest of the fried rice. My dad gets me a glass of water. I drain it in two gulps and stand, aiming for the hallway. My room. My bed.

"Keagan," my dad says.

I stop, look back. He's doing his discerning-parent face. Like he can see inside my head. Or like he's looking super hard but can't see because my shield's up. "Yeah?"

"You okay?"

Am I okay.

I—I don't know how to answer that. In all the most urgent ways? Sure, I'm okay. As in, I'm not bleeding. Or nauseous. Or being chased by a zombie.

But.

"Do you ever . . ." I don't know how to finish. My dad waits, patient. I swallow. "Are you proud of me?"

His eyebrows lift. "Proud of you? Keagan, of course I am."

Hearing that feels like a hot little flower blooming in my stomach. Weird, right? A little gross? But I don't know how else to describe it. I cross my arms to hold the feeling in. "Does it bother you that I don't have a . . . thing?"

He tips his head. "What do you mean?"

"Like, a passion. A dream."

"Oh." He shifts in the kitchen chair, making the vinyl squeak. "Maybe like how your best friends all want to be astronauts and famous artists and Olympic divers and, what's Nari always saying she wants to do, rule the universe?" He laughs. "Like that?"

I nod.

"Nope," he says. "Doesn't bother me."

"Aren't you worried?"

"That at eighteen you haven't figured out your life's passion? No."

I lean back against the doorway to the hall. Thirty percent asleep, remember? "Not even that I don't know what to do about college or jobs or whatever after school?"

"College isn't for everyone, Keag. And it doesn't have to be." He shifts again, crossing his arms like mine. Or mine are crossed like his. No, I did it first. What I mean is, you know how some fathers and sons or mothers and daughters or some other combo have that whole mirror-plus-thirty-years thing going on? Well, that's us. I will look exactly like my dad in a few decades, and a few decades ago, he looked exactly like me. But with, like, jorts or DayGlo or whatever shit was trendy in the early eighties. Big hair? Mullets? I don't know. Discerning-parent face back on, he asks, "Did Nari say something?"

"Sort of."

He sighs. "Listen," he says, and his face switches from discerning to gentle lecturing. "Knowing what you want to do with your entire life when you're seventeen, eighteen years old is incredible. And rare. And . . . how to say it?" He leans back in his chair and crosses one leg over the other. "Fleeting? I just mean it may not stick. People grow, Keagan. And they change. Not fundamentally, I don't think. Even now, I'm not sure about that. But their interests and, yes, their passions and goals. They evolve.

The stuff your friends are so passionate about right now might not be what they're passionate about in five or ten years. And you feeling like you don't have something like that?" He uncrosses his legs and leans forward, resting his elbows on his knees. "Take me," he says. "I thought I wanted to be a drummer. Or a lawyer." He makes a wide-eyed face. "And your mom? She did two years of an undergrad program thinking she'd go to pharmacy school."

"*Really?*" We don't even keep Tylenol in the house, my mom hates "Big Pharma" so much.

"Really."

I close my eyes, leaning my head back against the doorjamb and sighing.

"You'll figure your shit out, Keag," my dad continues. "In a few months or a few years. There's no rush. Try stuff out. See what you like and what you don't. You have some pretty exceptional friends. But having grand plans isn't what makes them exceptional. And you know what?" He pauses and I open my eyes to look at him. "Like calls to like. You're pretty exceptional, too."

I half smile. "In your unbiased opinion, right?"

"Oh, totally biased," he says, smiling back. "But that doesn't mean it isn't true."

I tell my dad thanks and shuffle down the hall and into my room, closing the door, shedding my shoes, jacket, and jeans before tripping onto my bed.

Eyes closed, I let my brain stumble along, ticking through a mess of thoughts like a scribbled to-do list—the stuff my dad said, stuff Nari's said, a slide show of images and snapshots from the past week—and finally devolving into a mess of surreal mash-ups of reality and dreams. The next thing I know, my room is dim and Nari's staring at me from my desk chair, which she's dragged over to the side of my bed.

"Hey," she says.

I roll over onto my stomach, arms folded beneath my chest, and turn my head to look at her. "Hey." I grin. "Gonna give me the Talk?"

Her brow quirks. "As in Birds and Bees? And"—she waggles her eyebrows—"ahem, Pollination?"

I nod, cheek against the mattress. "Re-pro-duck-shun."

She taps a finger on her mouth, considering. "Okay. Here's one: Zeus, after impregnating Metis, swallowed her up and birthed Athena from his forehead." She shrugs. "Good?"

"Perfect," I say, and stretch my arm out to her. She accepts the invitation and climbs over me into the bed, kissing the back of my neck as she goes. "They should use that story in sex ed. Like, 'Don't have sex, horny teens, or you may get pregnant and cannibalized.'"

She rests her head between my shoulder blades. I can feel her breath through my thin cotton T-shirt. "Or become a cannibal and push a baby out of your head."

"Exactly. Equal opportunities for horror."

We're quiet for a while. Nari slides her arm around my chest. I squeeze her hand between my side and tricep. "So."

She moves her head, rests her chin on my back. "So."

I roll over, and she shifts, too, until we're sitting on my bed, both cross-legged and not touching. "We're awkward," she says. "We're never awkward."

"Yeah, well, the past six weeks haven't been exactly normal."

"True."

She picks at a wrinkle in my comforter. Nari isn't big on nervous fidgeting because she isn't big on nervousness. It's the self-confidence thing. Like the idea of being nervous doesn't usually occur to her. Knowing that this makes her nervous, that *I* do? Let's just say that our dynamic has been a little skewed in the "nerves" arena. I mean, she's a badass while I'm . . . ?

Well, that's the thing, right? I don't know what I am. But maybe my dad's right and I don't have to know right now. Maybe I'll know next year or five years from now. Maybe I'll try carpentry or construction and hate it. Maybe I'll love it. I. Just. Don't. Know.

And you know what? That's okay. I get that now. Right now. That it's okay. That my dad's maybe right in a lot of what he said and definitely right about at least one thing: My friends are exceptional. And not because of their dreams, or not just because of their dreams, but because they're good, caring, determined, interesting, kind, accepting people.

But also, maybe he's right that I'm exceptional, too. Or maybe he's not, and I'm normal. But also good. And caring. And determined. And interesting and kind and accepting. Just without the cherry on top of some life–slash–world changing ambition. Which isn't a failure. And shouldn't make me ignorable.

Nari catches herself fidgeting, shakes her hands out, and arranges them neatly in her lap. "Say something."

"Something."

She glares.

"Sorry."

"I mean it. Tell me what you're thinking."

"Okay." I take a slow breath. "I'm thinking that not having some huge life passion like the rest of you makes me feel small and left out. And that being generally opposed to all the . . ."

"Grand theft and major cybercrimes?"

"Yeah, that. Has made that smallness bigger. Which is an oxymoron, but whatever, you get what I mean."

"I do." She chews the inside of her cheek, notices that she's chewing the inside of her cheek, stops, shakes her head, and asks, "Is that all?"

"No." I scoot closer to her on the bed, close enough that our knees are touching. "I'm also thinking that it's okay that I don't know what I want to do with my life yet. And that it doesn't make me smaller. And shouldn't make me easy to ignore."

"That's . . . a lot."

"Yeah. I'm feeling very perspicacious. Meaning, of course, that I now have 'a ready understanding of things.' "

"Keagan!" She beams. "All the points!"

"Like that? I've been saving it up."

"Brilliant."

I smile at her. The blip of normal feels nice.

Head slightly bowed, she looks up at me. "You feel ignored?"

I huff a laugh. "Well, yeah. Not sure if you know this about yourself, Nari, but you can be kind of a steamroller. But, like, in the best way."

She laughs, too, though a little sadly. "What's the 'best way' for a steamroller?"

I shrug. "Flattening things that really need to be flattened?"

"Har har."

"Narioka." I grab her hand. "You're amazing. And I love you. An obnoxious amount. But I think I can love you and still not want to be flattened."

She laughs again, small but for real. "And I can love you, an obnoxious amount, and still think you should yell a little louder

264

for me to change direction *before* it's too late and you're screaming about me flattening your feet."

"Right. Love and acceptance, but with, like, degrees. For example, 'I love you even though you like those horrible mustard pretzel things' versus 'I love you even though your kink involves a full-body hamster costume.'"

"'I love you even though you think the *Star Wars* prequels are better than the original trilogy' versus 'I love you even though you collect mannequins that you dress up, name, and talk to down in your basement.'"

"'I love you even though you hate peanut butter M&M's' versus 'I love you even though you spearheaded a campaign to get your boyfriend and three best friends to commit a major crime, which sure it was for the best of reasons and we all agreed to go along, so it's not like it's all your fault by any means, but it was still completely and terrifyingly illegal, and we still may get caught, and you basically ignored or glared down my every attempt at reason.'"

Nari goes back to fidgeting. She doesn't meet my eye. "Get you a girl who can do both." And I lunge for her, looping my arms around her waist and squeezing her to me as tightly as I can.

"Keag!" she laugh-screams.

I squeeze tighter. She squirms. I can feel her laughter in her throat, her chest. I kiss the space below her earlobe, rub the coarse stubble on my chin across the sensitive skin of her neck. She grabs my head and pushes it back so she can see my face. She's no longer laughing. In fact, she has tears in her eyes. "Tell me you don't hate me."

I loosen my grip but don't let go. "Five percent."

"What?"

"I hate you five percent. But I love you ninety-five. Even if you want to wear a full-body gerbil costume during sex."

She swallows hard. "Hamster."

"Right, hamster." I kiss her lips. "Promise you'll love me even if I start hoarding mannequin heads?"

She narrows her eyes. "Just the heads?"

I kiss her throat. "Torsos, then."

"Oh, okay. I mean, if it's just torsos . . ."

"Seriously, though. I love you. Your whole gray-area, Dr. Okada–slash-d0l0s-slash–Narioka Diane package. But I don't wanna be invisible. You don't get to ignore me. Or make me smaller when we don't agree."

She folds her arms around my shoulders, shifts her hips in my lap, and, brow curved, attention focused, says, "Deal."

I kiss her mouth again, longer, harder, and we stop talking for a while.

REESE

$0.00 ... $9,965.98 ...

Glaring at her phone, Nari paces the width of my room from the door to my bathroom past the end of my bed to my drafting table against the far wall and back.

"Trying to hit your step count?" I ask as she passes. My scalp, hair soaked with dye and wrapped in plastic overnight, itches. All over. If only because I can't scratch it and the power of suggestion is an asshole. Violet, in case you're wondering. The dye. Red may be the so-called color of victory, but been there done that, and I like purple better. Plus "Violet." Get it? As in my lovely cohort's recent pseudonym? Also, pride forever!

Nari looks up like she's breaking the surface after being underwater. "What?"

I poke at my head through the plastic wrap and mush of my hair. It doesn't help. "You're pacing like my mom worried about meeting her daily step count."

I could guess what she's looking at on her phone, what's making her so preoccupied. Not even guess, I *know*. The phone she's obsessed with is her prepaid, after all. But it's only Sunday morning. Not even forty hours since the deed was done. What is there to look at? Isn't this supposed to take months? Also, I'm still basking in the ombré pastel palette, the billowing, post-adrenaline-rush calm of our success.

My skull itches. Not even my scalp. My skull, the bone part, which I know isn't possible and is therefore not real, but whatever—I've waited long enough. "Okay. Can't take it any-more. I'm washing it out."

"Hooray!" Nari cheers. She locks her phone and leaves it on my drafting table. "Reveal time!"

And I let it go. Whatever she might've said, whatever else I could've asked, I let it go.

We walk into my bathroom, where I sit on the floor, unwrap the plastic from my hair, and lean my head back over the edge of the tub so my face doesn't end up purple, too. Nari pulls down the detachable showerhead and turns the water on, warming it up a few degrees above frigid but keeping it cold so my color will last longer. "So, uh, how's things?" I ask, looking up at her.

She moves the sprayer into my hair. The water filters through to my scalp for a long, quiet minute. "Things . . ." She uses her free hand to squeeze the water out of my hair, then starts rinsing again. "Um, my parents were grossly glowy after being Nari-free for five days. That's a thing."

"Sure, a deflection thing."

She sprays my face.

I cough. "Hey!"

"Sorry," she says, not sorry. "It slipped."

"Funny." I reach for a towel and blot my face. "Please, though, tell me more about your parents' sex life, 'cause that's totally what I meant."

She shuts the faucet off, squeezes the water out of my hair a final time, and hands me the bottle of conditioner. Still resting my neck on the edge of the tub, I squeeze out a palmful and comb it through my wet hair with my fingers, then twist it into a loose bun on top of my head and sit up, blood rushing out of my head. I lean back against the tub beside Nari.

"Things are things," she says. "Keag and I talked through a bunch of stuff yesterday."

I drape one of my rainbow hair-dyeing towels around my neck. "Which was . . . ?" I use a corner of the towel to dry my face again. "Really making me work for it today, Narioka Diane."

"It was good. Made me think." She looks at her hands, at the dye on her fingers, and grabs another towel to try to scrub it off. "Do you think it was right? What we did?"

I want to say, *Duh, of course!* But she's serious. So I say, seriously, "I don't think it's as simple as 'right' or 'wrong.'"

"Yeah."

"But," I say, "I'd rather do the wrong thing for the right reasons than the other way around."

"There needs to be a middle word. For the gray area in between," she says.

"Like midigood."

"Betwixtibad."

"Grawful. The mutant offspring of great and awful."

"Illeg-altruism." Nari tosses her towel into my laundry basket by the vanity, accepting her temporarily purple hands. "Except I'm not selfless. Keagan was right about that. Among other things."

"Well, you're not self*ish*. Or self-righteous or whatever he said."

She arches an eyebrow at me.

"Well," I say, "Keagan's . . ." I don't know how to finish that. Keagan had apologized for the Wednesday freak-out, and I would've forgiven him anyway. I, for one, am a fan of the occasional freak-out. Little freak-outs prevent mega freak-outs. A hypothesis Keagan proved by balling all his little ones into one over-compressed freak-out bomb.

"It's okay," Nari says. "And it's okay that Keag's right. I mean, not *okay*. But we're good. The way he said it last week was super shitty. But that—" She shrugs. "It's one moment in the middle of all the rest."

I frown and open my mouth to, I don't know, argue? Blame Keag? Though for what, I don't really know. Being an ass that one time? Like I've never been an ass? For hurting Nari? Sure. But they both hurt each other, and it wasn't exactly my business anyway. In any case, Nari reaches back to turn the faucet on again. "Let's rinse that goop out of your hair. I'm getting impatient."

Nari hangs out awhile longer. She watches me touch up the design I've shaved into the cropped side of my hair. Which comes out perfectly, by the way. Deep purple, near-black at my roots. She talks about summer and Berkeley and how she and Keag discussed her staying in the dorms and him finding an apartment with some roommates or something, then asks about my ever-upgrading itinerary for the fall—I've added Prague and Zagreb and Innsbruck—and how things are selling and so on and normal so forth, punctuated by a few gaping stretches of negative space. Ones we might've filled with blood packets and bank accounts and Bitcoins.

Except we don't. Then she leaves and I do some work; text

Maddie, who spent spring break in Vancouver; waste time online; eat dinner with my dad; then go to bed, where I think about all the things neither Nari nor I wanted to say.

I wake up in the morning to my phone screaming from the floor, where I plugged it in last night. Literally screaming. My mom's ringtone is a sample of some actress's horror movie shriek. Subtle, I know.

I don't answer. A week ago, that would've been obvious. Now, I hesitate. Hesitate to answer. To stop myself from answering? Both of those sound weird, but whatever. I count the screams. Three, seven, ten, then wait through the beep telling me she left a voicemail. In the quiet that follows, I pull my duvet up to my chin and stare at my ceiling. Two heavy cerise minutes later, my alarm goes off.

I wait to listen to the voicemail until I park my dad's car at school, half out of spite and half confusion. My epiphany about her hasn't worn off. But understanding and forgiveness aren't the same things. The morning fog hasn't lifted yet. People filter through the parking lot toward the building. "Reese," my mom's voice says. "It's Mom." Brilliance upon brilliance. *Thanks, Mom, for reminding me that I'm me and you're you.* I roll my eyes. "*Your dad says you got back from your camping trip early Saturday. Hope you guys had fun. I don't like how we left things last week. I*"— she pauses to heave a sigh—"*I don't like how we've left anything lately. I know you think everything's my fault, and I guess, for now, that's okay. But, if you'd consider forgiving me? Someday? Maybe before I'm old and frail and start losing my mind?*" Another sigh. "*I'm not perfect, Reese. I've never claimed to be. But your dad's not perfect either. Which isn't— Never mind. This isn't about that, it's about you and me.*

"Anyway. Your room here's all set up. Please let me know if you plan to use it."

And that's it. Click. The end.

I put my phone in my lap and stare out the windshield at the grille of the truck parked opposite my dad's car. Thing was, I hadn't even come home early that day. It was, like, five-thirty. FIVE-THIRTY. I'd even been kind of late getting home, having gone over to Nari's after school for whatever reason.

Basically, my mom wanted to get caught. By me? Doubt it. But she might as well have had the guy over for dinner.

Go big or go home, I guess. Or that morbid saying about cutting your nose off to spite your face. Except that this time, it was more like my mom didn't like the carpet so she set the house on fire.

Or.

Or she'd let herself get so bottled up, boxed in, *corked*, that the pressure built and, well.

Again, a week ago I would've said something snotty about her getting what she deserved. Shitty divorcee apartment, resentful kid, ruined reputation, etc. But now I think, maybe she is? Getting what she deserves. What she wants, at least. Not the pea-green muck of it, the hurt and loss and complexity.

But out. It's gotta be one of the most brutal ways to do it. I mean, when I came out to them at fifteen, I was like "Hey, I'm asexual and aromantic, any questions?" Get it? "Out"?

Anyway. My mom. She's . . . I don't want to say "free," but I will. She's free. She gets to decide who she is and what she wants without my dad's walls or my cork or bottle or combination of whatever. She gets to start over. Well, mostly over. And yeah, it's selfish. And yeah, the better time to have been selfish was twenty-odd years ago, though totally not wishing away my existence here, but.

Everyone deserves to make their own choices, to have their own life.

So that's why I text her: *Okay*.

The convo bubble with the three grayscale dots comes up immediately.

Okay?

Okay, I'll use the room.

I leave my phone in the car because I'd rather bask in that moment of closure than stumble through a dozen texts about logistics, and walk inside feeling lighter. More mature? Something corny and trite like that.

First period is AP English, then chem, then study hall, then lunch, which I'll skip to since who really wants a recap of the rest of it? After study hall I meet up with Bells and Nari in the hall outside their AP Physics class and we head toward the cafeteria. Almost there, I see Barret walking toward me with two of his interchangeable lackeys.

Five feet off, and he's laughing.

Three feet, and he meets my eye.

Two, and he winks.

One, and he's tripping.

Zero, and that piece of shit catches himself from falling by grabbing my chest.

"*What the hell?*" Nari yells.

I take an exaggerated step to the side. Barret rights himself, grinning. "Yeah, Barret," I say, frigid. "What the hell?"

He shrugs. "What? I tripped."

"That's sexual assault," Bellamy says loudly. Bellamy. *Loudly.* Last week really did something there.

"Aw, come on," Barret says. "Don't be a bitch about it. It's not like there's much to grab anyway."

And you know what? Fuck him. Fuck this. Fuck almost four full years of this asshat wasting my— Right. No more.

I wind up and kick him in the balls.

Hard.

Like, literally as hard as I can. Which is pretty hard, gauging from the way his face goes pale and he crumples to the floor.

His friends shout. Nari laughs. Bellamy smiles. An assortment of gasps, laughs, and groans comes from everyone else watching in the hall.

I lean down to where he has his face sort of mashed into the floor, hands gripping his groin, and say, "Don't touch me. *Ever.* I don't owe you *anything.* My time. My energy. My anger. And *certainly* not my body."

And I walk away with Nari and Bellamy trailing behind me. We might as well be in slo-mo with a muted explosion erupting at our backs, it's *that* awesome. Freaking Technicolor.

SANTIAGO

$19,937.15 . . . $28,012.51 . . . $37,890.65 . . .
$68,527.77 . . . $249,654.09 . . .

The ground is damp, the grass wet enough to soak through the old blanket we brought, but I don't care. Lying on my back, I close my eyes. A wave of sunlight pours over Bells and me as the clouds part, warming my face and arms, brightening the color of my eyelids to a vivid orange. Turned toward me, her body flush along the length of mine, Bells presses her cheek into my shoulder and squeezes my hand. I could stay like this forever, paused in this moment, folded inside the ease of our silence and the quiet warmth of the April sun.

But a shadow blocks the light, and I open my eyes. "I knew it!" Reese says. She beams, her sharp features bright with discovery, with being the first to know.

We sit up, Bellamy dropping my hand to remove her glasses and rub her eyes. She fixes her ponytail as Reese plops down across from us and dumps the contents of her bag out on the blanket. She smooths her deep purple hair over one shoulder.

"It isn't a secret. Just—" Bellamy shrugs.

"Hey." Reese sorts through her pile of art supplies. "I get it. Nari'll flip. In a good way, but still. I get it."

I pull my legs up and rest my forearms on my knees. My shirt clings to my back. "Well, Nari seems a little preoccupied lately."

Reese snorts. She pulls a black high heel and a gold Sharpie from her pile and gets to work. Bellamy and I share a look.

I'd expected it to be omnipresent, heavy and lurking, a rumbling shadow that dimmed every moment, but the truth was that I'd barely thought about Foster Innovations at all. All week, we'd gone to class, eaten lunch, worked, done homework, and hung out almost like normal.

Almost. *Almost like normal* because doing that changed each of us. It made Keagan sturdier, more assertive, from finally talking things through with Nari to declaring his love of diet soda one day at lunch. "I know it's disgusting!" he'd announced. "And probably rots your guts!" We'd all watched him proclaiming, emphatic, with our eyebrows raised. "But I love its numb aftertaste!"

"'Numb' isn't a flavor, Keag," Reese had said.

"Nonsense!" he'd cheered back, and chugged a third of his Diet Pepsi to prove a point no one cared he was making.

When he'd set the bottle back down, Bellamy had clapped a bit, murmuring, "Yaaaay." We'd all laughed.

Succeeding at her part had changed Reese, too, inspiring her to both quit putting up with Barret's bullshit and reach some sort of cease-fire with her mom. For Bellamy and me, it'd made us, well, an *us*. And for me? The feeling of invincibility had worn off, but my believing in myself had not.

Walking down the sidewalk back to Keag's car last Friday, I'd felt that wall of doubt in my head crumble. The plaster had cracked, the layers upon layers of paint had chipped away in flakes and sheets. I knew I could do anything. I felt as though, if I'd wanted it enough, I could've taken a running jump and leapt over a building. I clung to that, not the delusion but my optimistic determination. My parents' worries and doubts didn't have to be my worries and doubts, and if what they needed was proof and guarantees, then I was eager to give them both in the shape of my success. When I told them as much, for the first time both my mom and dad only listened and neither said no. It wasn't over, I knew that. I'd be pushing against their uncertainty as long as there was something to be uncertain about, as long as I was deviating from their prescribed plan, from their tradition and authority. But I knew their worry came from a place of love. And if I could respect their views despite that difference, I could also ask them to respect mine.

"So, it's not a secret," Reese says, concentrating on the creature she's drawing on the toe of the high heel. "But is it Breaking News?"

I smile like I always smile when I think about what Bells and I are now, like I can't help it, like what I'm feeling simply has to make itself known outside my head and heart, out on my skin. Bellamy and I share a glance, and I shrug. "We're seeing where it goes."

Reese nods without looking up. "Rad." And that's it. Bellamy looks at me again with eyes wide and an off-kilter grin, a look that I return because, that's it? But Reese is Reese, and her interest in concerning herself with other people's business extends only as far as knowing that the people she cares about are happy with that business.

I'm watching her add a detailed menagerie of insect-like

creatures to the strap and heel of the shoe when Keagan joins us. He walks over from the parking lot, passing among the other people out enjoying the nice day. When he reaches us, he moves some of Reese's stuff—pens, the matching shoe, a notebook—and sits between her and Bellamy on the blanket.

"No Nari?" Bellamy asks.

He shakes his head. "I got the same group text."

Park, 10:30, it read.

None of us asks a follow-up, I think because Keagan's face says he both does and doesn't know what this is about, which is a sense we all share. Instead, we ignore it, like we've been ignoring it, or not *ignoring* it but looking away, letting it happen, calling our parts done even though it's really only started, because we'd each rather bask in our positive change.

But, the thing is, Nari's changed, too.

NARI

$249,654.09

I walk to the park. It's . . . miles. And yeah, I know. I don't seem like the kind of girl who takes a lot of long, contemplative walks. Because I'm not. I like shoes where "comfort" is, like, the fifth descriptor and clothes you shouldn't sweat in. Clothes that would look at what I'm wearing (sweatpants, honest-to-goodness sweatpants) and laugh. Or gag.

My phone dings inside the pocket of my (Keagan's) hoodie, and I flinch.

Coming? Keag's text asks. I don't answer.

Things have gotten a little, uh, out of hand. To be totally glib about it. To put it *glibly*. It has been six days. Six, because after San uploaded my malware on the twenty-ninth, Foster began logging in to bank accounts on Sunday, the thirty-first, at 9:32 a.m., thereby activating it, and today is Saturday, April sixth. But my malware only ran for five. Well, five and a half. Five and a half, because I killed it last night. Five and a half, because when I logged in to Bells's bank account at a little after eight p.m. yesterday, I saw this number staring back at me:

$249,654.09

Yes. $249,654.09.

In five and a half days.

Or, better, in round about 131 hours.

We are so fucked.

How fucked? Well, here's how it went:

Sunday, Foster logs in to a few accounts, activating my pretty little bit of code. No big deal, right? Since, well, that was specifically The Plan. Except that within a few hours it'd already siphoned enough money to start the Bitcoin laundering business, ending the day with $9,965.98 in Bells's legit account. Which, okay. That was . . . a lot. More than I'd anticipated. By far. But not so much that I panicked. I'd just made some semi-minor ("minor" har har har) error somewhere. Forgotten to account for the nearly twenty-four-hour business day involved with international markets. Underestimated (okay, yeah, by a lot) how many accounts FI used and how much money they actually dealt in. But I still had it under control. Less than ten grand? Totally under control.

Then came Monday, and by the end of the day, the money had doubled-ish to $19,937.15 and . . . Again, it was way too much. The money was accumulating in the faux ID account, building to the Bitcoin cost threshold, and going through the auto-buy/sell system I'd set up at a drastically faster rate than I'd originally planned. But again, I didn't panic. We weren't there yet! This wasn't even a third of the way! And, dammit, I knew what I was doing! Ha ha. Ha. Aaah.

Tuesday: $28,012.51. I was starting to worry. But what was I supposed to do? Turn it off? We'd gone to all that trouble. All that mess. All that everything. For this. Couldn't I just, you know, wait it out? Nothing'd been flagged. Business was rolling (stampeding) along like usual, right? *What was the harm in letting it go all the way?*

Wednesday: $37,890.65. So, I reasoned, I'd let it hit the seventy-thousand mark. I'd go ahead and collect it all. Finish the job. And then I'd kill it. And, I guess . . . lie? To the others, I mean. About how fast the money was coming in. About how much was sitting in Bells's real account. The very thought gave me an ulcer. I mean, this was their thing, too. I knew that. I know that. They were along for the ride (as in, guilty, implicated, culpable) whether they knew how fast the car was going or not. But (and here's the kicker) I knew they'd tell me to stop. Keagan and Bellamy, definitely. San, probably. Reese, maybe. And what was I supposed to do? Quit now?

Thursday: $68,527.77. But then, nobody asked. Which isn't an excuse. I know that. And every day, every minute, every breath I breathed and every beat I heartbeated around them, I was sure one of them would ask. (Keag! Or, fuck, Bellamy at least!) BUT THEY DIDN'T. Four days passed, five, and still, *no one uttered a word.* Out of sight, out of mind, right? So I told myself, one more day. One. More. Day. Let it run for a final twenty-four hours, skid past that seventy-thousand threshold, then that'd be it. Done.

Well.

I don't know what happened. A few capital-M Major transactions? Foster logging in to a pile of accounts I'd never known about? But the number jumped. Almost two hundred grand in one day. And I . . .

I tried to fix it.

All last night. When I opened Bells's account and saw that

number, I killed the program. Right away. Closed the fake bank account, scrubbed what I could, going back through as much of Foster's computer and files as I still had access to, triple- and quadruple-checking that I'd covered every single one of my tracks, looking for warnings that someone, anyone, had noticed the missing money. Then I tried to put it back.

I tried.

But I couldn't.

I didn't even know where it'd all come from. I never thought I'd need to keep track. And I didn't have that kind of access anyway. Not to make hundreds of deposits across dozens of accounts without getting noticed. But I tried. Everything I could think of. Until, finally, this morning, I gave up.

Hence the hoodie. And stale sweatpants. And sneakers I haven't worn since my final gym class last year. Add in the hair I haven't washed and the makeup I'm not wearing, then subtract all the sleep I haven't gotten, and what do you get?

Another ding. Another text. My steps falter. But I don't take out my phone. I don't have any answers. I am so beyond excuses. We are so far past fucked.

I cross my arms and stare at the sidewalk in front of my feet, watching my toes poke into the scene: left, right, left, right. Cars drive by. A guy running with his dog jogs toward me, swerves into the grass of someone's front yard to pass, then steps back onto the sidewalk behind me.

Normal people. Doing normal-people things.

I've never been interested in being a normal person. Huge surprise, I'm sure. I'm different. I'm more. I'm d0l0s. Right?

Except what even *is* normal when *everyone* is different? With different wants and different goals and different things that make them happy or sad or bloated or satisfied or tired. Prom? Graduation? One last summer with your best friends before you all go your separate ways? College, dorm, roommate, classes?

Normal. Other people's normal, my normal, Reese's, San's, Bells's.

Keagan's.

Whatever it is, I want it. I want every average, cliché bit of it. The prom dress, the mortarboard, the going-away parties and buying extra-long twin sheet sets, FaceTiming with Bellamy as she shows me around her new dorm, Snapchats from Reese making inappropriate gestures with statues in Rome, a video of San's Olympic qualifying dives. Keagan's everything. Wherever he goes, whatever he wants, I want him. I want the picture, the one of the five of us posing around the statue at the Sea Lion Caves from the disposable cameras that I sent off to be developed when we got back. I want that smiling, simple reality. The one where five friends did a silly thing, and not as cover or an alibi, but just because. I want all of that so damn bad.

And I risked it all.

Like it was nothing.

Like I was different.

Like I was untouchable.

Because Keag was right. I was arrogant. I was self-righteous. And now, because of it, we're all going to jail.

BELLAMY

$249,654.09

"Abrir la caja de los truenos," San says, answering Reese's question about which idiom in Spanish does it better than the American equivalent.

"Open a box of . . . ," Keagan guesses. "What?"

Santiago smiles. Leaning back, propped up on his hands with his feet stretched out in front of him, he jiggles his right leg, bouncing it purposefully against my knee. "Thunder. 'To open a box of thunder.'" I pluck at the damp mix of old and new grass beyond the edge of our blanket and push down on his leg with my knee. "I don't know if that's the best," he says, "but it's one of my favorites. And thunder is inarguably cooler than a can of worms. I mean, what even is that? A can of worms?"

Reese takes her pen out of her mouth. "Right? Like how hard is it to put worms back in a can?" She mimes scooping up a pile of imaginary worms, then pauses, looking at something behind San and me with her cupped hands in the air. "Nari?"

We turn.

She's pale, and there are dark rings around her eyes. Her hair's a mess and she's wearing sweatpants.

Keag stands. "Nari, what's—"

She opens her mouth and closes it again, pulls out her phone, unlocks the screen, and hands it to Keagan. He frowns, reading whatever's pulled up on Nari's phone.

And recoils.

"What?" Reese asks, impatient. "You watching a snuff film or something?"

But she knows. She has to know. She gets up and takes the phone from Keagan. Her eyes widen. "This is Bellamy's account. The post-laundering one."

Nari nods.

"Holy shit," Reese breathes, and drops the phone like it's on fire. It lands with a soft bounce on the grass. "Holy shit. We are so fucked."

San stands, picks up the phone, blanches.

"*Nari!*" Reese screams. "*What the fuck?!*"

"*Hey,*" Keag snaps. He looks like he's going to be sick.

Nari's sobbing. "I—"

"Why didn't you kill the program?"

"I did." Her breath hitches. "I did kill it. Last night. Right away when I found out it'd taken so much."

"*Why didn't you tell us?*" Reese shouts.

"I—I fucked up."

"*Fucking obviously, Nari!*"

I haven't moved. Santiago stands beside me, Nari's prepaid phone in his hand, eyes unfocused and the fingers of his free hand digging into his opposite bicep. Keagan has paced away a few yards and crouches with his head in his hands.

"Put it back," Reese says. "The money. Just *put it back!*"

I stand and take the phone from San.

The bank account Nari made in my name is open on the screen. The balance, displayed in bold print near the top of the page, reads, $249,654.09.

Through her sobs, Nari says, "I can't. I can't put it back. All those accounts. I have no way—I don't know which money came from where. It's *too late.*" Then Reese shouts that she doesn't care, do it anyway, and Keagan shouts at Reese for shouting at Nari, and Santiago says something almost calm but I'm not listening because his eyes meet mine and they're bright with devastation.

I've ruined his life. This has ruined all our lives.

I waited until I was eight years old to finally ask my mom about my father. I wasn't a very fantastical child. I never believed in Santa or the Easter Bunny, so it wasn't that I didn't think I had a biological father or that I'd made up some convenient fiction to explain him away. But I'd never asked. And my mom had never offered. Even at eight, I figured it was better, *easier,* to look away. I figured if she'd wanted to tell me about him, she would have. I figured if he or my mom had wanted him to be a part of my life, he would have been. But in the third grade, the year after Nari claimed me as her best friend, I asked, and my mom answered by telling me some basics, and that together we were enough. That we were better off. That we didn't need him because I had her and she had me.

And we didn't. Need him. I say that with full self-awareness, with a complex understanding of need and want. I don't need him. Even as I stare at an account with my name on it full of his money, I know I don't need him. And I know that all of this could've been avoided if only I hadn't looked away.

It's what I do. What I did. I look away. When Nari suggested this plan, I figuratively put my head down, held my hand out, and said, "You lead, I'll follow." I looked away and waited for my friends to fix my problem for me. The unfairness of my mom's and my life is real, and undeserved, especially my mom's guilt about it. My anger and resentment are real, too. But I'd used them as excuses. And calling had been a stopgap, a way to absolve myself. I'd known when I called that if he hadn't answered, or if he'd answered and hung up like he did, if he'd done anything other than solve my problem with a snap of his fingers, I was prepared to label that experiment a failure, turn away again, and go back to waiting. Because I was always waiting. Waiting for that future moment when I'd finally have the right tools to change my mom's and my life. The classes, the competitions, all the extras I'd done, the things I'd accomplished, all the work; it was all parts, an assemblage of pieces that someday, once I had enough, once I'd reached some intangible concept of *enough*, I'd be able to build a new set of circumstances out of. Tools that didn't include Robert Foster because I didn't need him, I wasn't *supposed* to need him, to want someone who didn't want me.

And maybe that would've worked. Maybe five, ten, fifteen years from now, I'd have accumulated the proper components despite this. But what all of this has taught me, what saying yes and kissing San and getting Reese out of FI has taught me, is that waiting for some future moment when things are "ready," when they're "finished," is a good way to miss all of the amazing things I'm capable of right now.

It's taught me that the stopgap is never enough. That I'm done looking away.

I blink and take a deep breath, locking the phone and walking over to hand it back to Nari.

". . . keep it," Reese is saying, but I was so deep in my own thoughts I missed the first part.

Nari's eyes flick to me.

"No," Keag says at the same time San says, "Wait, let's—"

"It's the exact right amount," Reese interrupts. "It's what we were going to take from the beginning!"

"No," I say.

But Keagan and Reese start yelling over each other.

"How can you even *suggest* keeping it? How is that even an—"

"If seventy was right, why is two hundred and fifty wrong?"

While Nari cries.

"It's *all* wrong!"

"So going to jail for the rest of our lives is the answer? *They haven't even noticed!*"

And San stares silently at the grass, vision glazed.

"That doesn't mean they won't!"

"Stop," I say.

"Better to take the chance than guarantee being *fucked over for the rest of our lives!*"

"Perfect. That is just fucking *perfect*. More fucking chances. Haven't we taken—"

"SHUT UP!" I shout. Loud enough it makes my throat hurt. They do.

"Here," I say, handing Nari back her phone. I look between the four of them. "I'll fix this."

And I walk away.

It's a long walk. No one follows, not even San. And I'm

glad. I text my mom, telling her to come home, that it's an emergency.

Everything okay? she texts back a few minutes later.

No, I say, *but no one's hurt.*

Five minutes after that she writes, *On my way.*

My phone buzzes a few more times before I get home with texts from San, Nari, Nari, Reese, Keag, and San again, but I ignore them. By the time I reach the parking lot of my mom's and my apartment complex, her car's in her spot. I take deep breaths as I walk up the stairs and through our door. Standing inside with arms crossed and brow tight, my mom asks, "Bellamy? What's going on?"

And I tell her everything.

Afterward, my mom is silent. She listened the entire time without saying a word. Now she stares at the floor, expression stern. The light in the apartment changes as the Earth turns, shifting the placement of the sun in the afternoon sky. As the sunlight dims enough that we'll need to turn on a lamp, there's a knock at the door.

My mom stands to answer. It's Nari.

"Narioka," she says, "now isn't a—"

"It's my fault. Whatever Bellamy told you. It's my fault." I move from the couch and stand behind my mom. Nari's face is splotchy, her eyes puffy and red. She sees me and starts crying anew. "Bellamy, I'm so sorry. I thought I knew what I—"

"Nari," my mom interrupts. "Go home." I peer past Nari down the stairwell, at the bottom of which I can see the front of Keagan's car, idling in the handicapped space. "Bellamy and I need some time," my mom says. "I'll call your parents later." And she closes the door.

I go to the window that looks down on the parking lot. San stands outside the car by the rear passenger door. He sees me and lifts a hand, not a wave but an acknowledgment. I raise my hand to him in return. Nari comes into view, wiping her eyes, and climbs into the front passenger seat. I close the blinds.

When I turn back, my mom is on her phone. "Bobby?" she says after a moment. *Bobby*, because Robert Foster was young once. *Bobby*, because my mom knew him when he was young, a teenager, when they'd been teenagers together who'd hugged and kissed and laughed together, who'd liked each other and had maybe even been in love. "It's Lauren." And she shuts herself in her room.

Ten minutes later she comes out and tells me he's booked a flight. He'll be here in the morning.

I pass the rest of the evening lying in my room, staring at the ceiling above my bed. My mom took my phone, so I can't text the others. I heard her calling their parents but not what she said. Now the TV's on, playing a marathon of old *House Hunters* episodes, and she's banging around in the kitchen.

I keep my light off and drapes closed as the sun sets, and in the dim of my room I stare my new uncertainty straight on.

Facts are my comfort zone. I like certainty, or, the *pursuit* of certainty. The *possibility* of certainty. I like things that seem new and strange and incredible only because science is finally figuring out how to understand them, solving the strings of unknowns that lead to new knowns. Everything has an equation. Every equation has a solution. But this feels like staring at an equation I can't begin to know how to solve.

I'll take sole responsibility, but that won't erase Reese from the lobby's security cameras or San from the private camera feed in my father's office, or Keagan's license plates from the traffic cams if they trace Reese or Santiago or me back that far. And what about Nari? Not only d0l0s but Nari herself? She sat in that office, talked with Robert Foster the day before the program kicked on. And those variables aside, what about my mom? What about everyone else's parents? Even if I take all the blame, will everyone else let me?

My door opens. "Dinner," my mom says curtly, and turns back down the hall.

She's made lasagna. Real lasagna, not frozen. Which means she soaked the noodles, browned the meat, and grated the cheese. There's even garlic bread on the table, a loaf we've had frozen in the back of the freezer for I don't know how long.

"Sit," she says, opening a bag of salad. She dumps the lettuce into a bowl and picks through it, pulling out the bits that have started to go bad, then tears open the pouch of dressing that came with it and squeezes it over the top. She drops the bowl of dressed salad onto the table, a few leaves of lettuce spilling out, and gestures to the meal with her wineglass. "Eat."

She sits, and I serve myself a portion of lasagna, a pile of salad, a piece of garlic bread. My bite of lasagna is too hot and burns my mouth. I hold it on my tongue and blow air out of my mouth around it, trying to cool it down before I swallow. With my mom's work schedule, home-cooked meals like this are a rarity. If I were Reese, I'd say something like "What's the occasion?" But I'm me, so I eat quietly while my mom drinks her wine and frowns at me from across the table. Thinking of Reese makes me think about everyone, and I wonder what their evenings are like. Later, I'll find out. About Reese's shouting match with her dad, her *dad*, not her mom, including his threats to pull her Etsy storefront and cancel her plans for the fall. About Nari's tear-filled evening that ends with her computer, the one she lovingly built and rebuilt, in the trash. About Keagan's night filled with discussions of everything from peer pressure to the practicalities of life as an ex-con. And Santiago's, filled with silence.

Then my mom says, "I'm sitting here, looking at you, my *child*, who came from me, who's *part* of me, and I feel like I don't even know you."

I set my fork down and stare at my plate.

"Did Narioka make you do it?"

"*No*." I hate that she thinks that. I know why she does, but I still hate it.

"Then?"

I risk a look at her before focusing back on my plate. Her expression is livid.

"Answer me, Bellamy. And don't dare say that you don't know. You committed a felony. This is beyond serious. If your father decides to report you, which I can't imagine he won't, you'll—"

"I know."

"Of course you do." She takes a sip of wine. "You're *you*. You know it all. You *knew* it all. Risks and consequences and you did it anyway."

I take a deep breath, hold it, exhale. She waits. Finally, I nod. "Yes. I knew the risks and I did it anyway."

Her shoulders fall. I know I can't literally feel it. The molecules of nitrogen, oxygen, argon, carbon dioxide, and other trace gases including whatever chemical compounds waft off the cooling lasagna and garlic bread that make up the smells in the air aren't affected by my mom's emotions. But it's as though the space between us goes slack.

She sets her wineglass down and her expression sinks. An actual sinking. The tilt of her head, her eyebrows, the aim of her eyes, the corners of her mouth, all shift down. She shakes her head. "How could you—*you*, Bellamy—be so incredibly stupid?"

And I ask myself, *Was I? Was it?*

It was selfish. It was reckless. It was illegal. But I don't think it was stupid. Except for the oversight that led us here, it was smart and *bold*. And I realize in this moment that I don't regret it. That I can know I made excuses and mistakes, but that I don't feel guilty about doing it. If my father comes tomorrow with police in tow, I will spend the rest of my life mourning my dreams and regretting the consequences suffered by me and my friends. But I won't regret feeling like I've earned more than being screwed over by circumstances beyond my control.

Maybe that makes me a bad person. It certainly makes me an unrepentant criminal. But for the first time in memory, I don't think through every logistical avenue of this fallout. I don't second-guess myself, looking metaphorically to my left and right for co-conspirators to take both the lead and the blame.

Instead, I look at my mom, with my spine straight and shoulders squared. "It wasn't stupid," I say. "It worked." She meets my eye. "And no matter what happens tomorrow, you deserve to know it isn't you who failed me. And I deserve better than abandonment."

He comes anyway, of course. My bravado at dinner doesn't

change that. After dinner my mom shuts herself in her room and I wash the dishes, the *House Hunters* marathon switching over to a *Property Brothers* one that drones on beneath my racket. I catch the buzzwords "waterfall countertop," "bold fixtures," "quartz," and "open concept" on a steady rotation, and think, *Who are these people? Who spends tens of thousands of dollars on cabinets and countertops, backsplashes and smudge-proof stainless steel appliances?* They're useless thoughts, a pointless stream of consciousness to accompany the movement of my arm as I scrub baked cheese off the edges of the lasagna pan. But they're better than the cliché mess that fills my head after I finish and go to bed.

Will he recognize me? Will he see himself in the shape of my eyes and detached earlobes? If we hadn't done this, if I hadn't given us up, would he have ever wanted to meet me?

Does he think of me?

Does he hate me?

Will he report us and send my friends and me to jail?

I fall asleep at some point, because I wake up later and there's sunshine in my window. I hear the downstairs neighbors' TV playing cartoons. Through the wall behind my bed, Mr. Danson is opening and closing cabinets in his kitchen. I can even hear the condiments shift in the door of his refrigerator as he shuts it too hard. I used to think luxury was thick walls. Now I think, morosely, being accustomed to the noise will be a boon once I get to prison.

A few minutes later my mom opens my bedroom door. She's already dressed, wearing some of her nicest clothes, with her hair and makeup done, too. "He'll be here in half an hour," she says. I nod and she leaves.

I take a slow, deep breath. Half an hour.

I reach for my phone by instinct to text everyone, but my mom still has it, so instead I get up, take a quick shower, and get dressed, forcing myself to not care about which T-shirt I pull on because I don't care about it any other day, and I refuse to let today feel different. It doesn't need to matter that I'm meeting my father for the first time. It doesn't need to matter that my mom radiates nervous energy. It doesn't matter that I know that that feeling of "radiation" is caused by mirror neurons in the premotor cortex, that emotional contagion is the psychological phenomenon of one person's emotional behaviors, such as my mom scrubbing the sink that will never look clean or fluffing couch cushions that will never be fluffy, triggering a sympathetic response in another. And it can't matter that the way she feels right now is my fault, because my other faults are so much larger and need all the focus I have to give.

At 8:47 a.m. there's a knock on the door. My mom answers it and Robert "Bobby" Foster, CEO of a multibillion-dollar, internationally lauded venture capital firm, steps into our dingy apartment.

I stand.

And stare at him while he stares at me.

On an awkwardness scale of one to ten, this is debilitating. An integer raised to an infinite exponent. He's too real. Too corporeal. Too present. The air his mass displaces and the tightness in my chest make it hard to breathe.

I break my rule and wish. I wish for Nari's calm, her composure, her costume as she sat across from him in his office pretending to be someone else. I wish for Keagan's humor and Reese's confidence. I wish for Santiago's fingers woven with mine.

"Well," my mom finally says, and the stillness cracks. "I don't suppose traditional introductions are appropriate. But, Bobby—"

"Robert," he interrupts. "Please."

The muscles in my mom's jaw twitch. "Right." She waves a hand between us. "*Robert*, meet Bellamy."

He shifts his arms uncomfortably, like he might reach to shake my hand, then slips his hands into the pockets of his khakis. Reese would've had something perfectly snarky to say about his button-down shirt, ironed khakis, and brown leather docksiders, but all I can think is that he looks like someone's dad. Someone who specifically isn't me.

"Bellamy," he says, "it's . . ."

A *pleasure?*

His stumble gives me confidence. "Complicated?"

He frowns. "To say the least."

If the contagiousness of emotions had an off switch, I would flick it. Because this is unbearable. Literally. I cannot bear it: the way he looks at me with his mouth tight and brow creased; my mom's furious expression; my rapid pulse pushing heightened levels of cortisol, epinephrine, and norepinephrine throughout my body.

"Fine," my mom says, and I take a breath. She gestures for us to sit. "I'll start."

I sit back on the couch. My mom pulls a chair over from the kitchen rather than sit beside me. Robert sits in the lumpy old chair to my right. I feel light-headed, sick to my stomach, and, sunk low on the couch cushion beneath their attention, so very small.

Robert sits with his elbows propped on his knees. His gaze

flicks around our apartment, lighting on the many framed pictures of my mom and me on the walls, on our clean but worn furniture, our clean but cheap kitchen cabinets, clean but old appliances, clean but dingy carpet and linoleum kitchen floor. My mom watches him, brow tight, and I feel a jolt of defensiveness. I don't want him judging our life. He has no right.

"So," my mom says, addressing my father. "The way I see it, we have two issues. First is Bellamy managing to steal an incredible amount of money from you. Second is the issue of you being her father. But seeing how if the first hadn't happened, you wouldn't be here to address the second, maybe we start there?" Her tone is cutting.

Robert's focus settles on her. He laces his fingers together, and all I see is his wealth and power and largeness. The way wealth and power seem to make normal-sized people large. If he was ever a teenager with unstyled hair and an easy smile, I can't picture it. He arches an eyebrow and opens his mouth, but I interrupt.

"Is she wrong?"

His arched eyebrow falls as he looks at me. I swallow. Though I brushed my teeth less than an hour ago, my mouth tastes acrid.

I make myself hold his eye. I wonder if he can sense it, that phone call, the shared memory lingering between us. Even the financial aid paperwork, that reminder of my existence, his opportunity to claim me. "You've never shown any interest in the fact that I'm your daughter. And if it weren't for what I did, I doubt you ever would. So it doesn't seem like she's wrong."

"I don't think you're in a position to make accusations."

"I didn't make an accusation," I say, "only stated a fact."

My mom shifts forward, impatient. "Have you reported them?"

He clears his throat. "Not yet."

She exhales and leans back in her chair.

I ask, "Why?"

Robert unlaces and relaces his fingers. "I wanted to hear why you did it first."

First.

I look at my mom. She's closed her eyes and is rubbing her temples with both hands. "You didn't—"

"Nope," she says. "That's your job, Bluebell."

I glance back at Robert. He purses his lips. The searching way he watches me is unnerving.

"Okay." I want to pop my knuckles, pull my hair out, leap through the window. "I got into MIT. Early decision," I start. "But maybe you know that."

His brow creases and he tips his head. I wait.

"Financial aid paperwork," I say, and something clicks. His eyebrows and the muscles narrowing his eyes relax.

"My lawyer," he says. "He mentioned something in passing. Then sent it to my accountant." His gaze flicks around the apartment again. "I'm assuming you can't afford to go."

"No. I could have," I say. And I'm so angry. It surprises me, this anger, so intense I have to ball up my hands to stop their shaking. "MIT is need-blind with full-need financial aid. But there's . . . you. And they must've thought you'd help pay."

Which is why I called you, I think. But I don't say it. Let him say it. Let him say that I called and he hung up on me.

He nods, a vague gesture of understanding. Not sympathy or indignation, but basic understanding, as though this was the missing part of the equation he hadn't been quite sure how to solve. "How'd you do it?"

My mom lowers her hands and opens her eyes, focusing on me.

"You don't know?" I ask him.

He shakes his head.

"Would you have found out if I hadn't told?"

"Eventually."

I nod because I don't know how else to react. A quarter of a million dollars. In less than a week. And *he hadn't even noticed*.

"Malware," I say. "Code written to siphon a fraction of a percentage off of each of FI's financial transactions. Laundered through Bitcoin into an account in my name."

His eyebrows rise. "That's some sophisticated code."

"Yep."

"How'd you get past the firewalls?"

Again, he doesn't know. Incredible.

He doesn't know that we *didn't* get past all the firewalls. He doesn't know that we were in his building. Meaning he hasn't thought about security tapes. Meaning he hasn't added Violet Murakami plus the teenage activist in a black wig and fake blood plus the looped video plus a glimpse of San in a suit stepping out of his private bathroom before the feed paused and come up with grand larceny. Meaning . . . ? I meet my mom's eye, but the look she returns makes it clear I have to tell him.

"We didn't," I say. "We installed it physically on your desktop's hard drive."

His eyes widen, and I wonder if the pieces are starting to fit together. "We?"

Eventually I'll tell him everything. Eventually he'll even

meet everyone. Eventually he'll laugh at Reese's enthusiastic performance. He'll grill Nari on the code she wrote and shake his head thinking of her tenacious alter ego. But right now, as he waits for me to answer, all I say is "I'm sorry."

And I am. Not for the trouble I've caused him. Not even for doing what we did, really. Though if I could go back and do it all again? I don't know. Maybe I'd make different decisions. Rework the equation, change the variables. But right now, I'm sorry for something larger. Something indistinct. I'm sorry in a way I don't know how to articulate yet. In a way that has little to do with remorse or regret. Or at least, not my remorse or regret. Maybe I'll figure it out someday, but for now I just say, "I was desperate and angry. And I'm sorry."

He opens his mouth, then closes it. Twice. Finally, he says, "When you called . . ." He shrugs. "I panicked."

I blink hard. Tears of sadness have a different chemical composition than other types of tears. Prolactin, Leu-enkephalin, and adrenocorticotropic hormone all appear in markedly greater quantities in tears caused by unhappiness than in tears produced for lubrication only. Some theories suggest that apart from the social aspect of crying, such as eliciting sympathy, tears caused by sadness serve biochemical purposes, such as releasing certain toxins from the body and relieving stress.

But I don't cry. Not yet. I swallow hard. My throat feels thick. "Why didn't you call *me*? Why haven't you *ever* called me?"

It isn't the same. I know that. But he answers anyway, telling me about being overwhelmed and scared and shortsighted. He describes leaving for college before I was born and how each week, each month, each year away, charging forward through his life, made it easier to forget about me. Not entirely, he swears.

But I became an abstract concept. So intangible that when he did stop to think of me, I felt less like reality and more like some memory that might've gotten confused with a dream. "And I let you," he says. "I let you become a sort of figment." Because a figment, he tells me, a negligible child-support debit from one of his old and seldom-used bank accounts, a few forms passed from a lawyer to an accountant, was neater, *simpler*, than considering me as a reality. A person. His daughter. "As a toddler with my laugh." He looks up, meets my eye after having stared at the carpet between his feet for the past five minutes. His smile is small and tight, his eyes a little red and serious with that searching look again. "As a teenager with my nose and nearsightedness."

He almost called me after the birth of his first son, he says. But he realized that he hadn't had that feeling with me. That moment of instant "nearly debilitating love." And "Instead of trying to undo seven years of packaging you in that neat box of unreality, I gave in to my guilt and looked away again."

He just—looked away. Which might've sounded callous. Which was undoubtedly cowardice. But it's also something we had in common. *Had.* Because whatever else happens, we're both done looking away.

When he finishes, we don't do anything as succinct as hug. We only stare at each other for an elongated moment, his brow curved and my cheeks wet. We both know his guilt doesn't negate mine. We both know that part isn't over. We both know that this is only the start.

But we also know it isn't the only thing about to begin.

EPILOGUE

NARI

Saturday, June 8

All right. Picture this: Sun, grass, and a dome of blue sky. Poly-ester robes, each with our ace flag pin, decorated mortarboards, a heady dose of excitement, and a whole mess of pomp and circumstance because it's . . . graduation! I mean, of course it is! What better moment to go out on than the final one of our high school careers? Our last with literal ceremony? After this there's just summer with its five countdowns to five departures followed by the beginnings of five sequels.

So graduation feels right. Especially because we're here and, well, not in jail! Hooray! And I don't mean that flippantly. My exclamations are utterly sincere. Because instead of jail cells and jumpsuits and lawyers and court dates and bail and and and, we're sitting out on the lawn a few dozen yards off from the emptying bleachers and crumpled programs, post photo-taking frenzy, post proudly tearing parents and hovering, bored-ish sib-lings, for a few stolen minutes.

In other words, a moment of pure, unadulterated Friend Love.

"Well," I say. "It's been grand."

"It has," Keag says, "hasn't it?"

I rest my head on his shoulder. The bright blue polyester of his gown is warm from the sun.

Reese beams. "I feel like one giant smile. Like I might start seeping gooey optimism out of my pores."

"Satisfaction seepage," says San.

"Glee secretions," Bellamy adds.

Reese fake gags. We all laugh. I can't believe it's over. I mean, I know "over" isn't the right word. We all still have approximately 1,999,963 hours of community service (decided on by the tribunal of our parents, sans actual legal proceedings, thank every single iteration of god) to complete. Okay, I'm exaggerating. It's more like five hundred. Each. But seriously? I'd do the two million in lieu of juvie or jail, so kudos, Mr. Foster and the parents, for coming together on this non-life-ruining, extralegal consequence agreement. I may be grounded from all things tech until college this fall, and we all, except for this current celebratory moment, are forbidden from seeing each other for another few weeks. But again, NOT JAIL.

But averted penal consequences aside, we all know this is when things start to change.

Take Reese. Three months from now, she'll be off to Prague. Then Turkey. And Greece. Then on to Croatia, Italy, Austria, France, Germany, Switzerland. Basically, she's planning on wandering her way through Europe and wherever else strikes her fancy for as long as the money lasts. Which will be a while, because turns out people will pay out the ass for creepy-cute creatures drawn on various articles of clothing, and during our post-Event fallout, after her dad revoked his threat to trash her Etsy storefront, she used her sequestration to pump out an army of creepy-cute creatures. After all that she'll start college in New York. Where she's going to live with her mom (yes, her mom, for real) while she goes to school.

And San? Well, our beloved Santiago, man of many talents, air-duct contortionist, admirer of Bellamy, is still headed to Stanford in the fall and has already begun his Olympic-qualifiers diving regimen as laid out by his new Californian coach. His parents have also started speaking to him again, so, you know, progress? Oh, and I've given up asking him about him and Bellamy. All I've gotten out of either of them is a random "I don't know" or "maybe someday" despite the recent prevalence of shared smiles and elongated looks, *and* that one time when Bells, San, and I were all headed to clean the same stretch of highway and Santiago gave Bells a ride after school while I lingered for a few minutes with Keag before he drove me over, and we spied them both climbing out of San's two-seater looking a little ruffled, a little swollen-lipped and pink-cheeked. So, yeah, I feel pretty confident saying San's doing okay.

Next up: My dear, my love, my one and only, Keagan. Okay, for the record? I don't actually believe in soul mates. And Keagan might not be my One and Only forever. I can't see the future! But that doesn't mean I love him less than enormously. Just that this is life. And life changes. And we change. And we *have* changed. And I'm trying to be more realistic in my expectations. For him, for myself, for all of it. Anyway, Keags is fabulous. *We* are fabulous. We're also still headed in the same direction come this fall. He's been talking with a construction company that specializes in restoration about a job and looking into an apprenticeship with a woodworker, too. I like to picture him wearing flannel with sawdust in his hair. It's hot.

We've also been doing a lot of talking. At school between classes and at lunch; on the phone (landline) at night for the twenty minutes (seriously) we're allowed. We've talked about it all. The certainty of alien life. If Bells will be able to get us on the spaceship to our new planet when humans trash this one once and for all. Which is really better, Twizzlers (me, duh) or Red Vines (Keag, gross). How sometimes I let my brightness destroy my satellites like an expanding star, but also how I can't read minds and need said satellites to maybe do a little hand waving when my glow gets too hot. And how, okay, there was actually quite a bit of hand waving that I maybe chose to ignore but also that's over! In the past! And all I can really do is try to pay more attention and listen closer in the future while at the same time Keagan lets himself be a little louder. Thankfully that loudness sounds less like "I TOLD YOU SO!" and more like "You're amazing but imperfect and I love your amazingness *and* your imperfections but never ask me to commit a felony again because no."

As for me? Well. The tech ban has seriously cramped (read: nullified) d0l0s's style. But it's also allowed me to refocus my energies on things like roadside cleanup! Jokes (not really). Actually, it's been . . . I won't say good or liberating or anything else so painfully not true, but it has been, uh, healthy? Yeah, I'll go with "healthy." I sleep more, which is good. And my parents and brothers look at me differently, which is, well, different. But! All in all, I don't regret it. Should I whisper that? Maybe. But I won't, because I don't. What we did, what *I* did, was wrong. And that wrongness risked every good thing (both mundane and exceptional) in my and four other people's lives. So if I could go back, would I do it differently? As in, take international markets etc. into account? Ha ha, not answering that. But without all the illegal parts aka stealing loads of money and such? Yes. I'd still do it. It being the "fix Bellamy's problem" part. Because . . .

Bellamy oh Bellamy. Bells is . . . She's a foggy window scrubbed clean; a blurry screen protector swapped for a brand-new one. She shines. She glistens. Which I am so not taking credit for. Because it wasn't The Event (well, maybe a little) but the fallout that cleansed her tarnish. It's more like the Absent Father of it all was a sort of stain, a dampener. Confronting Robert Foster was Bells's version of shedding her too-small teenage skin, emerging from her chrysalis, spreading her wings and—

Yeah, okay. But really? She's the new Bells. Bells 2.0. A Bellamy who goes for it, who kisses San (undocumented fact but in this instance I'm cool with assuming) and calls her father Robert even after he asked her to call him Dad, to which she actually answered, "No, you haven't earned it." Legit fireworks.

But enough of all that, right? Because WHAT ABOUT MIT?

Well.

It's a go. Seriously. A Big Fat Go. And at the risk of suggesting that questionable behavior pays off . . . it paid off. I mean, okay. Keagan would interject here by pointedly clearing his throat because finally talking to her dad, not just the one nonstarter phone call, is what "paid off." But would that have ever happened without The Event? I don't know. Ifs, maybes, could'ves, would'ves, should'ves, whatever, I'm happy to leave that a muddle.

In any case. We gave it back. The money. All of it. (Of

course.) But Mr. Robert "Bobby" Foster did not report us, let alone press charges, and is still paying for Bellamy's tuition (plus housing and books), with the only contingency being that she calls him once a week and visits him this August. Oh, and that if she ever invents the means for near-light-speed interplanetary travel, he gets first investment dibs.

So, yeah, Big Fat Glitter Unicorn Win.

Which catches us up to today. To this bright and beautiful here and now. To a feeling in my gut like bottled sunshine as I open my bag and hand out four framed copies (mine's at home) of that picture of us posed around the statue at the Sea Lion Caves, as we laugh, then quip, then go silent as each of us stares at the photo and considers what it means, what we lost, what we changed, what we kept, what we gained, until Reese says, "Painted Pig!"

And Keagan says, "Okay, five teenagers, each with their own special skill set—"

Santiago groans. Reese throws her mortarboard at him, corners out, the black, gray, white, and purple stripes of the pride flag she painted on it spinning.

"Hey!" Keag laughs, hands up. "Kidding! *Kidding.* I swear."

Bellamy runs the strings of her tassel between her fingers and says, grinning, "I've got one. . . ."

The Friend Love glows. And we're basking in it.

ACKNOWLEDGMENTS

Reaching this page is utterly surreal. And I have so many people to thank for helping me get here. Because while writing is often a solitary endeavor, becoming a writer, finishing and publishing a book, absolutely is not.

To my agent, Melissa Edwards, thank you forever and always for plucking me out of the slush. Your keen eye, guidance, and unfailing support have meant more to me than I can possibly express. I am eternally grateful for your partnership through the ups and downs and everything in between in this business. Onward and upward!

To my editor, Kelly Delaney, thank you for falling in love with Nari, Reese, San, Keagan, and Bellamy the way I love them. From day one, you just *got it*. Working with you, with someone who so clearly shares my vision for this story, who has helped me make these characters and this book better at every turn, has been such an incredibly rewarding experience. I am so thankful to have you as my editor, so proud of this book, and I'm so excited for what's next!

To everyone at Knopf BFYR, to Angela Carlino, Jaclyn Whalen, Diana Varvara, Artie Bennett, and Renée Cafiero and all those who've had a hand in bringing *Immoral Code* into the world, thank you, thank you, thank you. This is a dream come true.

To Idris Grey and Laina, thank you! Your thoughtful feedback was crucial in helping me better understand Reese. I so appreciate the time you took and the insight you offered.

To my friends and family who've cheered me on through the decade-long process that led me to this point, to Laura, Carrie, Lacy, Mary, Devin, Reta, Brian, Jill, Greg, Amelia, Catherine, Bill, and the rest of my family, *thank you.*

To Maria, thank you. Thank you for being one of my very first readers. Thank you for listening to my book-related ramblings over the years. Thank you for all of your help with Santiago and the Spanish in this book. Thank you!

To the many teachers who've shaped my life and inspired me to pursue this dream, thank you. Thank you especially to Beth Loffreda for teaching classes that challenged me to expand my perspective, for hours of conversation, and for being one of the first people to call me a writer. And to the memory of Bob Torry, thank you. I'll forever remember sitting down with you the first time to discuss a paper I'd written for Freshman Honors Colloquium and you asking me what major I planned to declare in a way where "English" was the only right answer. What a remarkable turning point that moment ended up being in my life.

To Mark Spragg, thank you for the time you gave me at a crucial moment in my writing life. Your advice was invaluable and helped make me the writer I am today.

To Karen and The Second Story bookstore: Whatever I say

here will be insufficient. The nearly nine years I spent working for you, KK, will forever be some of my favorite. You were a fantastic boss and are a wonderful friend. Thank you. (Readers, if you ever make it to Laramie, Wyoming, check out The Second Story bookstore. It is one of my most loved places in the world.)

To Jim, thank you for years of interest and for always eagerly asking when I'd be done with the next chapter. Your encouragement has meant the world to me.

To the memories of my grandparents, thank you for giving me a childhood and adolescence surrounded by readers and books. Thank you for loving me and for believing in me. The day I got the call my book had sold, I missed you all a little extra.

To my dad: Thank you for telling me my entire life that if I wanted to do something, I could. Thank you for teaching me confidence and determination and for being there for me without fail. I could not have asked for a better father.

To my mom: Thank you for giving me a lifetime example of a strong, smart, driven woman. Thank you for motivating me to dream big and work hard and to always be learning. With your support and love, I know I can do anything I set my mind to.

To Owen: You can't read this yet, but someday you will, and I want you to know how wildly I love you, how full and vibrant you've made my life. I am grateful every day that I get to be your mom.

And finally, to Erik: How do I thank you for the last fifteen years? From those first scribble-filled spiral notebooks over a decade ago to today, you've believed in me, encouraged me, and taken my dream seriously. I could not have done this without you. Thank you.